As the Page Turns

by

Iona Morrison

This is a work of fiction. Names, characters, places, and incidents are either the product of the author's imagination or are used fictitiously, and any resemblance to actual persons living or dead, business establishments, events, or locales, is entirely coincidental.

As the Page Turns

Contact Information: info@thewildrosepress.com

Cover Art by *Debbie Taylor*

The Wild Rose Press, Inc.
PO Box 708
Adams Basin, NY 14410-0708
Visit us at www.thewildrosepress.com

Publishing History
First Edition, 2021
Trade Paperback ISBN 978-1-5092-3757-9
Digital ISBN 978-1-5092-3758-6

Published in the United States of America

Peyton awakened with a start. An odd scraping sound sent her imagination into overdrive. Was it outside? The scratching seemed loud enough to be coming from inside the cottage. Trying to focus in the dark, her eyes searched the room while she strained to hear the noise. The scraping sound came again. Nails on a chalkboard, tree branches against the cottage, or someone trying to force open a lock, back and forth it went, pausing only to begin again. She sat up quietly, swinging her legs over the side of the bed. Did Jessie hear it too? She reached for her phone. Slipping on her robe, she tiptoed over to the bedroom door to listen while reaching for a heavy vase on top of the dresser.

"Ouch." She heard Jessie yell out. Followed by something she couldn't hear.

Without thinking Peyton opened the bedroom door and raced toward the lightened living room, ready to go battle and save her cousin. Suddenly she was propelled backward when her body slammed hard into a solid object standing right in the way. The vase in her hand fell to the floor with a loud crash sending shards of glass in several directions. With the wind knocked out of her and no air to scream, she sprawled out helplessly on the floor imagining the worst. She was afraid to open her eyes.

Praise for Iona Morrison

Searching for Closure won 2021 Urban Fantasy at Speak Up Talk Radio

"[Only a Shadow] is another fun, fast moving, entertaining mystery. I love the character development and the twists and surprises in the plot."

~ *Tammy, Reader*

"With a compelling story line, relatable characters and mind-bending twists and turns, author, Iona Morrison, has delivered a truly remarkable book. [Key to the Past] is a page turner that will keep you on the edge of your seat from start to finish!"

~ *Review by the Book Excellence Awards*

Searching for Closure is a great book. A mystery is mixed with a great romance story and fantasy - it is excellent. The plot is compelling, the characters are interesting. I recommend."

~ *Julie, BookShelf Reviewer*

Dedication

Dedicated to my three special friends, Vickie, Judy, and Tammy. We have texted, Zoomed, laughed, and yes even cried our way through social distancing. Without you I might have survived but I wouldn't have thrived.

Acknowledgments

I would like to acknowledge the work of my great editor Dianne Rich, Debbie Taylor who designed the awesome cover, and the wonderful staff of The Wild Rose Press who made the production of this book possible. Thank you.

Chapter 1

Sneaking down the stairs, Peyton Reynolds made her escape through the back door. The beautiful day called to her all morning. Finally, she managed to slip out of the inn before Katie gave her another errand to run. The bride had her jumping alongside all the others, even though she wasn't in the wedding party. Turning her face toward the bright and glorious summer sun, she let it bathe her skin in its warmth.

"Freedom at last," she said putting on her shades. With a smile, she closed the door on all the wedding chaos.

Taking a leave of absence from her job to spend time in Blue Cove with her grandmother and cousin was one of the better decisions she had made. Her time here had not only given her new friends but all kinds of fresh possibilities for the future. She had to admit that sharing this special moment with Jessie and Katie was worth all the craziness of the past few days. Peyton would forever be grateful for the cove and the way people here embraced her. They played a big part in her recovery after being shot while in Arizona. Blue Cove was a godsend.

Inhaling a deep breath of fresh air, she hurried away from the inn before her absence was noticed. With a single destination in mind, she strolled through the gardens awash with color. Her senses were inundated with the sweet floral aroma. Pausing only long enough to smell one of the beautiful roses, she strolled to one of her favorite spots. Jessie had introduced her to the overlook with a private beach below not long after she had arrived in town. The two of them had chilled and chatted away many afternoons while plotting their futures together. At least Jessie plotted. She mostly listened or laughed. Her cousin was a trip. The smile on her face broadened when she thought about how Jessie handled Katie's theatrics only moments ago. Her cousin took Katie's bridal jitters all in stride and pushed back when she needed to.

How she loved this place. Standing near the edge of the bluff, she took in the ever-changing beauty of the bay. The tension of the last few hours seemed to melt away. With only the sound of the seagulls and the waves lapping the shoreline she savored a quiet moment in the picture-perfect day. She could breathe.

"Beautiful," she murmured. The vivid hue of the clear blue sky reflected in the deep blue shade of the water. The sun danced across the waves spreading sparkling diamonds and mini rainbows as if someone held a huge prism for the light to pass through. "Almost magical." She held her breath, releasing it slowly. Nothing she imagined could mar such a magnificent sight. At least for today, this was the best wedding venue ever.

A sailboat gliding across the gentle waves captured her attention along with her imagination. The boat skipped merrily over the water until it became a tiny dot on the horizon. How she wished she could go along for the ride. What romantic adventure were they off on? "Stuck on land at least for today." She sighed, clasping her hands behind her back. What did life have in store for her next?

Wistful, she reached out to straighten the wayward ribbons on a few of the multiple floral arrangements tied to the chairs on both sides of the makeshift aisle. The aisle where the white runner would soon be rolled out. The one Katie would walk down on her father's arm. Peyton sighed again. *Who would escort her on her wedding day? If she ever had one.*

She sat in one of the chairs giving her feet a much-needed rest. It was easy for her to picture Katie standing in front of the decorated archway with Dylan by her side, their love evident in the glances that would pass between them. With a bit of imagination, she could almost envision herself in a similar scene one day too. If she wanted to be. A question yet to be answered.

Jaxon Kincaid had given her cause for hope in that area, although she hadn't seen him since he went back to Arizona after his last visit. At least he called a couple of times a week which counted for something. Didn't it? He promised her that he would try to come to the wedding if he could arrange the time off. Her hope was fading fast because he hadn't called yet, and the wedding was only a few hours away. She would have to dance with some of the other guys, all the while wishing every dance it was him. Sighing seemed to be on tap for her today.

"Great minds think alike." Jessie squeezed her shoulder. "I was right behind you in escaping, and not a moment too soon, I might add." She laughed. "Katie was passing out more jobs that simply have to be done from her eternal list."

"Katie is a tad bit intense today." Peyton patted the

chair beside her. “Is that normal?”

“Duh, she’s always intense.” Jessie sat beside her cousin. “But today she’s taking intensity to a whole new level.”

“No kidding.” Peyton rolled her eyes behind her shades.

“On days like this, my friend could make coffee nervous.” Kicking her shoe off Jessie reached down to massage her foot. “This is the first time I’ve sat down since I arrived at the inn early this morning. I’m hungry,” she whined with quivering lips.

“Stop it.” Peyton stifled a giggle. “You look ridiculous. Matt would have second thoughts if he saw you now.”

“He’s seen me at my best and worst, and he still likes what he sees.” Jessie fluttered her eyelashes playfully. “I should go. I’m sure Katie is searching for me as we speak.” She groaned. “But I need a minute more.” She took a deep breath blowing it out slowly.

“All I’m saying is your friend may be a tad more passionate about wanting things done a certain way and as quickly as possible.”

“You’re too diplomatic, Peyton. Katie is acting nuts. She wants it done her way, and she wants it done as soon as the words leave her mouth. She’s not quite bridezilla but coming close to it. There, I’ve said it. It’s out in the open, and I feel better. How about you?” Jessie winked at her.

“Oh, yes. I’m glad you said what I was thinking. I wouldn’t want to disparage your friend. But I’m cool with you doing it.”

“Never. I love Katie. I would never say behind her back what I haven’t already told her to her face. That’s why I left before she could get worked up. She knows I'm right. But today everything must be perfect for her. She's dreamed of her wedding day since she was a little girl. I guess all of us have on some level."

"How can it not be perfect? Look at the setting." Peyton gestured toward the cove, changing the subject.

"Breathtaking. I told Katie this would be the ideal spot. Like a scene in a fairytale."

"Exactly what I was thinking, and the weather is cooperating too. Yay! Does all of this make you think about your wedding?" Peyton asked.

"Oh, heavens no. I'm happy to be engaged to my hunky cop for now. I'm not in a hurry to get married or have little Parkers running around. Could you imagine me chasing after them?" Jessie shook her head and laughed. "I want to enjoy this lovey-dovey stage first. Matt's good at it, and loving him comes with lots of perks."

"I'm in no hurry either." Peyton shuddered mentally at the idea of letting a man have any say in her life again. "Did you smell the flowers on your way here? A church filled with roses couldn't touch the beauty of this spot." Peyton stood. "I could look at this view all day, but I'm sure Katie will send someone to search for me."

Jessie pulled her back in the chair. "You! I'm the maid of honor, and she'll be sending a posse for me. I'll leave first. You can sit a little longer." Jessie slipped on her shoe and started to leave. "Nothing had better ruin her special day or heaven help us all." Jessie walked away.

As soon as the words left her cousin's mouth a strange foreboding came over Peyton. She shook her head trying to dispel the impression. The sensation wasn't leaving but started to intensify in strength. She had the same feeling a few days ago when she interviewed to fill an open Special Ed teaching position at the Pinedale Private Day School.

The building, originally an orphanage, opened its doors in nineteen-eighteen. Rumor had it that at one time the facility had also once served as an asylum with a dubious reputation. She wanted to find out more about that period in its history. The new owner rescued the building, renovating and transforming the historical structure into a wonderful space true to its period. The remodel was accurate, but the atmosphere seemed charged with some unseen presence. She had the strange sensation of being watched several times. At one point during the tour, she saw one of the reasons. A ghost, a little girl with braided pigtails, roamed the halls stopping to look in each of the classrooms. Her small boots clicked against the tile floor with each step she took. Of course, only Peyton could hear the opening and closing of the doors and the sound of her boots walking the halls. The spirit had intrigued Peyton when she saw her. There had to be a reason why she could. With no time to investigate she filed her concerns away. But they all came rushing back in with Jessie's words.

No longer comfortable sitting alone Peyton stood up to leave with the sense of prying eyes following her every movement. The urgency to hurry caused her to pick up her pace. Once safely inside the inn, she searched the gardens from the kitchen window. Frozen to the spot she watched for…what? She had no idea. Something or someone had decided to come to the wedding without an invitation. Hopefully Katie's perfect day wouldn't be ruined by the presence she felt out there.

"Are you, okay, cousin?" Jessie put her arm around her shoulders.

"I'm not sure. As soon as you spoke about not ruining Katie's day, I was hit with apprehension."

"I could sense it too as I walked back to the inn." Jessie shivered. "I'm sure I felt something similar once before. We'll talk about it later." Jessie pursed her lips when Katie called her. "Any ideas?"

"No, but I had a similar feeling the other day. I'm sure we'll know soon enough." Peyton rubbed her arms to chase the chills that were slowly creeping up them.

"This mystery is yours for now, cousin. You're going to have to keep watch. I'll be busy helping Katie get ready. Whatever you do, don't mention anything being odd in front of her. She won't take it well."

"Mum's the word. With a little luck, we'll get through this day without any problems to spoil her special moment." She smiled as Jessie rushed down the hall yelling at Katie she was on her way. Jessie had her hands full.

Peyton continued to look out the window lost in thought. In her heart, she knew the wedding would be all that Katie wanted it to be. No one in attendance would have any idea that this wedding had several uninvited guests watching the ceremony. Still, the reason for their presence left her wondering why they were there at all.

The loud banging at the kitchen screen door startled her. Standing outside was a young woman with blood splattered down the front of her clothes. Her face was ashen and wet with tears. "Call the police," she screamed. "There's a man stabbing people on the running path. I got away. Some weren't so lucky." She started to sob. "Please hurry!"

Peyton reached for her phone in her pocket to call the station. "Joe, we have an emergency on the path to the marina. Not far from the inn." She gave him the information as the woman told her. "Medical help is needed."

"You've got it." She heard Joe call the report over the radio. "We have a car in your area, and more are on the way. Peyton, sit tight don't try to be a hero."

"Hurry, please." Peyton disconnected the call when the woman ran toward the door.

"I need to go back. My fiancé was fighting him off." The young woman turned to leave.

"I can't let you go alone." Peyton reached for the stack of clean dishtowels on the kitchen table waiting to be put away. "We might need them." She rushed after her without closing the door.

"What would you do if it was the man you loved?" The girl glanced at her with tears streaming down her face. "Hurry!"

Peyton never answered as she ran beside her. The scene looked awful on first inspection and even worse the closer she got. Horrific didn't describe it as she counted the number of wounded from the jogging club writhing on the ground. One person was already dead. Peyton saw their spirit standing near their body as stunned as she must look at the moment. She didn't stop to consider the whereabouts of the attacker. She didn't think about her safety but simply got to work comforting those who were injured.

A man with blood flowing from a wound on his

thigh reached for her hand when she knelt beside him. “This guy came out of nowhere wielding a huge knife slashing anyone he could. There was nothing normal about him. He carried one of his victims into the woods. The man had to be high on something.” She leaned closer to hear him.

“Not like anything I’ve ever seen.” The man shook his head. “He picked the guy up like he was a rag doll and ran off into the trees. The man he carried was twice his size and had put up a hard fight. How is that even possible?” He groaned when she wiped the blood off his leg. The slash appeared deep. The wound was jagged and uneven making her wonder what kind of knife the attacker used.

“I’m sorry.” Peyton pressed the towel down firmly against his wound hoping to stem the flow of blood. “Help is on the way. Hang in there.” Peyton squeezed his hand. “Do you see your fiancé anywhere?” she called to the young woman.

“He’s not here. I can’t find him.” The young woman sank to the ground in a heap and wept uncontrollably.

Overwhelmed by the scene in front of her, Peyton did what she could until the police and medics arrived on the scene. Then she moved out of the way and let them take over.

“I thought I heard Joe tell you to stay put,” Kip, one of the officers she knew well, said as he squeezed her shoulder.

“I couldn’t let her face this by herself.” Peyton wrapped her arms around her middle. “She would have gone with or without me. Her fiancé fought the suspect, or this scene could be a lot worse. He’s the one missing.

What happened here is not normal from all accounts. Since you've worked with Jessie you'll understand when I tell you there is a ghost present, but there is something else more sinister at work too."

"A ghost is not new, but the rest of what I've heard is." Kip glanced at the medic bending near the dead woman. "Don't disturb anything." The medic nodded. "You did a good job here, Peyton, until we arrived. But I want you to leave and let us do our job. We have to secure the area. The suspect is still out there." He tapped her on the arm. "Don't you have a wedding to get ready for?"

"Yes, and so does he." She pointed at Matt, Jessie's fiancé. "You'd better find the suspect. Nothing can ruin Katie and Dylan's day. Especially considering what just happened here. Go find that girl's fiancé and bring him home to her." She motioned at the young woman talking to Matt.

"We'll do our best. Now get out of here." He nudged her gently. "Kenny, make sure she gets back to the inn safely."

"I hope he's still alive when you find him," she said to Kip as she turned to leave.

"I do too." Kip waved her on. "I'm not holding out much hope," he said under his breath.

"That's a heck of a way to start a day." Kenny walked beside her. "I've heard some strange things before from the guys when I worked the desk, but this one might top the list for a crime scene. Of course, most of my knowledge up until today is the classroom variety. It's a lot different when the scene is real."

"I can imagine. I don't know how you guys do it. At least you don't have crimes like this every day."

"Thankfully." They walked up the path by the cottage. "Be sure to keep the doors locked when you leave your place."

"I will. I guess I'd better check them now." She walked toward the cottage. "I usually lock them but not if I'm going to the inn. We were in a hurry this morning when we left."

"Let me check. I'll make sure it's secure. Stay here." Kenny opened the door and walked inside. "Well, the front door isn't locked as you can see."

Peyton waited outside while he checked. "Is everything okay in there?" she called in the open door.

"Yes." He grinned at her when he pulled the door shut. "The answer is no. You didn't lock either of the doors. Matt will need to lecture you both about safety. I'm constantly on Molly about it. It's easy to forget the important things sometimes. Small town doesn't always mean safer. By now you should know that."

"True." She patted his arm. "I'm sure I'll be fine from this point. You need to get back to the crime scene."

"My orders were to walk you to the inn and see you inside. That's what I'm going to do. You're stuck with me until you're back at the inn and you've locked the kitchen door."

"Okay, do your job." She smiled at him. Peyton tried to process what she had seen and heard. Only time would tell what they were up against. Yes, she had seen a ghost, but it was what she couldn't see that bothered her the most.

Chapter 2

Darn, she had left the door open at the inn too, and if Kenny's frown were any indication, he wasn't happy. Not in the mood for another lecture she spoke the first thing that came to her mind. "In my defense, I ran out in a bit of a hurry and didn't think to close it." She walked into the kitchen followed closely by Kenny. "Thanks for walking me back. I hope you can find him."

He chucked her on the chin. "Make our job easier and please stay put," Kenny told her as he turned to leave.

She nodded. "Since you said please, of course, I will." Jessie had trained them well. She smiled to herself.

"Be sure to lock the door after me and call if there's a problem. Jessie would have our hide if anything were to happen to you. In case you're wondering how I know, she yelled it loud and clear on the phone with Matt. Do us all a favor and don't let anyone leave the inn until you get an all-clear from us."

"I'm not sure how I can keep people from going out if they want without alerting Katie that there's a problem." Peyton walked with him to the door.

"Tell them the police are working a case and want to keep people out of the area. I don't think you should have a problem though. Dylan said all the guests at the inn were here for the wedding." Kenny walked out the door. "Remember to lock up," he reminded her.

Peyton watched the door close behind him, and she locked it. She turned around in enough time to see her cousin run into the kitchen at full speed. Her shoe caught the edge of the rug which sent her flying wildly out of control. The only thing that kept Jessie upright was the island her hand reached out to steady on before she went down.

"What were you thinking?" she yelled at Peyton. "You could've been killed." Jessie frowned.

"I could ask you the same question. You made quite an entrance. I thought I might have to pick you up off the floor." Peyton frowned right back at her cousin. "If you must know, I wasn't thinking, I saw someone scared and worried about a person she loved. I didn't want her to go back to the scene alone. I could hear the sirens and knew help was close. You would have done the same thing, and you know it."

"I suppose so. But when Matt called to tell me what happened and told me that you were there, I lost it. Still, I managed to maintain my dignity in Katie's presence. She doesn't suspect a thing."

"Well then, I'm glad she wasn't here to see you just now, or all your acting would have been in vain." Peyton pursed her lips causing her forehead to furrow. "The crime scene was horrific. One person is dead. I saw their spirit. Truthfully it's what I didn't see that has me most worried." Peyton told her about what some of the victims had relayed to her. "How could anyone pick up someone twice their size unless they had some kind of supernatural strength at the moment?"

"I don't know, but you can bet I'll be thinking

about it. Matt has called in a few extras to watch the area. Hopefully, the guy won't interrupt the wedding later."

"The wedding will go off without a hitch. I'm sure of it. Although several uninvited guests are present." Peyton pointed out the window.

Jessie walked over beside her and looked out the window with her. "Wow, when you're right, you're right. There seems to be a gathering of some sorts out there. I wonder what's up?"

"I have no idea. You're the expert. I still have my training wheels." Peyton couldn't believe all the spirit activity in the garden.

"In that case, we both will probably find out at the same time. It's bigger than what took place in the woods, and that is bad enough by all accounts." Jessie leaned against the counter.

"Do you think they're friendly?" Peyton glanced at her cousin.

"I sure hope so. If they're not, we're all going to be in big trouble." Jessie turned to leave. "Duty is calling." She smiled and saluted.

"Spend time with your friend. I'm not going anywhere." Peyton turned once again to the view out the window.

****

Jaxon turned off the highway onto the road into Blue Cove. He wanted to surprise Peyton until he saw several police cars speed past him. He pulled over and reached for his phone. The sound of her voice when she answered reassured him.

"Hi, how's everything in Blue Cove?"

"You'd never believe me if I told you." Peyton

watched the activity as spirits flew in and out of her line of vision. "Are you going to make it in time for the wedding?"

"I'm almost there now. I wanted to surprise you, but I changed my mind."

"Why?" she asked.

"I'll tell you later." He watched an ambulance race by him.

You'll be just in time," she told him.

"In time for what?" he asked.

"To help Matt. I'm sure he could use it and…" Her voice trailed off without finishing the sentence.

"What's going on?" he asked.

"What do you mean? We're getting ready for the wedding of course." She sounded preoccupied.

"I saw several police cars speeding through town toward the inn when I arrived. You're not telling me something." He pulled away from the curb and started driving again.

"Oh that. I'll fill you in when you get here. I can't say anything right now. I don't want to upset Katie with bad news on her special day," Peyton said.

"I'll be there in a few minutes, and we'll talk."

Jaxon didn't like the sound of their conversation. She sounded distracted, but he had also heard fear in her voice. He didn't like it one bit.

He called Matt Parker next. After a few minutes of talking to Matt, Jaxon understood why she sounded distant. He knew Peyton well enough to know she had a lot more she could add to the story. He turned onto the road to the inn. What started as a weekend to pursue the feelings he had for her was about to get far more complicated his gut told him.

****

Dropping what he carried, the man slumped to the ground sweating profusely with the sound of his own heart beating rapidly in his head. Glancing at the young man lying motionless at his feet he winced. Disgusted by what he saw, he wouldn't let himself turn away. The young man's face swollen and battered beyond recognition accused him. He fought to hold the contents of his stomach down. "Don't you dare turn away. You did this, you fool," he whispered aloud. The scratches and bruises on his hands convicted him. The bloody knife on the ground beside him told the story of his sick actions.

Frantically, he ran his fingers across the young man's wrists searching for a pulse. Faint but still beating. He felt a moment of relief. Damn, he didn't like to hurt anyone. *You're completely out of control. Why?* A wave of nausea moved the bile churning in his stomach up the esophagus, burning his throat as it came. Gulping, he took deep breaths trying to push the acid back down. The cramping and pain got worse. He was a man possessed, a predator who did not want to be and had no idea why he had become one. With one more excruciating pain, his stomach rebelled. Relieved of its contents he blacked out.

Chapter 3

Jaxon pulled into a parking space at the inn. Stepping out of the car, he grabbed his suitcase from the trunk. More determined now than before he had talked to Matt a few minutes ago, he wanted to have a discussion with Peyton about rushing into danger. He slammed the trunk harder than he had intended to. "*Slow down and take a breath,*" he reminded himself. Telling her anything would be one surefire way to end their tenuous relationship in the beginning stages.

He stopped on the huge porch, took a deep calming breath, and considered what he could say without upsetting her. If he said what was on his mind, he knew what would happen. What she had done was asinine, but telling her that would be a guaranteed trip to an argument. God knew he wanted to let her have it but only after he held her and made sure she was okay.

As soon as he checked in at the desk Jaxon went in search of her. Walking through the dining room he stopped at the entrance to the kitchen. His breath caught in his throat. She made a beautiful picture. Motionless, she stared out the kitchen window. Far away even though his hand was close enough to touch her with only a few steps.

He waited, not wanting to disturb the moment. The clock ticked away the seconds. He watched for any indication that she was in the room and not having one of her premonitions. "Peyton, are you okay?" he asked quietly.

He knew when she didn't answer that she was somewhere else. He would wait.

****

In the garden, amid the vibrant color and beauty, the stranger looked out of place. He beckoned her to come to him. The smile plastered on his face was at odds with his contorted expression and barely contained rage. He gestured again for her to follow him. Warning signs went off all around her. She shook her head and turned to leave, pausing long enough to check to see if he still stood there. His brown eyes filled with anger that flashed at her when she told him no. No ordinary man, this one could hurt her as he had hurt many others. How did she know that? He shouldn't be here, not on Katie's wedding day. Nor should all the spirits that watched him and buzzed around him. Was he at home among them, or did he even know they were present? He wasn't a ghost exactly, but he didn't seem normal either. Peyton memorized his face. They would run into each other at some point.

He turned to leave but not before he issued the challenge. "We'll meet soon. I'll get my way, and you can't stop me." His voice had an eerie, distorted quality to it. She needed to be ready for the moment which would come. Peyton could count on it.

The man left the garden as quickly as he had appeared. The disturbance he made among the apparitions was palpable from where she stood. Their deafening screeches grew louder as they followed him. Who was he, and why was he here? Only time would reveal the answers.

She inhaled a deep breath. “How long have you been waiting?” she asked, turning to look at Jaxon.

“Long enough to wonder where you were. Care to tell me about it?” Jaxon stood and pulled out a chair at the table for her. She remained standing.

“There’s a lot of activity out in the garden. But don’t tell Katie.” She placed her fingers over his lips.

He grabbed her fingers and held on to them. “I wouldn’t think of it. How could I, seeing as I have no idea what you’re talking about.”

She explained what she had seen. “He’ll be back at some point but not today. Today will be perfect for Katie and Dylan.” She stood beside him, glancing his way as she talked.

“Who do you think he is?” Jaxon asked.

“Good question. I have no idea. He looked like an ordinary man on the street. Average, not handsome. Normal height, not too tall, but with angry brown eyes. There’s something more. He’s extremely strong when he’s angry. Something I’ve never felt before surrounds him, emitting a strange kind of energy. I guess I’ll know soon enough.” Her voice softened. He leaned closer to hear what she said.

“Now I have another question for you.” His hand tightened around hers.

“I figured you might.” She tried to pull her hand from his, but he held on.

“What were you thinking when you went to an active crime scene with no police presence?” His voice had an edge to it. “I’m curious is all.”

“I can’t say that I was thinking at all.” She pulled away and sat in the chair.

“I’m sure you weren’t.” He frowned and mumbled

something under his breath. He reached for her hand again when he sat across from her.

She didn't want to know what he'd said. "In my defense, a young woman whose fiancé was in trouble was about to go back to the scene with or without me. I couldn't let her go alone. That's why I went. When I saw all the injured, I stayed and tried to help until the medics got there. End of story." She frowned.

"You have a kind heart, Peyton, which is one of the many reasons I want to get to know you better." His thumb stroked the palm of her hand. "But if you don't think a little about your safety you won't be around long enough for me to even try."

"You're exaggerating, but I can see how you might be worried."

"Might be, is an understatement. I couldn't rest easy until I saw for myself you were okay. Something tells me it won't get any easier in the future either," he grumbled.

"Probably not, but one can hope." She smiled at him and changed the subject. "I'm glad you're here." She withdrew her hand from his. The movement of his thumb was driving her nuts.

"I am too." He smiled and took her hand back. "What's the plan? I know the wedding starts at six o'clock. What should we do until then?"

"Rescue me from Katie. Lunch or anything will do. I'll let Jessie know I'm out of here." She sent a text to her cousin and got one back.

—Wait a minute we need to talk before you go—

"Hey, Jaxon," Jessie said when she walked into the kitchen. She squeezed Peyton's shoulder. "How is everything out there? You know what I mean."

"Active," Peyton replied.

"Matt told me about all the crazy stuff happening. He told me some of it earlier, but I got upset when he said you were there. I didn't hear anything else he said after that. If I remember correctly, I yelled at him to keep you safe and hung up."

"Give the poor man a break. He can't keep me in line any more than he can you." Peyton laughed. "Sadie passed her feisty personality to both of us it seems."

"That's true. Doesn't it freak you out how much alike we are?" Jessie shrugged her shoulders. "Stubbornness runs through our veins. We're like two peas in a pod."

"Freaky in a cool kind of way." Peyton smiled at her cousin. "Although it does make one wonder if the genes got carried away when it came to us." She stroked her chin. "Did Matt give you an update?"

"They still haven't found the suspect, but they did find the girl's fiancé." Jessie winced when Katie called her name.

"Awesome. How is he?" Peyton asked almost afraid to hear the response.

"Alive but in bad shape. He's on the way to the hospital. Kip is driving his fiancée there now." Jessie sat down on the other side of Jaxon.

"I'm glad they found him alive. I wasn't sure if they would. The scene was bad, really bad." Peyton closed her eyes and tried to shake the memory.

"Matt said that officers will patrol the area in case the guy thinks about coming back."

"I wonder," Peyton mused.

"What?" Jaxon and Jessie said at the same time.

"Probably not." She shook her head.

"Again, I'll ask what?" Jessie said.

"I wonder if the suspect was the man I saw in the garden with all the ghosts."

"You saw someone here? In the garden? And you didn't call the police?" Jessie sputtered jumping to her feet.

"Not literally, or at least I don't think it was literal. Then again, maybe it was. I thought it was one of my strange premonitions."

"We are a pair, aren't we?" Jessie rolled her eyes. "Who would have ever thought we'd grow up to see ghosts." Jessie shook her head when Katie yelled her name again.

"I can safely say, it wasn't on my radar." Peyton shook her head.

"Mine either." Jessie chuckled and looked at her ringing phone. "Katie will not stop until I answer," she said. The call was quickly followed by an incoming text. "It's her, and she's headed this way. You two get out of here, quickly. She'll put you to work if you don't. Don't be gone long though. You both have to get ready for the wedding." Jessie motioned them toward the door.

"We won't." She glanced at Jaxon. "Be sure to lock the door. Kenny made me promise to keep it locked."

"Whew, we just made it." Jaxon chuckled as he closed the door. "Katie was coming in as we were going out." He took hold of her hand, and they ran to the car laughing.

Peyton glanced out the passenger window as Jaxon drove toward town, happy to leave the heavy presence at the inn if only for a little while. The tension lifted, and her shoulders relaxed.

Chapter 4

The peaceful interlude didn't last long enough as far as she was concerned. Jaxon made her feel safe. Once back at the epicenter of spiritual activity, her stress level went up several notches. Jaxon checked her cottage when he walked her home and though no one could be visibly seen, there was something abnormal going on. In this case, out of sight did not mean out of mind. What she couldn't see worried her.

After a quick shower, she grabbed a glass of iced tea and began to dry her hair, a lengthy process combining a large brush and hairdryer that gave her plenty of time to think. She moved the dryer back and forth over the hair wrapped around the brush. Were the stabbings random? Maybe someone high on drugs went crazy slashing everyone on the scene, or was there more to it? Reaching for another strand of hair she began the process again. What did the ghost at the school have to do with what happened this morning if anything? She wanted to believe the first idea that the crime was random, but nothing was ever that simple. Sooner or later the connection would come to light. Slowly she worked her way through her wet hair until it was dry.

The man's appearance in the garden told her there was more to the mystery, and the ghost at the school did too. Arizona had changed everything for her. Her life had taken a turn in a whole new direction. Besides having to recover from being shot, which was no picnic, she also had to deal with the strange new world of seeing ghosts in which she found herself. She hoped this never happened to her sister, Madi. *Please don't let her have this so-called gift.* She would have never made it without her cousin's and grandmother's help. Until a few months ago she and Jessie had shared road trips, shopping, the museums, and theaters of New York. How their lives had changed in such a short period of time.

She ran the brush through her hair. Time to concentrate on the task at hand. Her job at the wedding would include greeting guests and handing them each a small bag of rose petals to toss at the bride and groom, only one of the many special touches the bridal party had worked on the past few months. She had done her fair share of work as she convalesced from her gunshot wound at the cottage. Jessie dropped more than one project into her lap to keep her busy. Peyton smiled. Secretly she had loved it, but she also loved grumbling at Jessie each time she brought one. Guilt is a powerful weapon. Jessie used it on her and vice versa. Did they get that from her grandmother Sadie or from her sons?

All the attention given to details was new to her. Thankfully, there wasn't a wedding in her immediate future. Unlike Katie and Jessie, she never created a book of wedding dreams when she was young. The thought never crossed her mind while she fought to keep herself and her sister safe. Jaxon made the idea almost tolerable, but she felt no desire to rush into anything. She wanted to be sure he wouldn't change on her.

"Hey, cous," Jessie called out as she walked

through the door and rushed to her room. “I have just enough time to shower and get back to have my hair and makeup done.” She kicked off her shoes, slamming her bedroom door. “Sorry,” she called out.

Peyton smiled at the closed door. Poor Jessie hadn’t stopped all day. She would probably crash tomorrow. Swinging her feet up on the coffee table with a glass of tea in her hand, she waited for what would happen next. Her cousin was always fun to watch. About fifteen minutes later Jessie rushed by her, her hair wound in a towel, waving with her free hand, carrying her dress bag over her other arm while a pair of heels dangled from her fingers. Closing the door with another bang she was off. Her cousin was a woman on a mission with no time to stop even if she wanted to.

The quiet of the room seemed soothing at first until the atmosphere changed and the walls seemed to close in on her. Thoughts of the awful scene earlier filled her mind. How were the victims? Would she ever get used to seeing blood? No! She laid her head back on the couch and closed her eyes. One by one the faces of the victims came through her mind followed by the shocked expression of the spirit. She had never entertained the notion of a person having emotions after death. The expression on the spirit’s face made her wonder. Between this event and her experiences in Tombstone, everything she grew up knowing had been turned on its head. The subject was too deep for her mind to wrap itself around now. She might need to have another talk with the pastors at the church where Jessie used to work. They helped her once before to make sense of the strange new world in which she found herself.

The woman who died was young. Life didn't seem fair at times. Sensing another presence in the room, Peyton opened her eyes to see the spirit watching her. "I'm sorry for what happened to you."

"You can see me?" she asked, moving restlessly about the living room.

"Yes, but I'm not sure why I can," Peyton said leaning forward in the chair.

"What happened? Why me?" The groans of sorrow rose with each question. "My family?" She sobbed. "It can't end like this."

Peyton had no idea how she could understand her. They were not words that she heard as much as odd sounds and thoughts filled with anguish. Much like a toddler expresses themself. Odd and yet she was drawn to the spirit's cries. "I'll try to find out who did this to you for your family." Peyton found peace in speaking the words aloud. Ripped from her life only a few hours ago by a murderous act, the young spirit had to make peace with the new world in which she found herself. Peyton shook her head. Fanciful thinking on her part or maybe not, only time would tell. A phrase that came to mind more often than she would like lately.

****

Jaxon reached for his tie. Not one of his favorite things to wear. A wedding or a funeral were among the only occasions he would pull the few he had out of his closet. Thankfully, he wasn't required to wear one on his job in Arizona. The FBI was a different story. He would need Peyton's help in picking out a new wardrobe as he started his new job.

Peyton still fascinated him. He was never quite sure what to think of her. He had talked to Matt several times over the past few weeks and twice today. He needed help in understanding the phenomenon of the Reynolds girls. Learning how Matt came to grips with Jessie's ability helped. Still, he found himself a bit nervous about the idea of a lifetime of upheaval which his life would become if he married her. For now, marriage was off the table. He wanted to get to know her. Everything about Peyton appealed to him, but he still didn't know what to think about this weird side of her.

Matt's experiences with Jessie were helpful but also gave Jaxon a few good reasons to take his time. The warning Matt gave him still rang in his ears. "If you pursue this relationship with Peyton, be prepared to come face to face with circumstances beyond your control. You'll find yourself feeling helpless trying to confront the challenge of something you can't see or even explain. Try to remember your logical approach to a case, and you should do fine." It was his chuckle at the end that had him second-guessing the whole conversation they had.

For now, it would be one day at a time, or maybe he should say one date at a time. Getting to know her ought to be an interesting if not a slightly disturbing time. What he knew for sure, Peyton was strong, kind, and generous to a fault. Easy on the eyes, she tugged at his heartstrings, and he thought a relationship with her worth exploring. Meaning he would have to convince her along with himself at the same time he could handle it. Okay, maybe it was a bit of a heavy lift even for him.

He slipped his arms into his jacket, straightened his tie, and splashed on a bit of cologne. Opening the door, he walked out into the hall. He had a wedding to get to and a beautiful woman waiting for him to escort her. He smiled, shutting the door behind him. Strange as it seemed, he considered himself one lucky man.

Chapter 5

Jaxon walked down the path to Jessie's cottage. The surroundings suited the Reynolds girls. He smiled at the image of Peyton in his mind. Her standing among the flowers would make a beautiful picture. He made a mental note to take one. His arms swung at his side in cadence with his stride. The painters were leaving the cottage next door. Peyton seemed excited to be moving into the place as soon as the renovations were done. Her eyes lit up at lunch when she talked about picking out the countertop and colors for the walls.

Liam, Katie's brother, and his friend Connor recently moved out of the cottage and into an apartment above their bar. They spent the past few months on the remodel, and the place looked terrific. Peyton took him on a quick tour earlier. She was proud of how Matt had put his touches in their place. Jaxon was thoroughly impressed with Matt's woodworking talents. The craftsmanship took the place up a notch. The entertainment center he had built along one wall was better than anything Jaxon had ever seen in a high-end furniture store. If Matt ever got tired of being chief of police, he could have a business in the remodeling industry. Peyton told him that Matt considered working with wood his therapy. All Jaxon knew was Matt's work was amazing. He would love to have his help in a place.

After all that happened to her in Arizona, he had worried that Peyton would be affected permanently by the experience. She seemed okay to him or at least attempting to come to terms with her new normal. Maybe a bit distracted by the events earlier in the day. At least she hadn't fallen apart on him. Which was a good thing because he never knew what to say.

Instinct told him trouble waited for them both right around the corner. He needed to stay alert. It could be today, tomorrow, or another day. There was no time to let down his guard. Peyton seemed to be in the center of it all again. Nothing about what Matt had told him about the crime scene spoke of normalcy or assured him that it would be simple.

He raised his hand to knock on the door when he saw her. "Wow." His mouth went dry as his eyes met hers.

"Wow, yourself." She held his gaze. "It's amazing how the right suit of clothes can transform a man."

"I could say the same thing about you, but you always look beautiful. That color suits you, and that dress, well I'd better not tell you what I'm thinking." He reached around her and pulled the door closed, checking to make sure it was locked.

"Thank you for noticing. I like it too." She leaned in close to straighten his tie.

He inhaled when her fingers touched his skin. The feather-light touch felt like fire against his skin. "Thank you. I never get the darn thing straight."

"My pleasure." She adjusted his collar in the back. "There, now you're perfect."

Jaxon reached for her hand. "I noticed the painters leaving. It shouldn't be long before you can move in next door."

"Only a few weeks, Katie told me the other day. The floors are being refinished, and the bathroom is getting its final touches. Then Jessie will move in with me for a few weeks while her cottage is remodeled. She's excited to have them get started. Jessie loves her place and can't wait to see it spiffed up a bit. She loves the whole seaside cottage vibe."

"How about you?

"I've always liked clean lines, wood, and chrome, not suited to the whole cottage look but more like my New York apartment. I have something in mind that I can live with and still have it appropriate to the beautiful surroundings of the inn. This will be a vacation rental when I no longer live here. Besides, I'm ready for a change."

"Sounds like a good idea to me. Change can be exciting and freeing." He stopped and held tight to her hand. "Look at this."

"What?" She glanced at him with a puzzled look.

"All of this." He motioned with his free hand. "Katie keeps the inn and grounds meticulous." Jaxon glanced around the gardens. "I'm sure it keeps the property values high."

"Spoken like a true man."

"What do you mean?" He grinned at her.

"Always calculating the monetary value alongside the ascetics." She smiled. "It must be that whole male need to provide thing." She glanced at him.

"Are you saying I'm exhibiting my caveman tendencies?" He chuckled.

"Who me?" She fluttered her lashes. "I guess I am. I kind of like it."

"In that case, I'm happy to oblige." He let go of her hand and flexed his muscles, making her laugh. "Stop right there. Don't move." He walked away and lifted his phone to snap a few quick shots of her standing where he envisioned her earlier. "Smile now. Perfect." He looked at the pictures, showed her one, and reached for her hand pulling her along.

"I need one too." She stopped and pulled him in the opposite direction toward the cove where the wedding would happen. "Stand still." She straightened his tie again, tugging his shoulders to get the right look. "Now it's your turn to smile." She clicked a few shots. He was handsome, and the view of the cove behind where he stood suited him perfectly.

"Did anyone ever tell you that you're bossy?" he asked.

"Shh." She placed her finger over his lips. "I'm not bossy. I'm a strong woman who is a leader. There's a big difference."

"You'll have to enlighten me. At this moment, you sound like my sister, and she is bossy."

"That's your description of her but not hers. She would call it survival. After all, she grew up with three brothers who I'm sure teased and annoyed her." She turned him around. "Isn't it beautiful?"

"Perfect." He reached for her hand never taking his eyes off her. "What's next on the agenda?"

"I have to go find Katie and see if she needs anything. You can hang with the guys. I see Matt has arrived, and I know you're itching to talk with him and get more details. It's that detective thing you have going." She tugged on his hand and got him walking toward where Matt stood with Kip and Gary.

He smiled, following her as she weaved in and out of people milling around. “Go do your girl thing, and I’ll do my manly stuff.” He enjoyed the view as she walked away.

“What was that all about?” Matt asked him.

Jaxon told him and then began to ask questions. The answers confirmed what his instinct had told him earlier.

****

“Oh, there you are.” Jessie turned to look at Peyton when she walked into the room. “That misty lavender is perfect with your coloring. Who would have thought it would make your hazel green eyes more vibrant?”

“I did. I made the right choice. Everyone thinks us green-eyed girls have to wear shades of green all the time, but we showed them didn’t we, Peyton?” Katie chimed in. “It fits you marvelously, darling.” Katie extended her hand, dangling her fingers. “I know Jaxon likes what he sees.” Katie chuckled.

“Stop teasing her, Katie. You’re embarrassing her.” Jessie tapped Katie on the shoulder with the brush in her hand.

“I’m stating facts. The man can’t take his eyes off her.” Katie preened in front of the mirror, turning to see another angle of her hair.

The heat began on Peyton’s neck, and she knew her face color wasn’t far behind. “I can’t wait to see you in your dress.” Peyton quickly changed the subject.

“I’ll be spectacular. You can count on it.” Katie smiled. “Peyton, would you do me a favor?” Katie quickly added, “please.”

“Of course, what do you need?” she asked.

“Go up to the attic. I left my Aunt’s handkerchief

on a trunk up there. It's the one she carried on her wedding day, and it's my something borrowed. Jessie and I searched the attic the other day for it. Then what did I do but leave it up there." Katie slapped her hand to her forehead. "Don't get your dress dirty. There's a lot of dust up there."

"I won't." Peyton walked up the stairs and down the hall to the door that led up to the attic. The door squeaked when she opened it.

The stairs creaked when she started up them. Each groan reminded her of an opening scene in a scary movie. Excited, she had wanted to see the attic since she first arrived at the inn. These old places had so many great antiques and collectibles stored in their attics. Stepping on the final step she knew this space would not disappoint, and she had to come back another day to explore the area more fully. She had studied antiques and knew the value of some of the things that others thought of as junk. Her hand reached for the doorknob and twisted it. A strange sensation shot through her fingers and up her arm as the door opened with a squeal.

The sunlight streaming through the small windows turned the dust to golden flakes floating in the air. Peyton maneuvered through all the items scattered about. Walking right past the old steamer trunk her gaze focused on the shelves filled with books along the back wall. Taking one of the books off the shelf she studied the copyright date. Nineteen forty-two. She ran her hand along the spines of the books. "I'll be back to explore you, my friends, another day." Peyton turned, picked up the beautiful lacy handkerchief, and carefully made her way back to the stairs.

"This is beautiful." Peyton handed the treasure to Katie.

"It is, isn't it?" She tucked it in a small secret pocket specially designed on her dress.

"That's the perfect place." Jessie studied the small pocket. The lace made the spot invisible. "The seamstress did an amazing job."

"I know. When I told her what I wanted to be added to the dress she knew just what to do. It didn't cost that much either."

"Let's get you dressed." Jessie held the dress so Katie could step into it. As soon as the dress was buttoned, she turned Katie toward the mirror. "You are beautiful, my friend." Tears filled Jessie's eyes.

"Katie, you're stunning." Peyton watched as Jessie added the veil, adjusting it on her head. "I'd better get to the garden. The guests should be arriving soon, and I need to do my job. I hope you don't mind if I come back while you're on your honeymoon and go through your attic. It's filled with amazing treasures. I want to explore it. Especially the books."

"Be my guest, and have fun. If you find anything of value let me know."

"Thank you. You'll be the first to know." Peyton turned to leave. "I can't wait to see Dylan's face when he sees you. You're perfect." Peyton closed the door with a smile on her face. Dylan was in for a real treat.

Chapter 6

"There you are. I've been waiting for you." Jaxon walked up beside her. "I missed you," he leaned close and whispered in her ear. "You're better looking than these guys."

"Thank you." Her skin grew warm under his intense gaze. Yep, she was blushing. Another Reynolds' trait that she wished she didn't exhibit so often.

"I'll save you a seat. It looks like you're about to get busy." The first guests were headed their way.

"Sounds good. Sit toward the front on the right. It has the perfect view." She pointed to the area.

He nodded. "Seats are filling up fast. I'd better grab ours."

It was time to do her job after the first guest signed the guestbook. "Hello, and welcome," she greeted the guests.

Liam and Connor escorted them to their seats. It didn't take long for the chairs to fill in with family and friends while a few of the uninvited guests of the ghostly variety looked on. Happy no one else knew they were there, she kept busy until there were no empty chairs but the one next to Jaxon. Liam added another row of chairs for last-minute arrivals.

As the wedding party began to line up her emotions began to build. The guys were handsome in their tuxes, and the girls' dresses were the colors of the flowers in the garden. Katie looked gorgeous, dressed in a simple but elegant gown with a fitted waist, perfect for her petite figure. Katie's dad glanced at his radiant daughter with a look of pride on his face. That look made her long for a father who cared even a little for her. *Don't go there.* She shook her head trying to get rid of the wayward thoughts. She made her way to where Jaxon sat and slipped into the seat beside him as the music began to play. Glad she had grabbed a tissue, she dabbed at her eyes already getting misty with tears.

"Weddings always make me cry. I have no idea why. I don't know if it's because they make me happy or sad," she whispered. She wiped the tears rolling down her cheek.

Jaxon reached for her hand as the wedding procession began. "I'm sure it's a girl thing. My sister does the same thing. I'd say today it's because you're happy."

Pastor Kevin, Dylan, and Matt got into position near the arch at the front with the cove as the backdrop. As the music began, the procession of groomsmen with a bridesmaid on their arms started. Peyton knew the minute Jessie started down the aisle because Matt's eyes lit up exposing his feelings for her cousin for all to see. The love exchanged in their glances filled Peyton with hope.

Jessie looked gorgeous, and Matt gazed warmly at her. But it was the look on Dylan's face when he saw Katie that sent the tears that had been building in her eyes spilling down her cheeks. Katie beamed and sparkled. In her heart of hearts, Peyton believed there was nothing as romantic as the look on a groom's face seeing his bride coming toward him for the first time. Dylan's love visible on his face made her sigh within. Katie had been adamant about not having pictures of her and Dylan taken together before the wedding. She wanted this moment. It was worth it.

She wiped her happy tears away and noticed Jessie was busy doing the same thing. Katie spoke the vows she had written, while Dylan set every woman's heart aflutter with his promised words to his bride. A romance novel couldn't get much better than this. The setting, the flowers, the music, and the couple made it one of the most memorable weddings Peyton had ever been to. The only thing missing to make it perfect was her sister Madison. She was on duty at the hospital this weekend and couldn't get away.

In the end, it was the kiss that stole the show. Dylan got more than he bargained for with his pint-size bride. He bent his head to give her a chaste kiss, but she would have none of it. She pulled his head down and planted a big one that went on until all the guests were chuckling. Peyton could relate to the rosy blush that Dylan sported as he walked the aisle with his wife by his side.

Katie stopped at the edge of the runner and turned around. "He's all mine!" she shouted. "Now it's time to party."

"I'll be back in a few minutes." Peyton slipped out of her seat past Jaxon. "I have to give Katie's list to the photographer.

"I'm not going anywhere." He touched her hand.

While the photographer checked off Katie's list and took pictures, the guests were encouraged to make their way to the reception and enjoy the appetizers that were waiting for them.

Peyton laughed at the antics of the groomsmen making the photographer's job a bit harder. The pictures would be awesome with the cove as a backdrop in some and the gardens in others. She had to have a copy of the picture of Katie and Jessie together by the roses. Their friendship was a special one. Every girl should be so lucky to have a special best friend.

****

Jaxon walked up behind her leaning close. "What are you thinking about?"

She leaned back against his chest while encircled in his arms. "How fortunate my cousin and I have been to have a best friend that knows and loves us. Our lives have been richer for it."

"Friends are good, but do you know what's even better?" he asked.

"What could be better than a best friend?" She turned in his arms to glance at his face.

"Take a look at Matt and your cousin or Dylan and his bride. I'm sure you'll catch my drift. At least I'm counting on this evening to give you a clear picture." He winked at her.

"Am I allowed to grade you on how well you get the message across?"

"That depends." He grinned.

"On what?" she asked.

"Well, let's see. It depends on if you're a stickler for the perfect answer, or will you grade me on a curve?"

"Hmm, I'll have to think about it." She smiled at him coyly. "If you were one of my students"—she tapped her fingers against his chest—"and if you did your best, I would take that into consideration."

"No sweat, you can count on it." He grabbed her hand. "What's more romantic as a setting than the wedding of your friend?" He let her turn and watch the photographer finish the photoshoot. The woman was taking some great shots, Jaxon thought. Content to hold Peyton in his arms, he was happy to stand there and watch with her.

"When do you have to go back to Arizona?" she asked.

"I'm here for a few weeks. I have to look for a place, find out the office I'll be working out of, and spend some time with you if you don't mind." He rested his chin on the top of her head. "Why, are you in a hurry to get rid of me?"

"Not at all. I have some places I want to take you if you want to go with me?"

"I'll go with you anywhere. Right now, we should probably follow the wedding party to the reception." Reluctantly he let go of her as he let his arms go slack. Then he reached for her hand. "My car or yours? Technically it belongs to the rental company, but for now, it's mine."

"I don't have one of my own. It looks like it will have to be yours. I would offer Jessie's car, but Matt is driving it. He does every chance he gets."

"Hey, it's a classic. What guy wouldn't want to drive it?" Jaxon whistled as Jessie's red convertible passed them with Matt honking the horn and Jessie waving at them. Jessie's convertible followed the line of cars behind the bride and groom's limo.

"Matt reacts the same way. It's her car. Maybe that's the real reason he wants to marry my cousin."

She glanced at him and laughed. “If you like Jessie’s car, you’ll love Matt’s old pick-up that he restored. I don’t remember the year. But all I know is every guy at the station drools over it every time he drives it to work. All of them have tried to get him to sell it to them.”

“I’m game to see it. What I can’t believe is that you’ve never wanted a car. I couldn’t wait to get my first car. It spelled freedom. She was a beauty.”

“She?”

“A car is always she.” He smiled. “The lines, the chrome, the shine—it all says she to me.”

“It must be a guy thing.” She glanced at him out of the corner of her eye, shaking her head at him.

“You’ve got that right, sister. That first car was my baby. She got tender loving care. I washed her every few days and waxed her until she shined. There was nothing like the feeling of driving into the school parking lot and having the other guys drool. She was a chick magnet.” He grinned. “Sorry, but that’s the extent of my deepest thoughts in high school.”

“Is that right?” Her brows rose. “I had a car in college but sold it when I moved to the city. It was just a car.”

His hand flew dramatically to his chest, and he took a step back. “It’s never just a car, sweetheart. I can see I need to explain the male mind when it comes to his wheels.”

“You can try.” She laughed. “But before you do can I first explain that living in New York I never needed a set of wheels as you call it. The transit system and subway took me everywhere I wanted to go. Besides, I didn’t want to drive in city traffic anyway. Jessie only used hers when we left the city. We shared the cost of the parking permit and insurance. It saved us both a bundle."

"Did you live with your cousin in the city?"

"We lived in the same building. She already had a roommate when I moved there, but we spent a lot of time together. My apartment, a small studio, was on the floor above hers. It was all I could afford. Rent is high in New York."

"So I've heard."

She nodded. "The parking space in the garage was a premium and came with a high price tag too. It took both of us to pay for it. As you can see, two cars were not an option. That's why I've been using Sadie's or Jessie's car since I've been here. But it's one of the things on my agenda to buy. Maybe you could help me pick it out."

"Now you're talking. I'd be happy to." He opened the car door for her and closed it when she was in. He glanced at her while he latched his seatbelt.

"I wouldn't want to be taken advantage of." She fluttered her lashes at him.

"I doubt you'd be in danger of that happening. You're too tough to let it happen. You could always threaten to use that high kick of yours. It's lethal. Do you have an idea of what you want?"

"I have an idea. Something sporty but still gets good gas mileage. I have done my homework. I'll show you my list tomorrow, and you can tell me what you think."

"Of course you have a list. Me, I choose a car by its looks and if it appeals to me."

"I'm looking for reliability as well as the car's appeal. I like my cousin's convertible but not if I have to ride in the backseat. It's not easy to get in and out of. I try to think of all the details." She paused when she saw his smile. "Are you making fun of me?"

"Who me? Never. You're efficient is all, which is something that I'm not."

"That's not true." She shook her head. "Your job demands that you give attention to details. Now I know you're teasing me."

"Honest, I'm not. I'm good at my job, but when it comes to other areas not so much. Look, you saw my condo."

"You hadn't settled in yet is all."

"Sweetheart, I lived there for years and didn't do more than I had to."

"Well it looked okay to me, and it was neat and clean, which is at the top of my list." She paused. "Maybe an interior decorator could have helped you out a bit." She laughed.

"Neat I can do, decorate not so much. I'm ready to celebrate. How about you?"

"I'm ready for the meal. I'm hungry." She slipped off her heels, wiggling her toes for a moment.

"I could use some food too." He started the car and followed the other cars toward town and the reception. He glanced at his beautiful date. The guys would be lining up to dance with her, but not tonight. This evening belonged to him, and he didn't want to share. He didn't have much time, and he still had some work to do to convince them both.

Chapter 7

The marina lights cast a warm golden glow, welcoming them as they pulled into a parking spot. Peyton stepped out of the car when Jaxon opened the door. She took a deep breath. "I love the ocean air. I can sit here by the hours and watch the boats be rocked back and forth by the gentle waves. Of course, in a storm, it's a different story," she said as she exited the vehicle.

"I get it. I spent lots of time at the beach as a kid. I haven't got to the shore often enough the past few years. My family used to spend most of our summer vacations at Cape Cod or the Jersey shores." Jaxon reached for her hand. "Of all the things I missed the most living in Arizona it was this." He took a deep breath. "There's nothing like the smell of the sea and the sound of the waves lapping the shore." He smiled at her. "We should join the party. It sounds like it is going strong already."

She stopped abruptly, tugging on his hand. "Look at the sky." She pointed skyward at the last shades of intense pinks and oranges of the setting sun. Peyton snapped a picture of him and slipped her phone into the small evening bag she carried.

"I've got used to the sun setting over the desert with the cactus and palm trees. There's something to be said about an Arizona sunset. The sky is amazing there."

"I remember how beautiful they were." She glanced at him. "This is an ideal night for a wedding celebration." Peyton tilted her head to look at him. "Sharing it with you makes it even better." She waved at Reba, her grandmother Sadie's best friend, getting out of her car. Her husband Lawrence looked handsome in his suit as he held the door for her.

"From where I'm standing, it's perfect." He glanced at her.

"Wait until you see the inside." She held tight to his hand and pulled him along beside her. "We worked hard."

The reception had all the earmarks of a well-planned event. She knew because she had worked alongside her cousin to bring it about down to the last detail. The ballroom sparkled with flickering candlelight against cut crystal, while the view of the cove from the floor-to-ceiling windows gave the room a romantic setting. The wedding cake was a work of art created by Molly, along with the cupcake tree on each side of the cake. The flower arrangements brought the fragrance and colors of the inn's garden to the tables.

Locating their name cards, they had no sooner got seated when they stood again to cheer the arrival of Mr. and Mrs. Dylan Mitchel. Katie worked the room greeting guests like a pro until the evening's festivities began. The Chowder House catered the meal, and Roger Blackman was there to make sure everything went smoothly. The food was superb. Peyton's chicken was excellent, moist and not dry. If an empty plate was any indication, Jaxon also appreciated his prime rib.

Peyton found herself crying when Katie danced

with her dad and Dylan with his mother. Grateful for the tissue Jaxon pressed into her hand, she wasn't sure if the tears were because of the dance or seeing both parents happy for their children's happiness. Reminding herself once again of something else she would never experience. She dabbed at her eyes and forced a smile.

Between toasts, great music, and lots of dancing Peyton enjoyed herself. Watching Katie and Jessie taught her the lesson of how to let herself go and have a great time. They wouldn't let her retreat for a minute, and she was having a blast. The only issue she had was Jaxon had been commandeered by Sadie, Reba, and several others. He wasn't living up to his promise. Of course, it didn't help that every time he wasn't dancing she was. It was time to take matters into her own hands.

Peyton strode toward him, grabbing his hand when she reached his side. "I do believe this dance is mine." She tugged him away from the group of young ladies who stood around him.

"Thank you." He pulled her into his arms when the band began to play a slow song. "Someone up there is on my side." He gazed into her eyes. "All night I've watched you dance with every single guy in this room. Finally, when I get you in my arms the perfect song is being played."

"You're such a romantic." She playfully swatted his arm. "It didn't look to me like you were suffering or wanted to be rescued. You had your own fan club." She smiled despite the stab of jealousy clouding her thoughts.

"I could say the same thing about you. Truth is the only girl I wanted to be with tonight was you. Everything seemed to be against it, but now I've got you, and I'm not letting go. I have something to prove." He turned her and pulled her back in close.

"I've been waiting. Prove away." She laid her head against his shoulder and swayed with him to the music. His arms tightened around her, and for now words were no longer necessary.

As the song ended Jaxon held on to her hand. "Let's go for a walk. It's warm in here."

"Looks like everyone has the same idea." They followed a group of couples heading outside to cool down. The slight breeze blowing over the water felt wonderful against her clammy skin. They sat on an empty bench with a view of the water shimmering in the moonlight.

"Matt is concerned about what took place today. They have no suspect. Do you think it'll be safe to stay in your place tonight?" Jaxon asked.

"I won't be alone. Jessie will be there. And besides, you're staying at the inn. I can call if I need you." She rested her head against his shoulder. "It's a beautiful night isn't it?"

"Are you trying to change the subject?" he asked.

"Yes. It's been a strange day. I saw a lot that I'm trying to forget and some that I'm still trying to figure out. Right now, all I want to do is to enjoy getting to know you. We can talk over everything else tomorrow."

"Sounds fair enough. I should be the one saying those words to you though. I can't promise I won't stray back to shoptalk as the evening wears on. It's the cop in me, and I'm used to hanging around other cops." He put his arm around her shoulder and pulled her close. "When it comes to dating it's safe to say I might be a bit rusty." He grinned. "What do you want to know about me? I'm an open book."

She asked questions that he answered candidly. He took his turn asking her too. Comfortable with him she shared parts of her life with him that she had never told anybody else. Except for maybe her best friend Destiny or her sister Madison. After they danced a few more dances, Peyton was sorry to see the night end. She liked him. He made her want to dream and believe in the impossible. A good feeling for a girl who had never seemed to measure up to the high expectations that she placed on herself.

Chapter 8

Later, back at the inn, Jaxon walked her home. He checked the cottage out of his concern and then kissed her goodnight. And what a kiss it was. She sighed, leaning against the door reliving the moment when he framed her face with his hands. Never taking his gaze from hers until his lips claimed hers. Wowie, zowie she could still feel the effects of his kiss down to her toes. Peyton kicked off her shoes, walked dreamily into her room, and changed into some comfy clothes. Grabbing a glass of iced tea from the kitchen, she sat on the couch reaching for the remote when Jessie came in the door.

"I'll join you in a few." Her cousin raced into her room closing the door behind her. She returned a few minutes later wrapped in an oversized pink, fluffy robe and plopped down on the chair across from her.

"Are you cold?" Peyton snorted.

"Are you kidding me? I'm burning up."

"Then what's with the robe?"

"Once I got the dress off, I didn't have the energy to put anything else on. Katie gave me this. I think I look like a big serving of cotton candy in it." Jessie laughed. "I have no idea what she was thinking."

"It's unusual, especially for summer. Still, you're pretty enough to pull off the look."

"Thanks, I think. Is that what they call a

backhanded compliment? I'm not sure it's a good look for me anytime." Jessie leaned her head back against the chair, rubbing her temple.

"Maybe it would be okay in a blizzard." Peyton chuckled. "One thing for sure, you look warm,"

"I won't be for long. I cranked up the air. You'll be wishing you were wearing it soon."

"Jess, you did a great job as maid of honor. The wedding was perfect down to the tiniest details." Peyton curled her legs under her. "I had a great time."

"It was exactly right for Katie in every way. I had fun watching her. It will be strange to see my friend a married woman. I'm happy you're here. I love late-night chats, and I'll miss that most with Katie."

"We've had some great times, but if I know Katie, she'll have those chats with you—" Peyton paused. "—speaking of Katie, do you think she suspected anything that happened earlier?" She rubbed her arms while pulling the throw around her.

"See what I mean. I'm comfy now." Jessie paused. "Katie knew something was up but not any of the details. I know she had no idea that there were ghosts at her wedding. She would have come unglued if she had." Jessie grabbed the pillow and hugged it to her chest. "What do you think is coming? It has to be big. The supernatural activity in the garden was seismic."

"Don't ask me. I'm new to this, but I have plenty of questions. For example, when I went to my job interview this past week, I saw a ghost there. The spirit was a little girl, and she seemed to be lost and looking for something or someone. Is she connected with what happened today, or is it something else altogether? Another thing, earlier when I went up into the attic for

Katie, I felt something there. I can't explain it, but part of the answer is in the attic. I'm sure. Although I have no idea what I'm looking for."

"Smart thing that you got Katie's permission to snoop around up there. Have you talked to Jaxon about it?" Jessie asked.

"I haven't had the time. I mentioned a few things I saw, but I haven't discussed much with him. We're going to spend the next few days together. Hopefully I'll get a chance to talk to him about it. I want to know what happened to the guy that stabbed those people today. I'd also like to know, how could one of the suspects in our last case have the same DNA of a man who had died months before?" she mused. "Mysterious."

"I might have an answer for you on your last question." Jessie stood and walked to the desk. She pulled several papers out of the drawer. "This is the report from our last case when I went through the portal. Remember I told you about how Skylar jumped into another person's body. Here is a copy of the report that we couldn't add to the police file. No one would ever believe it. You can ask the men listed in this report. They know what they saw. The doctor that declared Garrett Massey's death at the hospital is major. He has no idea how the man walked out of there alive. He also had no idea whether it was Massey or Skylar in Massey's body. He only knew both men had died."

Peyton read the report. "Wow, what do you think this means? Is Skylar still jumping from body to body or is it Garrett? This is way too weird for me. It makes the coroner's report in Phoenix important. I'm curious to hear what comes out in his report."

"I wonder what people would think if they heard our conversation. Do you find it strange that we talk about ghosts like some people talk about going to dinner?" Jessie asked.

"They would lock us up. I wonder about it every day. Like you, I still find it hard to believe. These last few months of spirits and murders have been strange. Not something I could have imagined at the beginning of the year. But I'm coming to terms with it." Peyton rested her head against the back of the couch. "Only think, a year ago all we had to talk about was Broadway shows and where to go for dinner or maybe our next road trip. Now look at us," she said with a tinge of sarcasm.

"Sorry, cousin. As far as the coroner's report you're waiting on, I have no idea what he'll find or if he'll even tell you. But I think this current case is yours and not Matt's and mine. Maybe it's the welcome message to Jaxon and you to the area. I'll be here if you need me. Right now, I'm too tired to think. This wedding kept me busy for the last couple of months, and what I want now is a break and to take a step back. I need time to hang out with Matt without any ghosts, wedding plans, or anything else. Just so you know, this wedding makes me want to stay a fiancée for as long as I can without all the work of marriage."

"I hear you. I want to enjoy getting to know Jaxon to see if there is anything between us. Plus, with all these new ghost sightings, he had better be sure he's okay with it. The ability or curse, depending on how you look at it, doesn't seem to be going away any time soon." Peyton shivered. "It's freezing in here."

"What? I'm not cold at all." Jessie laughed. "Seriously, I know my guy has his struggles with it. We have worked through a few issues and probably aren't done yet. That's another reason I'm in no hurry to get married. I don't want to ruin Matt's life. He's a great man, and I don't want him to wake up someday after another strange occurrence and wonder what he got himself into."

"What are we going to do?" Peyton sighed.

"What do you mean we? I'm going to do nothing but go to bed and rest for at least a week." Jessie stood.

"I don't believe you for a minute. You're like me. You won't be able to let it go. If I know you there will be no sleeping for you until you figure it out." Peyton turned on the TV. "Please turn the AC down. "It's cold."

****

He slithered through the darkness having no idea where he was going. His legs were losing strength, his palms were sweaty, and his heart was beating too rapidly. If he didn't do something soon, it would be all over for him. Like the blood that dripped from their bodies, life was fading in his. He had the answer at his fingertips, but he couldn't get to it. Even after he had killed for it. When had he got a conscience? Damn. Why did it have to be now? He should have taken from the body what he needed. Instead, he beat the guy senseless and left him to live. The way the young woman looked at him made him have to face what he had become. Not a pretty image, a sewer rat roaming and stealing what didn't belong to him.

****

Jaxon leaned back against the headboard and

flipped through the channels on the TV looking for the sports channel. He stopped channel surfing when it landed on the shopping network. He paid no attention to the host or what he was watching. His mind was lost in thought. At the top of the list was the night he had shared with Peyton. No amount of planning could have arranged a more perfect evening. Especially the kiss. It had dazed her, she trembled in his arms, but her response surprised him. He couldn't stop smiling. The evening worked out the way he had hoped. Even though the day had strange elements to it, he was happy with the progress he was making with her. Peyton trusted him and told him more about herself than she realized. The more he got to know her the more he liked her.

Chapter 9

Peyton's phone woke her up. She glanced at the clock. Almost ten. She shoved her hair out of her face as she answered. "Hello." She sounded groggy, maybe because she was.

"Good morning. I hope I didn't wake you," Jaxon said.

"I needed to wake up. It's getting late." She sat on the edge of the bed.

"Is it safe to assume you haven't eaten yet?" Jaxon asked.

"You'd be correct in your assumption. I'm still half asleep. Why?" She looked at her disheveled appearance in the mirror.

"There's quite a spread at the inn for Sunday brunch, and I thought you might like to join me."

"Not cooking sounds good to me. I'll meet you as soon as I can. If you're hungry start without me." She made her way toward the bathroom. "I'll hurry."

"Take your time," he told her.

"I'm hungry. Hunger is a great motivator for me." She reached for her brush, working the tangles out of her hair as they talked.

"I remember that about you. In that case, I'll see you soon." He chuckled.

"In a few." She hung up and continued to work on her appearance. A while later and one last glance in the mirror she was ready to be seen. She almost walked right past him.

"I thought I would wait for you out here," he called out.

She jumped at the sound of his voice. "I didn't see you sitting there. I was in a hurry to find you." She stopped.

"I noticed." He stood, walking toward her. "Besides it being a beautiful morning, it's a bit quieter than the inn right now."

"I forgot all the wedding guests are still there." She patted his arm. "I often come out here or down near the cove when I need a moment to myself. The inn has a private beach area for its guests. I'll take you there later. It's a beautiful place to relax and so are the gardens—except for when it's filled with unwanted guests," she muttered under her breath. Spirits were still active this morning.

"I know I'll regret asking this question, but here goes anyway. Who are the unwanted guests? Bugs or pests?" he asked.

"Yeah, something like that. Of the spirit variety. You can't swat them with a flyswatter to get rid of them. I can't figure out why they're here."

"I knew there wasn't going to be a simple answer." He frowned.

"Sorry about that. These strange problems seem to come with me. Do you still want to have breakfast with me?" She gave him a sheepish look.

"What do you think?" He grabbed her hand. "You can't scare me off that easily. Remember, I'm a big tough guy here to keep you safe." He flashed her a smile.

"It's not like I couldn't use a big strong man in my life right now." She glanced at him. "Jessie and I agree. Something big is about to happen. She seems to think the case is yours and mine. I guess we'll see about that."

"I'm not sure how that can be. I'm only in the process of moving here." Jaxon shrugged his shoulders.

"Your guess is as good as mine. Jessie seems to think it is, and she usually knows. I'll tell you everything we talked about last night. We were up late going over everything. That's why I slept so late this morning." Her stomach gurgled.

"Sounds like the perfect excuse to sleep in. I'm sorry that I woke you, but I'm not sorry that you're here." He held the inn door open, and they walked into the dining room.

"It smells heavenly and as you've already heard I'm hungry."

"Our secret." He smiled when her stomach growled again. After looking over the buffet tables, they started filling their plates. Peyton followed him to two of the empty chairs.

"The inn is known for its amazing Sunday brunch. I've eaten here a couple of times." She placed her napkin on her lap.

"You won't get any complaints from me. Everything I've had here has been great." He smiled at her. "I will miss the hot and spicy food from the Southwest. It's not readily available on the east coast."

"I know one thing you won't find is a Navajo Taco. I've looked." She sipped her coffee. "I still think about the place you took me to for my first taste in Phoenix. I loved the frybread."

"One of my favorite places." Jaxon took a bite of an egg casserole. "Dylan and Katie should be on their way to Hawaii by now."

"How did you find out where they were going? Dylan didn't tell anyone so Katie would be surprised."

"Matt told me. He said it was hush, hush. He had to work to keep it from Jessie because he was afraid in her excitement she would let it slip. She tried hard to get it out of him."

"My cousin is good at ferreting out information, but so is Katie. She's a master. If Jessie knew, then Katie would have found out for sure. I'm amazed Matt could hold out against her pleas and blue eyes." Peyton popped a grape in her mouth. "Which reminds me, I need to fill you in on what's been happening to me the past few days." She explained about the ghost at the school and all that she had talked over with Jessie. "Remind me to let you read the report that Jessie let me read last night. It left me with more questions than answers."

****

After they finished eating, Jaxon's mind shifted into overdrive. Their conversation continued as they walked to the cottage. He sorted through the story she had told him. He was intrigued, but he had no idea how he could help. This was Matt's case. He needed to talk to Matt and Tom Maxwell, his new boss, about what she told him. What he wanted right now was to read the report. There didn't seem to be an easy way to distance himself from any of this if Peyton was in the center of it.

"You're quiet. Is everything okay?" she asked as they walked side by side.

"What you told me has me thinking is all." He took a quick look at her. I'm curious about that report."

"Why don't you sit here on the bench and I'll get it for you. It's too nice of a day to sit inside."

He watched her walk away. She was a mystery to him. Normal, beautiful, and strange all at the same time. He wasn't ready to run yet, but he wondered at times like this what he had gotten himself into.

"Did you miss me?" She sat beside him and handed him the papers.

"Of course." He began to read the report. When he finished, he remained silent.

"Well, what do you think?" Her foot tapped impatiently on the ground.

"Wow." He shook his head. "I didn't see that coming." Truthfully, the report blew his mind, to put it mildly. Matt had mentioned some of it to him in a previous conversation, but the details were astounding. How did any of it fit into what Peyton had told him? "Remember, I have to go back to Arizona to finalize my move in a few weeks." He reached for her hand. "But until then if Parker and Maxwell say I can, you can count me in. I'm hooked." He handed her back the report. "What's next on our agenda?" Did he want to know?

"I think we should chill and watch a movie. Tomorrow looks to be a busy day for both of us."

"Works for me." He stood when she did and followed her to the cottage.

****

Hidden from view he watched the young couple. How were they connected? The woman concerned him a lot. Unusual energy seemed strong around her and the other woman who lived in the same house. He knew one of them had crossed through the portal. With his great attention to detail, he had learned about it. She had outmaneuvered another traveler before him. The voice in his head warned him about her. Was it possible there were two of them now? It seemed strange to think of others. But there were none like him.

He still wasn't sure how he had become this person. The last memory he had before he awakened to a new reality was feeling dizzy, hot, and stopping his work to rest. When he awakened, it was like that person never existed. He didn't know what happened or why he had this constant voice in his head telling him what to do the last few months or had it been longer? Maybe it had been years. He had no idea. All he knew was that he went from a law-abiding citizen to a person whom he no longer recognized. Powerless to stop what was happening to him, he had become complicit and guilty of unthinkable crimes. With strange memories all jumbled up in his mind he had no idea who he was or where he came from.

Chapter 10

The next day, Peyton needed to run by the school in Pinedale to drop off a copy of her college transcript and job history that they had requested. Jaxon wanted her to wait for him to go. He had left early for an appointment with Tom Maxwell. She wasn't sure if he wanted to go with her or he was concerned for her safety after their talk yesterday. Although she loved the school in Hanover, Pinedale called to her. Maybe it was what Reba said about situations making room for her gift. It was still hard for her to think of these experiences as a gift. Being positive in the face of her new normal was something still to be learned. One minute she felt okay with her ability to see ghosts, and in the next she was certain she had lost her mind.

The reason the school at Pinedale piqued her interest had to be the little girl's ghost. She intrigued Peyton. She made her think of her sister when she was younger, fueling the protective nature in her, compelling her sense of duty to help the little girl just like she had watched over Madi for all those years. She shuddered to think what would have happened to Madison if she had been on her own.

The school building itself was old but architecturally interesting. Three stories of red brick with a tan brick framing out the windows, it was an imposing structure. Several eaves in the roofline and chimneys added to the mystery of its appearance. Built in the early nineteen-hundreds, the history behind the building and when it was remodeled into the present-day school for special needs kids and adults piqued her interest. Maybe the library or even one of the books in the attic at the inn could fill in some details. Beautifully maintained, the lush green grounds were tended with care and welcomed visitors. The atmosphere, however, was a different story. Charged with a strange presence that Peyton couldn't name. The whole ambiance should be a deterrent for her, but it wasn't. If they offered her the job, she would take it in a heartbeat. Jessie would get it, but Jaxon probably wouldn't. If she accepted the position, she'd be off to the races again. Only this time she didn't want to get shot. She winced even thinking about it.

The tea kettle whistled, and her toast popped up at the same time. Placing the bread on a plate, she buttered it and topped it off with strawberry preserves. Yum, her favorite. All normal morning activities for her. But today a different sensation crept over her while she worked. Someone or something was observing her, and they were nearby. A man. She could feel his thoughts even if she couldn't see him. Grabbing a cup, she placed her favorite tea bag in and poured the hot water over it. The smell of cinnamon soothed her rattled senses. There was nothing she could do until he showed his hand and revealed his purpose. She would have to wait. Maybe it wasn't even about her. Adding a few fresh strawberries and a banana to her plate she sat down to enjoy her breakfast. She had a fruit theme going this morning.

"Good morning, cousin," Jessie said cheerfully. "I

need to get to the store early. We've been busy the last few weeks, and I've taken off a lot of time for the wedding. Anytime you want to work, just say the word."

"Busy is good." Peyton took a sip of her tea. "Until I get a job I would love to help out once in a while."

"What I think is we should become partners in the bookstore, or better yet you could rent the building on the other side of my store. The tenant is moving out. You could turn it into a small daycare for special needs kids. That would be perfect." Jessie looked over Peyton's shoulder at her cup of tea. "Think of the fun we could have and all the world's problems we could solve."

"Enticing, but it sounds expensive to me. Besides, I wouldn't have the first idea how to go about it."

"You could learn, and in the meantime you could work for a while to see if you like teaching. And if not, you can work with me." She inhaled the spicy aroma of the tea. "That smells good. What kind of tea are you drinking?" Jessie asked.

"My favorite, cinnamon apple. Something is soothing about it. I like coffee, but some days I want a cup of tea, and nothing else will do." Peyton took another sip.

"You and Reba. Anyway, you've sold me. I'll give it a try. What's on your agenda for the day?"

"I have to run by the school in Pinedale to take them some paperwork. Jaxon is going to take me, and then we're going to look for a car for me. I'll need my own if I start work."

"How long is Jaxon here for?" Jessie poured water into her cup, pushing the tea bag down into the hot water.

"For a couple of weeks, I think."

"I hope he's here long enough to help Matt and especially you with this case. Matt called Tom Maxwell and Captain Stolberg to request permission for Jaxon to help on the murder case while he's here. He wants to find the guy before he hurts someone else. Although, I'm not sure it will be that simple. I let him believe it is until I have to tell him more details. If you get anything, let me know. Between the two of us, Matt's sensible world is liable to explode. That's why Jaxon would be good. He can keep Matt grounded."

Peyton laughed. "One can hope it will work that way. At the very least they could exchange their weird stories about us over their beers."

"Yes, I can see them now crying in their beer." Jessie laughed. "I know logically this case should be mine. I live here, and Matt is on the case already, but there is nothing logical about this one. Don't ask me how I know. I just do." Jessie tossed her hair over her shoulder and out of her face.

"Remember who you're talking to. I get it. I sense it too. At least what I can understand at this point." Peyton used the quiet moment to take a bite of her toast.

"Good, because it's yours. I'm sure I'm right about that little tidbit. I might be pulled in for a moment or two, but it's yours to solve." Jessie shook her head. "I can't believe I'm even saying this to you after what you went through in Arizona. If I were you, I'd get on a plane and go anywhere from the cove and your crazy family." She poured her tea into her travel mug. "I had better get going. The mystery book club meets after the children's story time today. This is one of my favorite days of the week. There are several book clubs scheduled this summer, but this group is so much fun. I love to be around whenever they're in the store."

"Oh, I like that group. They have lively discussions." Peyton smiled.

"That's an understatement." Jessie paused. "Someday you have to hear the story of the book club and a ghost in my store at the same time. It was quite entertaining. She was a whimsical ghost with a sense of humor who could pitch a book like nobody's business."

"This one I've got to hear. Your life should be a novel. I might have to write it." Peyton waved at Jessie as she rushed to the door.

"Have a good day with your hunky cop." She banged the door on her way out.

Peyton sighed, her lips turning up at the corner. Her cousin was a hoot. She loved being near her again. Especially now.

****

Jaxon still couldn't believe what Tom Maxwell had told him. Matt not only gave him a high recommendation but had requested that Jaxon work with him on his case and was granted permission. Technically he still had a few weeks before he was an agent. Tom had heard all about Peyton and the case in Arizona from the agents who had worked it with them. Tom told him that Jessie seeing ghosts he considered an anomaly, but two from the same family changed his theory altogether.

Jaxon had concerns after his conversation with Peyton yesterday. The news today came as a relief to him. He could watch over her for the next couple of weeks. The captain also okayed him to stay extra time if needed. Maybe there would even be enough time for him to take her to meet his family. He would love for her to meet Emmie. He knew Peyton would love her and his family would love Peyton.

It seemed strange to want to take a woman home to meet his mom. He had avoided it for years. Peyton was a different story. Although, he wasn't ready to tell his family everything about her yet.

Chapter 11

The drive to Pinedale took about fifteen minutes. Jaxon thought the surrounding area was beautiful—another small coastal town with lots of charm. The east had plenty of pretty little gems perfect for calling home. Something he thought about a lot more since Peyton had come into his life. He glanced at the lovely woman in the seat beside him. The excitement was written on her face, in the sparkle of her eyes and the smile showing off her dimples to perfection.

"You can make the next left. You'll be turning into the parking area." She unlatched the seatbelt the minute he turned into the school parking lot. "See what I told you. Doesn't it look great?"

He took in the monstrosity as he approached a parking space near the entrance. The foreboding building would be scary if seen in the dark. Though the updated grounds were nice, nothing could change the building's institutional appearance. He didn't want to dampen her enthusiasm while still letting his caution remain in place. His hunches didn't usually lead him astray, and something felt off about this place. Maybe the inside would be better. He would reserve judgment until he checked it out.

"What do you think?" she asked breaking into his thoughts. "You're too quiet."

"You're right. They did a nice job on the remodel."

He paused. “Can I ask you something?”

“Of course, but now you’ve got me worried.” She scrunched her face, glancing at him.

“You don’t need to be concerned. I’m only wondering, why do you want to work here? Is it the only open teaching position available in the area?” His hand tapped against the steering wheel as he talked.

“No. I’ve interviewed at a couple of schools. Why? Something is troubling you. I know that look.”

“Nothing…well that’s not exactly true. It’s a hunch is all. Something feels off about the place, and I have no idea why. I might feel different about it once I get a look inside.” He opened the car door. “As a kid, I would have thought that it was haunted.”

“That’s exactly why I’m drawn to the site. There’s a history that is hidden out of view and a small girl’s ghost that roams the halls. I’d say from the feel of the place there might be more than one.”

“And you still like the idea of working here? Why?” His brows rose with the question.

“I’m intrigued by the idea. I know that might sound odd to you. To me, there seems to be a greater purpose. I saw the little girl because she’s looking for something. It’s no different than seeing the ghost of the murder victim in my room. I’ll do all I can to help her. Neither of the incidences has any connection, or maybe they do and I don’t know why yet. I simply must follow where this takes me. Of course, I might not be offered the job, but I still want to find out the history of the building. It interests me.”

Once inside, the school didn’t make him feel any better. With its freshly painted walls and shiny tile floors it was almost too sterile to be considered a happy place for kids. It seemed like the complete opposite. He leaned against the wall while she handed the envelope with her transcripts to the receptionist.

"I'll see that they get these, Ms. Reynolds."

"Do you feel any better?" She looked out the window as they pulled away from the school.

"Not really, but I'll listen to your reasoning." He stopped and waited for an opening in the traffic.

"To me, it's like a giant puzzle, and I'm working my way around the edge so I can fill in the center."

"Good enough. Unless it becomes dangerous." He would leave it there for now. He turned onto the highway leaving Pinedale behind. Maybe they wouldn't offer her the job and he would have nothing to worry about. "Are you ready to look for your new wheels? I have an idea in mind after looking at your list."

"I'm ready, but I'll probably be doing this for days."

"You want to have a friendly wager?" He grinned.

"I'm listening."

"I bet you'll be driving your new car home tonight. I'm sure I found the one for you."

"What's in it for me when you lose?" She reached for her purse beside her. "Do I need to get this on the record?"

He shook his head. "No need. I'll take you out for a night on the town."

"And if I lose?" She glanced at him and still wore that silly grin. "Should I pay for the night out?"

"Impossible. I can't let you pay for our night out. My mother would never let me live it down. I'll have to think about it." He stroked his chin.

"You can't expect me to wager if I have no idea

what it may cost me."

"I'll think of something. How about a quiet night in at your place? You make dinner, and we'll watch movies."

"You're on. I hope you like to shop until you drop. I love to comparison shop." She heard him chuckle. "You seem sure of yourself."

"When it comes to cars, I'm good. I mean really good." His hand tapped on the steering wheel.

"You'll be losing then because I want to see several of the cars on my list."

"We'll see," he told her.

"Yes, you will."

****

Her famous last words were ones that in retrospect she wished she had never uttered. The first dealership and the first car they looked at had her sold. There was no way she could find a car more perfect for her. Midnight blue, sleek body lines, plenty of chrome, and a plush interior was enough. But the backup camera and the fact the car could parallel park itself put it over the top. He sealed the deal when he told her she was as beautiful behind the wheel as he thought she would be the minute he saw the car. Vain. Jaxon was right—she was driving it home with him following behind her. How was it possible he could know her so well? Right before they got to the dealership Jaxon changed the wager. If she lost, she would have to let him drive her new car for their night on the town. The night out would happen either way.

The car drove like a dream, and she was excited to show it to her cousin. He had been right, but in his winning she had won twice. A beautiful new car and a night out on the town. What an awesome day. The voice message she listened to after she pulled her car into the space beside Jessie's made it a trifecta. The school in Pinedale offered her the job.

"Did I do good?" He smiled at her when he opened her door.

"You know you did. How is what I want to know."

"You inspired me. "He reached for her hand. "I picked the best one imagining you behind the wheel. The minute I drove by the dealership on my way back to the cove after my meeting with Maxwell this morning I knew this had your name on it."

"It's perfect." She traced his lips with her finger. "Just like you are." She stepped back from him. "I was offered the job."

"If you're happy then I'll find a way to live with it."

"At this moment I couldn't be happier." She gazed into his eyes.

"Carry on, you two. Don't mind me." Jessie slipped past them and opened the car door. "Wow, this car is sharp. I can see you in this. It's perfect for you, Peyton. The way you shop I didn't think you would find it for days."

"Jaxon found it." She smiled at him.

"Man, did you do good. Before I forget, Matt wants us to meet him at Angelo's, and he said to be sure you both come." Jessie got in the backseat.

"Sounds good to me." Jaxon glanced at Jessie. "I'm hungry. How about you, sweetheart? Are you up for a little celebratory dinner?"

"I could eat crow." She gave him a flirty smile as she strutted past him.

He reached for her hand and stopped her. Leaning close he whispered in her ear, "I'm thinking of a few more ways that we could make our wager a bit more interesting. Do you trust me enough to jump into the game?"

"I'll think about it. Is there a chance I could win this one?"

"With any luck, we'll both come away winners." He winked at her.

"Okay let's go, guys." Jessie motioned to them to get in. "Get a move on. Matt's waiting, and he'll want to see this new car."

Peyton handed the keys to Jaxon. "I know you want to drive it. No scratches, please."

He shook his head and handed her the keys back. "Not tonight. Blue Cove needs to see you behind the wheel. We're in your hands." He closed the driver's side once she got in. After he got in the car, he looked at Jessie. "It suits her doesn't it?"

Jessie nodded and gave him a thumbs up.

Peyton put the car in reverse and drove past the inn to the road into town. The perfection of the moment wasn't wasted on her. Life could be filled with highs and lows all in the same day and from one moment to the next. But right now, with Jaxon beside her and her cousin in the backseat, this was a high. A day she would remember for a long time. The reason why it had been perfect was because of the man beside her, which both thrilled her and scared her at the same time.

Chapter 12

Peyton awakened with a start. An odd scraping sound sent her imagination into overdrive. Was it outside? The scratching seemed loud enough to be coming from inside the cottage. Trying to focus in the dark, her eyes searched the room while she strained to hear the noise. The scraping sound came again. Nails on a chalkboard, tree branches against the cottage, or someone trying to force open a lock, back and forth it went, pausing only to begin again. She sat up quietly, swinging her legs over the side of the bed. Did Jessie hear it too? She reached for her phone. Slipping on her robe, she tiptoed over to the bedroom door to listen while reaching for a heavy vase on top of the dresser.

"Ouch." She heard Jessie yell out. Followed by something she couldn't hear.

Without thinking Peyton opened the bedroom door and raced toward the lightened living room, ready to go battle and save her cousin. Suddenly she was propelled backward when her body slammed hard into a solid object standing right in the way. The vase in her hand fell to the floor with a loud crash sending shards of glass in several directions. With the wind knocked out of her and no air to scream, she sprawled out helplessly on the floor imagining the worst. She was afraid to open her eyes.

"Peyton, are you all right? You could have killed

yourself." Jessie looked over the top of the chair at her.

She held up her hand trying to catch her breath. "I heard you yell. I thought—I had no idea what was happening to you out here."

"I'm sorry. I couldn't sleep, and I needed to stay busy to keep from thinking. I stubbed my toe." She grinned sheepishly.

"Are you kidding me? You rearrange the furniture in the middle of the night. Is there any other strange or wild behavior you have that I don't know about? I was imagining all kinds of awful things. You need to come with an owner's manual." A giggle wiggled its way out of her mouth despite the angry words right on the tip of her tongue.

"Sorry about the vase. Do be careful getting up. There is glass everywhere." Jessie reached her hand down over the top of the chair to pull Peyton to her feet. "I'll buy you a new one."

"Why? It's yours," she sputtered. "I came this close to knocking out the chair." She snapped her fingers and then dissolved into laughter. "I heard a scraping sound and well you can imagine what I thought," she managed to explain between laughter. "Your life wasn't in danger. You were moving furniture in the middle of the night. In the future could you please warn me before you have one of these moments?"

Jessie nodded. "I tried to be quiet, but I guess I didn't do a good job of it. I often clean the cupboards or refrigerator. Consider yourself lucky."

"Let me help. I'm up now." Peyton helped her move the couch and chairs around. "Whew, I'm done." She plopped down in one of the chairs. "What's troubling you? I do the same thing when I'm worried. Another Reynolds' trait we share. Right up there with blushing and ghosts. Do we have any good qualities?"

"I think we're both nice. That should count for something." Jessie sat on the other chair. "I tried not to listen to Matt talk with Jaxon at dinner, but I still heard what they were saying. I'm tired of cases and seeing things that no one should. I can't turn it off, and I want to. There is something strange going on here. I know you're aware of it too. How is the inn involved? Katie would freak out. All the spirits have gathered here, and this isn't the first time. But I have no idea why."

"Neither do I. One of them was inside the cottage." Peyton rubbed her arms, wrapping them around her middle.

"I know. I've seen her too, and I'm not supposed to. This is your case." Jessie tossed the pillow on the couch.

"Maybe it's our case. It would be nice to work with a pro." Peyton smiled at her.

"Don't go there." Jessie waved off the idea.

"All I'm saying is you might have to help, whether you like the idea or not. Like you've said, you can't turn it off even if you want to."

"What facts do have you right now that I need to know?" Jessie asked.

"Not much." Peyton explained what she knew so far. "I sensed something in the attic at the inn when I was up there the other day. Tomorrow Jaxon is going to spend some time with Tom Maxwell again, and I'm going to explore the attic. Katie told me I could."

"I might have to tag along." Jessie stood. "We should probably get some sleep after you clean up the glass." She laughed.

"Me." Peyton stood, placing her hands on her hips. "Who is cleaning it up?"

"Okay, okay, I'll help." Jessie handed her the dustpan and began to sweep.

****

Matt brought Jaxon up to date on the case at dinner last night. He wished Peyton had paid closer attention, but she couldn't stop talking to Jessie long enough to listen. He couldn't blame her. Between the new car and the job offer, she was flying high. What the investigation had turned up at this point gave him little assurance that this case would be normal. The evening got off to a bad start after Peyton told him she had decided to take the job at Pinedale School. A sinking feeling hit the pit of his stomach at that point, and nothing set well with him after that.

He spent the night tossing and turning. It's not that other cases he had investigated over the years had never bothered him or kept him awake nights. But this one had all the earmarks of becoming stranger by the minute. He went over one scenario after another. How could anyone with a rational mind anticipate the irrational or supernatural? One and same to his way of thinking.

The school troubled him, and he needed to understand why. Determined to find out more information, he wanted to talk to Tom Maxwell. Peyton would be on her own for a few hours. If he found any negative information regarding the school, he would discourage her from working there. She promised him last night to hold off accepting the offer until he had time to check it out.

After arriving at the field office, he spent the morning poring through records on the school for complaints or problems. Nothing stood out. He did learn that Pinedale wasn't just a day school for special needs kids and adults, but several kids and adults lived on the premises. Had Peyton mentioned that to him? He couldn't remember her telling him about people living in the school, although the size of the building could accommodate both easily.

Two more cups of coffee and an hour more digging through historical records he found an interesting tidbit that Peyton would love to know. He made photocopies of the pages. Now to get this back to her. Maybe she would decide not to work there. If he knew her, she'd look at this as the main reason why she should work at the school. Hell. He rubbed his temple. This part of her would probably drive him nuts for the next many years, but he would go there happily.

Chapter 13

Peyton walked into the kitchen dressed and ready for a morning of rummaging in the attic at the inn. “Hmm, the coffee smells good.” She reached for a mug and started to fill it.

“It’s decaf. If you want caffeine, you’ll have to make it.” Jessie reached for her bagel that popped up in the toaster.

“I’ve known you long enough to know it’s decaf in your cream, and by now you know you’ve converted me. I can drink coffee either way depending on who I’m with. Usually, I prefer tea.” Peyton poured in cream and stirred. “Me, I’m what you’d call a versatile coffee drinker. Not a serious one by any means.” She cut a cinnamon bagel in half and put it in the toaster. She lifted her heavy hair, fanning her neck. “It’s already a warm one.”

“It is summer after all, but autumn will be here before you know.” Jessie wiped her mouth with her napkin.

“Then we’ll be complaining about the cold.”

“You’ve got that right.” Jessie pointed to the small jar on the counter. “Be sure to taste the fresh blueberry preserves. Reba gave us a couple of jars of her homemade jam. Wow is it ever good.” Jessie took a bite of her bagel loaded with cream cheese and blueberry goodness. “Made from Maine blueberries. One of these days I might try my hand at making some. Reba said she would teach me. It might be fun and a welcome change of pace."

"You must be tired. I would love to be a spectator when you do." Peyton reached for a napkin. "I love blueberries in any form." Peyton buttered her bagel, spooning the blueberry preserves on the top. She sat across from Jessie with a cup of steaming hot coffee. Taking a bite of bagel, she closed her eyes. "You're right. This tastes yummy."

"I swear we're more like sisters than cousins. I make that same look when I taste something I like. Matt always teases me." She sipped her coffee. "Well, cous, are you ready to do some exploring today? I can't wait to see what's waiting in the attic to enlighten us. Audrey is opening up for me this morning, and Grams will help her hold down the fort until I get there." Jessie took another bite, and the blueberries squirted down her chin. "It's messy but good."

"Doesn't Audrey work at the church?" Peyton asked.

"She does, but only part time. She helps me out whenever I need her and switches her hours up at the church. Today she is going to work there in the afternoon, so it worked out perfectly. I have until noon, which gives us a few hours."

"Sounds good. I know there is something there. Whether we'll find it today I have no idea, but at some point, I know we will.

The gardens were filled with life and something extra that made the hair on the back of her neck stand up. "I'm not sure what we'll find in the attic, but enough is going on out here to keep us busy for a while." Peyton swatted at the fly annoying her.

"Which has me wondering why there's so much activity. Why now?" Jessie asked.

"It has to be connected to the murder, but there must be something we're missing. Unless, of course…" Peyton mused.

"What? Don't leave me hanging."

"What if they're all victims of this guy in whatever time period and form he took?" She shook her head. "Forget what I said. That's even too crazy for me to think possible."

"Not so fast. You might be onto something. We'll have to consider the idea and think outside the box. Nothing that's happened to either of us has any basis in reality. At least in the world we grew up in. From this moment on, we have to think differently about this case."

Peyton laughed. "I knew you couldn't walk away and leave this to me."

"Not entirely, but I still think this is your case to solve. I have no idea what that means for you or me." Jessie patted Peyton's shoulder, her words hanging heavy in the air.

Peyton shivered. An odd sensation filled the pit of her stomach. Nausea with a dose of fear. Whatever awaited her it was bound to be dangerous. "You don't suppose I can toss this one off to somebody else. Anybody?"

"Let's not think about it anymore. The attic and antiques are waiting. Maybe we'll find something of value." Jessie linked her arm with Peyton as they walked toward the inn.

"Have you ever noticed the struggles we often have

to face seem to help shape us for our greater purpose in life? I mean if I had grown up with no obstacles in my path would I be the person I am now?" Peyton opened the backdoor at the inn and waved at Katie's assistant working in the kitchen.

"I've often thought that, but I think the verdict is still out on the person I'm becoming." Jessie laughed. "You're being way too serious for me, cousin. Let's go exploring."

****

Hidden from view, the man followed their progress through the garden. He smiled when they laughed. A rare joyous sensation filled him for a moment. What women found to talk about was always a mystery to him. Mary, his wife—or at least she used to be—could talk for hours. If he were honest, he missed her constant yammering and felt lost without her. She was not beautiful as some men would describe beauty, but to him she was perfect. Her smile could light up a room, and her heart overflowed with kindness which she readily shared with all she met. Hell, why she loved him was another one of life's mysteries. No one knew better than he did that his looks were tolerable at best. Romance, loving words, and appreciation had not come easily to him, but now he longed to tell her those words she always wanted to hear. But there would be no going back now or ever. Even if there was the slightest possibility, he was unworthy of her now.

How had this happened to him of all people? He had always lived a simple life, kept his nose to the grindstone, and out of everyone's business. The first on the job in the morning and the last to leave every night and always invisible when awards for discoveries in his field came around. That was then, but now he was a man possessed, and he had no idea by what or maybe he should say by whom.

In quiet moments like this, he could remember some details of his past. The house—not fancy but he held the mortgage on it—and his wife standing at the door to greet him. Strange scenes of an accident and a minor explosion of some kind with no details of how it impacted him. Disjointed images that made little sense to him but spoke to him of another time when he was a different man. Peace washed over him when those memories came to him, but they were often followed by murky images at the edge of his mind so dark they frightened him. He tried never to go there in his thinking. Still, the memories would come roaring back when he least expected, and then the monster within would rear its head and begin to prowl.

He watched the women until they went inside and of his view. The aura around them was strong. Could they sense him watching them? Why couldn't he move on? Maybe tomorrow he would be free again. But it did not matter anymore. He would never be free from what he had done.

Remorse filled him all over again, but he had no more tears to cry. This was his lot in life for whatever reason. More than anything he wished he could go somewhere and die. He could not even do that right. He had tried more than once, and the beast would not let him.

Chapter 14

"These old stairs are creaky." Jessie took another step, and it groaned too.

"They add to the atmosphere of sleuthing don't you think?" Peyton stepped on the step behind Jessie.

"I can live without sound effects. My nerves are on edge as it is."

"Get with it, Jess, there's always creaky steps or doors in a movie when it gets to the scary part. The music builds, the dumb heroine grabs the first thing she can find to use as a weapon, and then she goes searching the dark house for an intruder. What's up with that? Not me. I would hide."

"No, you wouldn't. You came out of the bedroom with a vase. Remember." Jessie reached for the doorknob at the top of the stairs.

"Oh, yeah. You're right. I should be the heroine in a B movie." Peyton laughed and reached to steady Jessie who yanked her hand back and almost fell down the stairs taking Peyton with her. "Sorry. I forgot to warn you about the zing that comes when opening the door."

"It didn't do that when Katie and I were up here searching through the trunks for the handkerchief."

"Who opened the door?" she asked.

"Katie did." Jessie wiggled her tingling fingers.

"Mystery solved." Peyton stepped in front of Jessie

and opened the door. "Now you can understand why I want to search up here. The atmosphere is zipping, and there is bound to be a good reason." Peyton opened the first trunk and went through it carefully. "Some of this stuff is cool."

Jessie opened the doors of an old armoire. "Peyton, you've got to see this. We could have a costume party. Would you look at these clothes?" She wrapped a feather boa around her neck and placed one of the vintage hats on her head.

"I'm not a fan of the feathers, but the hat is you with your golden curls spilling out. You look like you could be one of the women in Monet's famous garden painting except for your clothes of course." Peyton jumped when the attic door slammed with a loud bang. "Zip, zip, zip. See what I mean."

"I wonder what that's all about." Jessie took off the boa and hat. She bent to open the drawer at the bottom of the armoire, but it wouldn't budge. A second attempt and one hard pull sent her falling backward onto her derrière. The drawer was still firmly closed. "A slamming door and a drawer that won't open has me more curious than ever. How about you?"

Peyton nodded. "Oh, my. Look! Peyton pointed to the shelves filled with books. Books were spinning, dancing, and moving around. Mesmerized, she was drawn toward the motion. One large book flew off the shelf propelling toward where she stood, picking up speed as it whirled closer to her. She reached out to grab it before it hit her in the head.

"Don't open it whatever you do. Something isn't kosher." Jessie yelled out the warning.

"Oh, goodness. What is happening to me?" The

book flew open, and Peyton's words slowly faded as she was sucked into the pages of the book. It fell with a thud to the ground, opened to a page somewhere in chapter one. Jessie dog eared the corner of the page. It might be important at some point.

****

Jaxon had been trying to get the story straight since he had arrived back at the inn and was met by Matt. Jessie fell apart every time she tried to tell the story again. How could Peyton be sucked into a damn book? The whole thing sounded preposterous. He didn't want to call Jessie a liar, but how could something like this happen? If he did say what he was thinking Matt would probably punch him out.

"Jess, sweetheart, you need to stop crying and explain to Jaxon what happened." Matt squeezed her shoulder, hugging her.

"I'll try." A hiccup followed the sob that came out despite her best effort. Matt continued to pat her shoulder. She told him what happened with the armoire. "When I looked at Peyton, she pointed to the books spinning and dancing in the air. Suddenly one flew off the shelf aimed right for her. She snatched it from the air before it hit her in the head. I yelled at her not to open it, but the book flipped open on its own accord, and she was gone. Sucked right into chapter one. This is the book. Once she disappeared, the book dropped to the ground and opened to a page in the first chapter." She handed it to Jaxon. "I marked the page at the corner. This might be a portal that she has passed through, and she may need it if she is going to come back to us." The groan escaped her lips and then the crying began again.

"How is it that she went through a portal and no part of her remains here at all?" Matt looked perplexed. "When Jessie went through the portal she was also here." He paused and then added, "Jessie was stuck in two dimensions."

"That doesn't help. I have no idea what you're both talking about." He frowned. "Words fail me." Jaxon shook his head. He had never heard of anything like this before. "Jessie, give me something to hold onto here. I feel like I'm in the twilight zone. Give me something rational to work with. I'm drowning."

"If I might venture a guess." She glanced at Matt who nodded at her.

"Please enlighten me." Jaxon raked his hands through his hair and plopped down in the nearest chair.

Jessie took the book from him. "I think Peyton has been transported through time. This book holds the key to where and when. As odd as this sounds it may be how she comes back to us too. I'm taking this to my cottage, and I will make sure it stays open on this very page. I'll bookmark it securely, but I'm also going to read it, because the answer is somewhere in its pages."

"Start reading aloud. Three heads are better than one. I've got to know where she is and if she's all right." Jaxon rubbed his temple area. The tension was causing his head to throb.

Jessie began to read. "The year was nineteen-eighteen, and the country was in the midst of a World War that seemed would never end. I found myself the proud owner of a draft registration card along with millions of other men." Jessie jumped up, excited. "Listen! I think this might be a historical story of Pinedale in nineteen-eighteen." She continued reading while Jaxon and Matt listened for some clue as to what happened to Peyton.

****

She had no idea what had just happened. The woozy feeling in her head wasn't helping either. Running her hands up and down her side gave her the proof she needed that everything seemed to be in place. She was standing on her legs—another good sign. Although they didn't feel right. She was afraid to look. Instead, she checked her hands. Her arms were in working condition. She could still raise them above her head. Taking a deep breath, she worked up the nerve to look down at her legs. "Oh my goodness," Peyton said under her breath. Where were her legs? They were hidden under layers of clothing she had never seen before. Not a personal fashion choice. *Think Peyton.* She tapped her forehead. She touched her hand to her hair, and there seemed to be a hat perched jauntily on top of her head. Unpinning the contraption, she held the hat in her hand. Moving it back and forth, she studied it from every angle, running her fingers over the funky feather adorning the top of it. Probably the height of fashion in its day, but why was she wearing it? Through the fuzziness in her head pictures flashed through her mind. Jessie wearing a similar hat and falling on the floor. Followed by disjointed pictures of books whirling and buzzing through the air with her hand snatching one of them before it hit her head. Slowly her memory started returning along with the voice warning her not to open the book and then…she was sucked into the pages. Impossible! Why oh why hadn't she listened and simply tossed the stupid book aside before it opened? No, not her. She had to keep holding it. And now here she stood. Wherever here was. How would she ever get back? She didn't have the book anymore and didn't even know the title.

"Listen to me, girl, you didn't get here by ordinary means. You're here for a reason, and the sooner you figure it out the better you'll be." She gave herself a pep talk. It wasn't helping. Alone, and from the looks of the clothes she had on in a different era with no Jaxon beside her to talk her through the danger, she could easily lose it. The sob caught in her throat. No Jessie or Reba either. She had no choice. Discover the purpose or never make it back to Blue Cove again, which wasn't an option.

Taking stock of her surroundings, she looked for a newspaper to know what day and year it was. What she read in the store window changed everything for her. And when she found herself standing across from Pinedale School the small light that turned on was overshadowed by the fact that it all seemed completely wrong.

****

"Jessie, you understand this better than either one of us." Jaxon motioned between him and Matt. "Tell me what we are up against."

"If it is anything like what I went through, she'll be there as long as she is needed to solve something that has to do with your investigation." She shook her head. "Or what one of the ghosts around her wants."

"Keep reading. There has to be a clue in there somewhere." Jaxon pressed his hand to his chin. "I wonder—no, it's ridiculous to think of it—but no stranger than being sucked into a time portal through a page in a book."

“Can anyone join this conversation, or do you want to continue it on your own?” Matt asked him.

“Jump in at any time.” Jaxon stood and started to pace. “Is there is anything in the book about Pinedale?” he asked when he stopped by Jessie’s chair.

“Why?” Jessie glanced up at him.

“Call it a hunch. I read something earlier that I wanted to tell Peyton about when I got back.” He explained to them what he had learned about the Pinedale School. “There has to be more to the history of that place than what I’ve found out so far.”

“I know just the person who can help. You remember Jeremy. He helped Peyton with your murder case in Arizona.” Jessie picked up her phone to call him.

“Why didn’t I think of him?” Jaxon started pacing again. His mind raced forward with questions he wanted to be answered.

“Sit down. You’re making me nervous. I imagine you didn’t plan on being involved in a case yet nor having your girl disappear in such an unusual manner. Hell, I was a mess when it was Jessie, and part of her was still here. Consider this your new normal.”

“Call him, Jessie. We are going to need all the help we can get with this one.” Jaxon sat down in the empty chair. How was any of this even possible? His job was stressful enough without any of the crazy elements of ghosts and a girlfriend lost in the pages of a book. Hell. Who would ever believe him anyway? He raked his hand through his hair and listened to the conversation with Jeremy as Jessie put her phone on speaker.

Before Jeremy hung up, he promised to get back to them as soon as he found out any valuable information.

In the meantime, Jaxon had to do something. He stood, knocking the chair off balance and grabbing it before it hit the ground. “I can’t sit here and do nothing. Maybe a drive to Pinedale and an afternoon talking to some of the locals might help.” The door closed on his final words. “At least I hope it will.”

Chapter 15

News of the war glared from the headlines of several newspapers ready for purchase at the corner stand. When Peyton stopped to read the column, a man grabbed the paper from her. "Lady, if you want to read it pay for it. A man has got to make a living. No one will ever buy one again if I let them stand here and read it for free."

"Sorry." She opened the ridiculous looking purse she carried and extracted three cents. Two for the cost of the paper and one to be nice. He smiled at her. At least she thought he had, but she couldn't tell because he was wearing a mask. His eyes smiled, and that was good enough for her.

The date of the paper told her everything she wanted to know. The year was nineteen-eighteen. Good heavens. At least her clothing made sense along with the crazy purse. The paper also had plenty of news about the Spanish Flu that was ravaging the country. What purpose could there possibly be for her to be here on this day and at this time? Yet here she stood across the street from the newly built Pinedale Orphanage. She couldn't fathom the answer, but she would soon find out.

Never one to be shy and as long as she was here, she might as well check the building out. After all, it would be her secret that she saw the original back in the day. Who would believe her anyway? Possibly the reason for this adventure would be discovered behind those walls. She took a deep breath, pausing long enough to consider her next move. As an outsider in the year nineteen-eighteen, she had no idea what she would find, but she planned to take plenty of notes.

Starting with the cars. Wow, Matt and probably Jaxon too would go nuts over them. From the small trucks to a classy-looking tour car complete with a backseat, there were some interesting cars. Not one could hold a candle to her new car. A rush of emotion caused her to gulp back the sob threatening to rush out. Gosh, she hoped she would get back to drive it again.

The book was the portal at the inn, but she had no idea if there was one here. She could be stuck in this year forever. The thought stopped her in in tracks. "Don't go there. You'll find a way. There has to be a way back."

The town of Pinedale seemed quiet for the time of day. It could be because most all the stores remained closed due to the pandemic. The same sign appeared in almost every building she had passed. "This business is closed until further notice by order of the Mayor." She looked both ways and crossed the street to be closer to the building. There seemed to be more activity there than any other location in town. According to the paper churches and schools were closed also. Why all the activity at the school then? An ambulance pulled into the parking area, and several people ran out to unload the stretchers in the back. Was it possible the orphanage was used to care for an overflow of influenza patients? She moved closer to the gate to get a closer look.

A car pulled in behind the ambulance. Not just any

car but a black beauty with a cream-colored soft top and a familiar name that she quickly jotted down that caught her eye. One look told her the occupants must have money. The woman who got out was dressed to the nines. Unlike the functional dark skirt, white blouse, and dark stockings that Peyton wore, the woman's clothes were stylish. A little girl tried to get out behind her and was quickly restrained by her nanny's hands. The woman turned and said, "I have to stay with Daddy. Be a good girl for Nanny Fran."

"Don't go, mommy, please don't leave me." The cries became louder as her mother walked away and followed the stretcher. The car turned around in the parking area and drove down the street past where she stood. Peyton could hear the girl's heartbreaking cries for her parents.

She understood her mission. The little girl crying was the ghost she saw walking the halls of the school. That had to be her—and Peyton's purpose for being here. She needed to find out the girl's story and what was going on inside the building. Without further thought, Peyton walked through the gate and into the front doors of the building. The inside looked the same as the Pinedale School in her own time. Newer, of course, but the same drab colors and super shiny floors.

"Thank goodness you're finally here." A large woman dressed head to toe in white thrust a mask into her hand. "Put this on, and don't let me catch you without it on again. We thought you would never arrive. Mrs. Woodson from the boarding house called to tell us about the small situation that had detained you."

Peyton had no idea about anything happening around her or who this woman was. Something told her to go with it, and she would soon find out. "I'm glad she called. I'm here now. What do you want me to do?"

"I want you to sit at this desk"—she pointed to the one by the door—"and stay out of the way. There are too many sick and dying patients in all the rooms. Contagious, you know. You'll have to answer questions for the families coming to check or calling. They cannot visit. Some will be cranky, but there's nothing to be done about it. Rules are rules. You can call a constable if necessary. As I told you during your interview, they're on every floor in the building. I will bring you an updated list of the patient information each morning. There's the phone. Get busy, girl. Don't forget to answer how I told you during the interview. The information is on the desk in case you've forgotten." She pointed to the desk. "I hope you remember the switchboard. I'll take this call so you can get settled, and then you're on your own. You do remember my name is Irma from your interview, don't you?" Irma rushed to the phone, flipped the switch, and began to talk. "You've reached Pinedale Orphanage now being used for Spanish Flu patients. How can I help you?" She looked at the patient sheet. Gave the caller the details about a patient, and then she was off and running.

Peyton took off her coat and hung it on the hook beside the desk. Surreal described her morning. A fish out of water came to mind. The ringing phone took her out of her thoughts and kept her busy for the rest of the day. Everything hurt from being hunched over the desk in the most uncomfortable contraption she had ever had to wear. A corset, better known as a torture device with strings. She had been shocked to see it when she went to the restroom earlier. Sitting all day laced in the blasted thing had been sheer agony. One more reason she couldn't wait to go home to Blue Cove. For now, walking to wherever the boarding house was located sounded perfect to her. How long did she have to sit at this desk? Thankfully at five minutes to five her replacement arrived.

"You're the new girl. My name is Emily Smith, and I'm living at Woodson's boarding house too. I saw you there this morning when all the commotion was going on. Everybody was in a flap if you know what I mean. Sorry I didn't get a chance to introduce myself. I just know we're going to be good friends. Poor Miss Ruth was so sick, and I thought the ambulance would never get there. Kathryn, Mrs. Woodson told me to remind you how to get back since you're new to the area." She stopped talking long enough to take a breath.

Her name was Kathryn. She would have to get used to that. "Nice to meet you, Emily. I would appreciate any directions you can give me. I can't remember the names of all the streets yet."

"Of course, you can't. I'll be happy to help." Emily drew her a map listing the streets and where to turn. "Mrs. Woodson said to go straight home because dinner is almost ready. That is a joke." Emily smiled. "There is nowhere to go right now. Do not get too bored, Kathryn. I'm sure you'll find something to keep you busy."

Peyton put on her jacket and walked out into the fresh air. It felt heavenly against her skin. She adjusted the mask on her face. She followed the directions toward the boarding house wishing she were heading home to Jessie's cottage. What today taught her was that the orphanage was being used for an overflow hospital for influenza patients. They lost several people that day. The nurses and doctors were doing their best, but no one knew how to treat the patients. She also learned she was here for the little girl. Her daddy was one of the patients, and her mother refused to leave his side. Irma, the woman who had hired her, told her the woman would probably get the illness too. What a sad time to be alive. For now, she was Kathryn, and she could not wait to be Peyton again. Oh, and comfortable clothes would be nice too.

Chapter 16

The earth moved beneath his feet. Someone had gone through the portal. How? He had no idea of its location though he had looked for what seemed a lifetime. The monster within him stirred to life demanding, cursing, and commanding him to do what he could not do. Longing many times to go back, he had looked for the way over the years. He would do anything to return to his quiet life. His dreams were becoming more vivid with each passing day. Bits and pieces of memories were returning. Still, he had yet to figure out what this entity living within him was. When did it take over his life? Think, man, think. *You may not be able to go back, but possibly you could find peace and be free*. Vulnerable and lost with only pieces of his past life he wandered doing the bidding of God only knew what. Oh, how he wished he could see his Mary one last time. Pity from others—he did not want any or deserve it. He had shown no mercy on anyone. But deep inside he knew he once used to be a good man.

****

Jaxon left the cottage walking in the garden back to the inn. He had spent the day in Pinedale and learned more about the history of the area. Peyton seemed close to him there. It was as if she was aware of him searching for her. Fanciful thinking for a realist like him, and he couldn't afford it. He needed to think clearly now more than ever. Her life depended on him keeping his wits about him. Sitting on one of the benches, he sorted through what he had learned earlier.

"It's a beautiful evening, isn't it?" A couple staying at the inn stopped to talk.

"Yes, it is. A nice time for a walk," he replied.

"That's exactly what we thought." The woman smiled at him. "Have a good night." They followed the path toward the cove.

Jessie and the ladies had read more of the book. Jessie made notes and gave him a copy. Reading over the notes at dinner, Jaxon had found confirmation of some of the information he had learned throughout the day. He sat back on the bench and looked up into the starry night sky. He could not believe any of the events of the morning were real. Where was Peyton, and how would he ever get her back? Damn. He balled his fists in frustration. Would their relationship always be fraught with strange occurrences? His feelings were already attached, and he could not see himself walking away. And yet this wasn't easy to dismiss. He had to solve this puzzle, but there wasn't a bit of rationale to grasp at.

The cop in him said the picture was all wrong and that she wouldn't return. How could she? His heart was another matter. He wanted to believe the crazy story. Leaning forward on the bench, he rested his face in his hands. "Keep her safe and tell her I'm looking for a way to bring her back," he whispered determinedly into the night. "I promised her I wasn't going anywhere." He stood and walked back to the inn.

Opening the door to the room almost overwhelmed him. Jaxon prided himself on being strong and independent, but at this moment he felt lost. Stretching out on the bed, he laid his head on his hands stacked behind him. "Love has a way of sneaking up on you," his mother used to tell him. "When you least expect it you suddenly meet that one person who sets your heart on fire and you know this is the one." He used to laugh at his mom when she told him that. *Well, Mom, I'm not laughing now. I get what you were trying to tell me. I would do almost anything to get her back. I could use a bit of your motherly advice right now, but I have no idea where to even begin.*

He reached for his ringing phone sitting up as he did. "Hey, Jaxon, it's Matt. Checking to see if you're okay. I know it's hard for us guys to share feelings. If I were you, I'd need someone to bounce ideas off about now."

"You're right about that. There isn't anyone I know who would believe me if I told them anyway."

"Look, it's unconventional, and I had plenty of doubts at the time, but Jessie amazed me with what she found out. I think you'll be surprised when this is over is all I'm saying. I'm here if you need to talk, but in the meantime you need to keep busy. Come to the station tomorrow, and I'll put you to work. You can investigate from this end while she's doing whatever it is she's doing. Dylan's on his honeymoon, and I can use the help."

"Sounds good. I'd like that. Too much time to think is never a good thing. There are too many troubling scenarios. My gut tells me she's okay but my head not so much. None of this is normal. What troubles me the most is I'm concerned the murderer is still in the area. Peyton can ID the suspect. I'm sure of it. And he knows it. He probably is watching the inn, so give Jessie a heads up. He has a vested interest in being here. The question is why?" Jaxon frowned. "Nothing about this case makes sense."

"Welcome to my world. Jessie keeps telling me to keep my eyes on what I can see, and she'll take care of what I can't. Hell, I have no idea what she means half the time. But it's worked out all right every time, and she's persuaded it will this time too. That makes me convinced. I'll see you in the morning. I suggest you get some sleep, and we'll hit the ground running as soon as you arrive."

"Thanks."

"Hey, Jaxon, welcome to the real Blue Cove. Our peaceful little town is nothing like how it looks." He chuckled. "This past year has proven that to me on more than one occasion. At least we can still host a beautiful wedding." Matt paused. "Two things I need to tell you before I forget. Reba told me when I was going through a similar situation with Jessie to listen for her and that she'd find a way to tell me she was okay."

"And did she?" he asked.

"Yeah, she did. Jessie wanted me to tell you to stop by the store tomorrow at lunchtime, and before you ask, I have no idea why. I'll say goodnight. It's time to call it a day,"

Jaxon turned off the light and stretched out on the bed. Closing his eyes, he took a deep breath and pictured Peyton in his mind. I'm listening if you want to talk. His last thought as he drifted off to sleep made him smile. *Damn, but she has pretty eyes.*

****

For a moment as she laid back on the bed, she

thought she could hear Jaxon talking to her. How she wished it were him. She sighed. Today she had seen a few actions that deeply troubled her, and she didn't know how to process them. Jaxon would know. She focused on the chair across the room and imagined him sitting there. She began to tell him about her day and all that she had seen so far.

"I'm not sure how to deal with any of it." She explained what had her troubled. "I can't erase the visual from my mind. What would you tell me to do? Probably you'd say that I need to investigate the situation further," she whispered. Tears fell from her eyes as she recalled the numerous incidents she witnessed over the day. "I have to go back tomorrow and every day as long as I'm here. What I saw is heartbreaking. I wish you were here." She rolled over onto her side. How could people treat others that way? Hopefully, she could remember the details to tell Jaxon when she saw him. Not seeing him again wasn't an option she would entertain. She closed her eyes, but sleep evaded her. Peyton spent a restless night talking to an empty chair. She shared everything she could think of along with a few of her personal feelings for him.

Chapter 17

He awakened humming a favorite tune as he sat up. Cheery wasn't a usual morning feeling especially before coffee. He smiled at his reflection in the mirror. Happy is exactly how he felt. Peyton filled his dreams with conversation most of the night. Dreams vivid enough to convince him she was talking to him. As strange as it might seem it brought him peace. A sign that Peyton was very much alive and staying in touch. Exactly what he had needed. Now he would be able to concentrate on helping Matt until Peyton came back in whatever means she would arrive. He wasn't about to second guess how. Hell, he had done that already. He wished he could remember what she told him. Maybe what she talked about wasn't as important as the fact she was talking to him.

He made his way to the dining room for breakfast. Another great spread. He spooned some of the hash brown casserole on his plate, followed by a slice of ham and an egg dish of some kind. Coffee and a blueberry muffin rounded it out to be followed later by a workout at the gym. Either that or with all this good food he was eating every day he would be packing on the pounds. Opening the notes Jessie had written for him, he began reading. Her handwriting, unlike his, was neat and legible. Jaxon had no idea what he was looking for, but he would know it when he saw it.

He walked into the station a while later ready to get to work. “Good morning,” he said as Kip approached him.

“The chief said to send you back the minute you got here. There’s a fresh pot of coffee if you want some.”

“Thanks.” He walked down the hall toward Matt’s office. He knocked on the open door.

“Come in.” Matt motioned to him. “I was waiting for you to get here. The hospital called, and our witness is well enough to talk this morning. I figured you would want to come along.”

“You figured right.” Jaxon sat in the chair in front of Matt’s desk.

Matt leaned forward in his chair. “I can’t wait to hear his story. The other witnesses’ descriptions have told us a lot. Almost hard to believe, but they were all consistent on how it went down. This guy’s story will likely take it over the top.”

“I guess we're about to be educated.” Jaxon stood when Matt did.

“More like confused. I have to always remind myself some things have no logical answer and then go about trying to rationalize it.” He chuckled. “Common sense may not be applicable when the Reynolds girls are involved.”

“I’m beginning to find that out.” Jaxon shook his head.

“You’re still an amateur. I’ve seen Jessie in action for over a year, and my head still spins each time. The phrase ‘nothing shocks me’ is no longer in my vocabulary. I’m shocked regularly.” Matt pushed the door open, and they walked out of the station.

Jaxon asked questions about the case, and Matt filled him in on the evidence they had to date. "I wanted to thank you for the call last night. Peyton showed up in my dreams. At least for the moment I know she is okay. That's the best I can hope for right now. You take what life gives you I guess."

"Believe it or not I know what you're feeling. In some ways, it's a great relief, and at the same time you feel nuts for thinking that way. Hell, your girl was sucked into a book. That tops Jessie and the girl in the mirror. I keep wondering where the next case will lead. I long for the day of a simple arrest or rescuing a cat from a damn tree." He started the car and pulled out of the parking lot.

"You would be bored in a matter of days. Admit it, man, this tests everything you know and stretches how you view the world. Things aren't always black and white. There are lots of shades in between. I found myself wondering last night if I could follow her to wherever she landed. Would I know her? Is she still Peyton, or did she become someone else living during that time?"

"All interesting questions, which leads to a few interesting theoretical possibilities." Matt explained what he was thinking. He pulled into a parking space at the hospital.

"Something to let Jeremy take a stab at for sure. I would be interested in seeing what he comes up with."

"Let's roll. This ought to be an interesting conversation."

****

Peyton looked at her image in the mirror. Hair was neat and tidy and pulled tightly off her face except for two small tendrils left down for softness. There couldn't be any free hair like a ponytail hanging on her shoulders. A big no-no, as Irma had told her several times yesterday. "It makes a young woman look wanton. We can't be a temptress, now can we?" Wow, how times have changed. At least the hat on her head was more to her liking. She still didn't like wearing the darn corset. A form of torture for women. It must have been designed by an angry man. The long skirt and stockings were hot but at least functional for moving around. Not an inch of skin below her waist showed. Good grief, what would these women think if they saw how she really dressed? Modest compared to some, she would still be considered a loose woman by their standard. Peyton glanced at the clock. She had better get a move on or she would be late again. Besides, she had a plan today to investigate a bit. Her smile broadened as she walked down the stairs. She sounded like her cousin. Irma would play a big part in the success of the said plan, and hopefully she would not catch on.

"You look happy today. Have a nice day, Kathryn. Be sure to come right home after work. Dinner will be waiting."

"I will, Mrs. Woodson." Emily was ready to come in the door as Peyton was on her way out."

"Long night," Emily moaned. "I can't wait to eat and go to bed. See you later." Emily gave her a tentative smile while rubbing her eyes. "I hope your day is better than mine was last night. They lost quite a few patients. The numbers are still being tallied, and families will have to be notified, which will keep you busy today."

"Get some rest." She patted Emily's arm as she passed by. "I'll see you later." She walked down the steps out to the walkway. Following in reverse the same directions Emily had given her yesterday, she walked to the temporary hospital and her job. As each block passed, she couldn't help wondering what happened to the real Kathryn whom she had become. There seemed to be no end to the craziness of the situation in which she found herself.

****

"What do you think?" Matt asked as soon as they were both in the car.

"I don't know what I expected to hear, but it wasn't what he told us. The guy had guts after what he had been through to feign being out to hear what the suspect said and did. I'm not sure how you proceed with knowledge like that. Is it possible like Peyton said someone else has been yanked from their life into another time and place?"

"How would I know? I'm as perplexed by this as you." Matt scowled.

"I'm not saying that's what is happening here. I think this guy gave us some information that doesn't fit into a normal situation is all." Jaxon latched his seatbelt. "I wish I knew what Peyton was up to and how it corresponds with what the victim just told us."

"If you think your head is spinning now just wait." Matt started the car. "Jessie made me promise to bring you by the store on our way back to the station. Reba is there and has a few words to say to you. Get ready! You're in for one hell of a ride."

Chapter 18

"Hello, sweetheart." Matt kissed Jessie. "Ladies." He nodded at Reba and Sadie, Jessie and Peyton's grandmother. "I hope your day is off to a good start. I have delivered Jaxon to you as requested. Take it easy on him. Remember, he's a newbie." Matt chuckled. "I'll bring you a coffee, Jaxon. Something tells me you'll need it." He cuffed Jaxon on the shoulder.

"Don't let his teasing concern you, young man." Reba patted the chair beside her. "I don't want to scare you, but I do want to talk to you."

"I'm listening." Jaxon sat in the chair and stretched his legs out under the table. "This may be new to me, but I've seen Peyton in action once before. And as strange as this may seem I'm convinced she is all right."

"Yes, she is. Jessie and I have been talking all morning, son. The book is central to what happened to Peyton but not necessarily the page. I consider this to be important. Please listen carefully. It would be easy to get stuck on the page where Peyton went through the portal, but we must keep turning the pages of the book. There is more to the story than a single page. And with each turn of the page, something new emerges. She will have lived too much of the story to come back at the beginning." She glanced at him. "Do you understand what I'm saying?"

"I think you're telling me to keep searching through the story for the answers. What she is doing is written on the pages of the book. She will return as the page turns or as the story progresses. On her return, we'll understand the whys."

"Our dear girl may have become a character in the story, living it out and discovering as she goes along. Which you must admit makes for a strange twist in the case. Believe me when I say this story may have several surprises for you both. I can't tell you how this adventure ends, and neither can the book because it's only part of the story. The rest will be discovered by you on this side of the book."

"I guess I need to get a copy of the book."

"It's old, and as of yet I haven't found any other copies in print." Jessie handed him the book while she stapled two stacks of paper.

"What's all this?" he asked.

"I copied several chapters this morning for us so you could have the book. Now get busy reading. I've scanned a copy for Jeremy too. We have a mystery to solve. I want to bring Peyton home."

"You're getting bossy, sweetheart." Matt handed Jaxon his coffee. "Are you thoroughly indoctrinated in their theory?"

"I'm up to speed." Jaxon stood. "We can go anytime you're ready."

"I think operation 'As the Page Turns' has a good ring to it." Reba smiled at him.

"Oh, Reba, I think you've been watching too many soap operas." Jessie laughed.

"I like it," she said.

"Works for me. Straight and to the point." Jaxon

nodded at her.

"You're a wise young man. And catching on quicker than this one did." Reba patted Matt's hand. "When he fell for our Jessie it was fast and hard." She smiled at Matt. "They were fun to watch, and now Sadie and I get to watch you and Peyton. It gives us old ladies something to talk about."

Matt kissed Reba on the cheek. "You girls stay out of trouble. Speaking of Sadie, where is she?"

"She went back to her apartment to get her knitting project. We'll fill her in on the details. She loves to knit when she listens. The more eyes and ears we have on the story the better." Jessie glanced at Matt. "See you later." She waved.

"Keep those pages turning, ladies." Matt opened the door, and Jaxon followed him out. "What do you think about their theory?" Matt asked as soon as they were in the car.

"Makes as much sense as being sucked into a book does. One thing I do know—at this rate I'll never have a chance at a normal relationship with Peyton. If you want me, I'll be doing some light reading." Jaxon shook his head looking at the thick book in his hand. He frowned every time Matt chuckled. His fist twitched at his side. "You seem to be enjoying my discomfort."

"Ever hear the saying 'misery loves company?' Hell, I'm glad not to be doing this alone anymore. It will be a pleasure to watch someone else get blown away for a change. Maybe you'll get lucky and Madison will be another one of the Reynold girls with this strange ability. For her sake, I hope not but for yours, it might not be too bad. You might be entertained like I am now."

"I'd rather watch an awful movie or sleep on a bed of nails."

"I'm kidding of course. I know how tough this is on you. My best advice is to keep a sense of humor because you're going to need it."

****

Emily's warning to her was right. Peyton spent the morning contacting several families on Irma's list. She read the handwritten message Irma told her to tell them about their loved ones. Two different messages in all, depending upon the situation. The process was simple enough. All she had to do was go down the list and fill in the name of the patient and share the right message with each family. The easiest calls were updates on the condition of a patient. The hard ones were about the death of their loved one and where the hospital sent their body. Cut and dry, except when it wasn't. The broken families tore at her heart, and the calls were not getting any easier. The last one had been the worst. She wanted to console the wife. Her words seemed inadequate to meet the overwhelming grief. How do you tell a woman with five children depending on her husband that everything will be okay? It would never be fine. The woman knew it, and so did she. Women had few rights or opportunities for jobs that paid enough to take care of a family. A large family took a man's income. She wiped the tears from her eyes. *Kathryn, I can't imagine how you did this every day. I am not here to get entangled in the emotion of the time.* She sniffed. *Yet how can I not?* Searching through her purse she pulled the paper with the plan she had worked on most of the night. More thoughts needed to be written down to document what she had witnessed.

Words spilled out from her heart reminding her no matter what else she learned kindness to others and treating people right had to top the list.

The clock above her desk ticked away the minutes at a slow pace. When the hands reached noon, she knew Irma would be there soon. Time to enact stage one of her plan. She placed the lunch Mrs. Woodson had packed for her on the desk and waited until she could go to the dining area. As soon as Irma arrived, Peyton pointed to the place on the list of names where she had left off.

"Goodness, you are fast. Hurry off then and eat your lunch. Our list keeps growing. I will polish off more calls while you are gone." Irma put her glasses on and waved her on.

Grabbing her lunch, her feet carried her toward the dining room only veering at the last minute to the stairs that led to the basement. She opened the door a crack. Wide enough to see and confirm what she had heard was true. Racing up the stairs and out the door, she leaned against the side of the building gulping to get her emotions under control before anyone could see or question her. Was Emily aware of this?

The sandwich Mrs. Woodson made for her felt like a big lump in her throat. One bite was all she could tolerate as she fought back the sob threatening to escape. "You, my dear, have had the privilege of a life-changing wake-up call." She wrapped her sandwich again. Not even the bright red apple could tempt her to eat another bite. Maybe later, on her way home from work, she could eat the apple and finish the sandwich. She didn't want to hurt Mrs. Woodson's feelings.

Peyton got back to work making calls as soon as

she returned to her desk. The afternoon passed by quickly. "You're early." She smiled at Emily as she walked in.

"I had to run an errand for Mrs. Woodson and decided to come straight here." She pulled up a chair and sat beside her. "Emily Smith isn't my real name. It's a name I made up to start a new life," she said speaking in a hushed tone. "I am a Mrs., and my husband is missing." She glanced around to make sure no one was near and proceeded to tell Peyton her story. "You have to keep calling me Emily. I think you can see why."

"Yes." The chills started at the base of Peyton's spine and crawled up her back. "And you have no idea where he is?" she asked.

"No, but I keep this with me always." She pulled the chain of a heart-shaped locket hidden under her blouse and opened it. "This is my John. He was a decent sort of guy. A real dollar a year man."

Peyton managed to keep her voice normal or at least she hoped she had. "He is a nice-looking man." Where had seen his face before? She had to write these slang words down so she could look them up at a later time.

"I know he is not much to look at, but he was good to me. Legally I am still married to the man, and I guess I will die that way. I have no idea what happened to him. They could charge me with murder for all I know. A man does not just disappear unless something bad happened to him. I guess he could be living somewhere with another woman. Either way, I would pay the price. It simply became easier to sell the house, move here, and change my name than to face all the questions. He worked here at the hospital. So I came to Pinedale and got a job answering the horn. I guess I hoped if he were still working here that I would see him." She swiped at the tears forming in her eyes.

"I am sorry, Emily." Peyton tried to recall where she had seen the man before. His face was familiar. The question to be answered, was he recognizable to her or Kathryn?

"My John wasn't a grifter. He was a real straight shooter. You know what I mean?" She looked at her locket and sighed. "He didn't drink giggle water except for a glass at home." A smile lit her face. "And boy was he a great hoofer. He took me out dancing on Saturday nights. I miss those times together. We were the best dance pair on the floor." She sniffed.

"I can't imagine how hard it must be for you." She reached for Emily's hand and patted it.

"I miss our mornings over a cup of joe the most." She paused to compose herself. "I can only jaw with you like this. You, being young and all. Mrs. Woodson is too proper. She doesn't like when I use slang. She thinks I'm a dumb Jane. Listen to me go on about myself. You have your own sad story according to Mrs. Woodson. Your fiancé, Stewart Gimble, fighting overseas has to be tough on you." Emily pulled a hankie from her purse and dabbed at her eyes. "Now both of us have to work to make jack."

Go with it she told herself. "Yes, I don't like to talk about it much. I guess I think if I remain quiet it makes it seem less real. I am afraid for him every day. I haven't had any letters for a couple of weeks now." She knew when the words left her mouth that it was Kathryn's reality, and she was worried. They talked until five came and Peyton could leave. Two things needed to be added to her notes. She had to find out who Kathryn Campbell and Stewart Gimble were. Thanks to Irma and Emily she learned their names. The full effect of what Emily Smith told her about her husband hit her. She remembered where she saw his face before. Now all she needed was to interpret what Emily had told her.

Chapter 19

After spending time with Mrs. Woodson, Peyton climbed the stairs to her small room. Even with the windows open, the room was hot and stuffy from the heat of the day. The lightning streaking across the sky followed by the rumble of thunder accounted for why the air felt muggy. A storm was rolling in, and the sky seemed darker than usual. Standing at the window she mused, what an interesting day this had been in every way. She discovered small details with big implications, and at dinner she learned more about Kathryn and her fiancé Stewart Gimble. The conversation had challenged her comprehension of life as she knew it. How was any of this possible? She couldn't imagine loving someone and seeing them go off to war, wondering all the time if they would come home to you again.

When Peyton looked in the mirror, she only saw her face staring back. True, the hairstyle might be different, but it still was her face. Others saw Kathryn when they looked at her. Was it possible they looked alike? Not likely. Still, she wondered about Kathryn's appearance every time someone called her by Kathryn's name. Was her face altered to look like Kathryn's when they saw her? Impossible. It was all too crazy to consider.

Which left her with a big question. How did

Kathryn and Stewart fit into her investigation? Slowly the pieces were starting to form the border of what seemed like a gigantic puzzle. They were tied in some way along with the little girl to her present, and she wanted to find out how. As soon as she did, she would be on her way home to her family and Jaxon. If he were still there.

She could only hope Jaxon would be happy to see her. A man could only take so much. “Don’t go there, Peyton. He’s not your father,” she said staring out into the darkening sky.

It was time for her to have another chat with Jaxon. She walked away from the window as a bright flash lit the dark sky again and sat on the bed and wrote a few more thoughts on her paper. Hopefully, the notes would return with her. Every experience needed to be documented. She didn’t want to forget the smallest details. Each one might be crucial to solving the case or at least understanding it. The murder was only one layer of something that went much deeper. In her heart, she knew it. She would need to raid Mrs. Woodson’s paper stash again. The pages she had were filling up fast. Each time a memory of her day popped up she wrote it down and any details of the event that came to mind.

A while later she lay back on the bed closing her eyes. Today had brought many sights and emotions that left her reeling. The longer she lay there the louder the approaching storm became. The dark room lit with each flash of lightning. “Kathryn,” she whispered. “Tell me who you are. For some incredulous reason, we are sharing this moment of life.”

As rain pelted the window, the wind howled, and the stormy night sky unleashed its fury. But in the tiny room a strange and sweet peace prevailed. Suddenly several pictures of family, love, and passion rushed through Peyton's mind. Not one belonged to her personally but each one a treasure from Kathryn's thoughts. Her memories to guard but shared with Peyton in one unique moment. Two women from different generations sharing a miraculous experience in time. One image after another played through her mind like a movie until the tears filled Peyton's eyes in wonder at what she viewed. An amazing woman no longer on this earth from a few generations before her now openly shared her life with her. Peyton saw Stewart and the family they had together. Two fine sons and a daughter, who looked much like her mother and had the same spunky personality. She grew, married, and in time also had a daughter. From Kathryn passed the gifts of a passion for justice and sight to her daughter, Evelyn. And she passed it on to her daughter. Tears flowed from Peyton's eyes as she realized who and what she watched. At least now she understood there were others besides Jessie and herself. Kathryn had lived an extraordinary life, and she got to share in it for a moment. Peyton was living Kathryn's life and seeing it through her eyes. Another piece to the puzzle. She had to tell someone. Jaxon needed to know even if he couldn't hear her. One by one she recanted the events of the day. Starting with her visit to the basement at work.

****

Jaxon read until his eyes could no longer see the words on the page. If Peyton went back to nineteen-eighteen, she had to be viewing some harsh realities. Damn. Not being there made him nuts with worry.

What was happening to her? The war and the Spanish Flu were both devasting events that took a great toll on the country. The loss of life was astronomical. What did he need to see in this book that would bring her back? He rubbed his eyes, growing more tired with each word that he read. His phone signaled a text.

—Hey, Jaxon, if you're still awake call me.—

He immediately called. "Jeremy, I'm awake. What did you find?" he asked.

"I found a few things of interest. Pinedale is in the story. On page 207, the orphanage is mentioned. They were ready to open with a celebration, but it became an emergency hospital overflow for flu victims." He read some of the details to Jaxon.

Jaxon flipped through the book until he found it and read along with Jeremy. "At least there is one connection. No wonder I was so concerned when she told me she was taking the job at Pinedale. Maybe my gut warned me of the trouble that would be ahead for her."

"Could be. On the other hand, there has to be more to the story, or she wouldn't need to be there. I think we're all about to be knocked out of our comfort zones again. A portal in time is fascinating on its own, but through the pages of a book it becomes mind blowing. What she is seeing in real-time is liable to top anything we might come up with. Jessie's time in two dimensions was fascinating, but Peyton went physically through the portal. I want to know—is she observing unseen or is she a part of the story? It's awesome to think about."

"All I want to know is how do we bring her back? Is it even possible?" Jaxon stared at the words on the page without seeing them.

"My answer would be if she left through the pages of the book that she'll return in some mind-altering way. Anything is possible." Jeremy chuckled. "Get some sleep. I bet she'll be back before you know it with quite a story to tell us."

"We'll talk again soon," Jaxon said. A thought took root in his mind, and he went off on a new train of thinking. What if? He stretched out on the bed and closed his eyes. Hey, like Jeremy said anything is possible if she went through a portal in a book. The idea formulating in his head made at least as much sense. He needed to talk to Jessie and keep reading the book.

Peyton talked with him in his dreams. Her presence danced at the edge of his mind, their conversations vivid and filled with details from her day. But with the light of day, his memory seemed patchy at best. He missed her, which didn't seem an adequate way to express the ache in his heart. Every song he heard and each picture he saw reminded him in some way of Peyton.

He got ready to meet Matt at the station. Reaching for his phone, he removed the charger and placed the phone in his pocket. On impulse, he opened the book to a series of photos he had seen last night. Dang, his mind hadn't been playing tricks on him. The woman in the photo really did look like Peyton, or maybe he should say Peyton looked like her. Remarkable. He wondered if Jessie caught it.

They could almost be twins except for the clothes and hairstyle. And of course the year. There had to be something important about the photo, but he had no idea what. With the murder case getting stranger the more facts they learned, he was convinced that what she was seeing was important. Why couldn't he remember any of the details she had told him? Instead, each night he wanted to wrap his arms around her and wipe away the tears in her eyes. They fell on a regular basis, a detail he had no problem remembering. He would have to do a lot better job of keeping his head in the game or this case would get away from him fast. Matt would want to send him packing and rightfully so. He would never get anywhere if he couldn't hear what she was trying to tell him. From day one he lost coherent thought whenever he saw her. He wondered what that said about him. He grinned at his reflection in the mirror. "You have it bad."

Chapter 20

By lunchtime, Jaxon and Matt had turned up few leads and more questions than answers, although the morning hadn't been a complete loss. Through data mining, Jaxon had found a cluster of felony cases in the area. All had been committed over the past few years with similar crime patterns in the category of spree killings. Jaxon introduced Matt and Gary to the new software that Phoenix PD purchased from the New York PD. They had developed the program in-house out of necessity. His boss had sent him to New York to be trained. The software program, now widely used by police departments in Arizona and other states, made investigations less time-consuming. Previously, he would have had to go through mounds of physical files and police bulletins. Their department's time spent contacting other police departments looking for information was cut in half. With a few clicks of his mouse, it became easier than ever to connect crimes that had similar evidence and patterns in the area or state to state.

"It reduced the amount of time we spent searching for crimes or suspects with similar MO." Jaxon clenched and opened his hand, moving his fingers. "The only drawback is someone has to enter the data upfront, and it needs to be maintained with new interstate information coming in. We hired someone who does all the data entry. After training, each officer files their own reports online."

"I can see how once you learn the program this makes short work of gathering information. I am going to work the cost of equipping our computers with this program into next year's budget before I send it to the town council next week. Budgets." Matt frowned. "My least favorite job." He stood and stretched his arms over his head. "The time it would save in man-hours makes it worth the up-front costs in the long run. Even when you add the salary for the person needed to do data entry. Thanks for showing us. It made the morning somewhat productive."

"At least we know there have been some similar crimes in the last few months in other towns near yours. If they are connected to this one remains yet to be seen." Jaxon closed his laptop. "I'm hungry. I think I'll stop by Joe's for lunch and talk with Jessie about something I saw in the book."

"You said the magic word." Matt chuckled

"Food?" Jaxon asked.

"Hell no. Jessie, man. Have you learned anything about me?" Matt grinned. "Food sounds good too. Gary, are you coming?" Matt asked.

"I could eat." Gary followed them out of Matt's office. "When you've been here longer, you'll figure out that for the chief the sun rises and sets in Jessie. It was touch and go in the beginning. We were all placing bets on whether they would or wouldn't ever get together."

"Gary, you have to finish the story, and don't spare Kincaid because he's a visitor."

"I was getting around to it." Gary laughed.

"Spare me what?" Jaxon latched his seatbelt.

"We're all placing bets on you and Peyton now. It seems with the Reynolds girls it's never about if the guy is willing. It's more like can he even get out of the batter's box and will she or won't she." Gary smiled. "I hear Peyton's sister is a knockout too.

"Do you see what I have to put up with? Jessie's been a good sport about the guys teasing her."

"Good sport my foot. She doesn't put up with much from us. She's intimidating, and so is Peyton."

"Why?" Jaxon and Matt asked at the same time.

"For starters, they know things. It's like they can read your mail before you've even opened it." Gary tapped Matt's shoulder. "You remember how she knew before we heard the gun she was in the crosshairs. For most of us normal guys, that's scary." Gary explained about the case with the Harvest Club. "It was Matt and Jessie's first case together. A group of civic-minded doctors and politicians decided to become rich by trafficking in organs. Pastor John's son was one of them. Jessie was always one step ahead of the bad guys."

"What a case. A lot of good people were tangled up in that crime, and it all started because Jessie saw the ghost of the murdered associate pastor on her first day in town. The Harvest Club, as they liked to call themselves, had been working under the radar for a while." Matt shook his head. "Damn, she was something."

"From what I know of Peyton she's the same way. How does one find a portal into another time in a book? You have to admit they may be gorgeous but they're not normal."

"Jessie's gift has shaken me a few times," Matt said. "But not enough to deter me."

"I'm right there with you, Matt. How about you Gary? Are you willing to set your cap for Madison?" Jaxon teased.

"No way. Not me. I want a girl that finds my jokes funny, likes pizza, and stays put with no strange notions and premonitions."

"Sounds boring, eh Matt?"

"You've got that right." Matt pulled in front of Idle Time Books.

While they waited for lunch Matt went into the bookstore to talk to Jessie. Jaxon opened the book to the page with the old photo outside the orphanage. "Gary, tell me who does she look like?" Jaxon pointed to the picture.

"Wow, she could almost be Peyton's twin. That's freaking weird." Gary took a closer look.

"My thoughts exactly. I wanted to make sure it wasn't my mind playing tricks on me. In case you're wondering, I have no theories." Jaxon studied the photo, lifting it closer to get a better look at it. "Unbelievable."

"Matt, you've got to see this," Gary told him as he sat down at the table.

"See what?" Matt looked at the photo that Jaxon pointed out.

"I say it's Peyton, but it's impossible." Matt shook his head. "We need Jessie's take on this one. I've got nothing." He motioned for Jessie when she looked at him.

"What's up?" She leaned against Matt's side, and he put his arm around her hip.

Jaxon pushed the opened page toward her. "Have you seen this yet?" He pointed at the photo.

"Wow, can I just say wow! That's Peyton except it's not or is it? I'm going to have to think about this for a while. What's the page number?" Jessie went and grabbed something from behind the counter. "I have a magnifying glass. We should take a closer look."

"There's no number. It's a series of pages with photos," Jaxon told her.

"Bummer. I didn't copy the photos, so this is my first time to see any of these old pictures. She looked at the photo through the glass to get an enlarged view. "Amazing. I want to scan this into my computer. Do you mind?

"Be my guest. Jeremy called me last night, and Pinedale and the orphanage are listed in this book on page 207."

"This changes everything. I'm going to have to talk to Reba and think about the possibilities. Could it really be her? Has she changed history? Or…"

"Or what?" Matt asked.

"I have no idea. This is going to take time. Peyton is the only one who will know. Now more than ever we need to get her back here. Maybe there's another way. I'll tell you later." She walked back into her store.

"Here you go, guys. I hope you enjoy your lunch." Molly placed their meals in front of them.

"Thanks, Molly. I'm sure we will." Matt kept glancing at Jessie. "She's up to something. I can see the wheels turning in her head from here."

"I'm glad she is. I don't know how they do it, but something tells me different and unusual is what we need now. We are too logical for this moment." Jaxon watched Jessie rushing about with a phone in her hand talking to someone. Reba, he hoped.

Chapter 21

Another day at work was almost over. Peyton glanced at the clock for the first time all afternoon. The days were not getting any easier. The death toll was mounting, and the bodies were stacking up down in the coolest part of the building waiting for the undertakers or families to get them. Someone had mentioned today they might have to bury them in a mass grave, number the sites, and keep a record for families who wanted to rebury them later. The heat would become a problem before too long.

The hardest part of the day was when the little girl was brought in as a patient. Peyton cried when she saw her carried in on a stretcher with her nanny by her side. Her sweet little face was flushed with fever, and her long golden hair braided and pulled off her pale face.

"Irma, will they put her near her father?" Peyton asked.

"No, she will be in the children's ward. Their care and needs are different. I will try to wheel her mother in to see her later. She has a lighter case than her husband. I'm not sure if he will make it."

"Please let me know how the little girl is doing. She has captured my heart." Peyton dabbed at her eyes.

"Oh, Kathryn dear, this job has enough pain and sorrow that comes with it. You'll seldom be without tears." She handed Peyton an updated list to pass on to

Emily as soon as she arrived. She gave her shoulders a quick squeeze. “You do such a nice job. I have had many of the families of our patients compliment how kind you were to them when you called. You’ve gone the extra mile to get them the information whenever you could. You are one of their main links to their loved ones. We all are trying to make a difference in our small ways. Such sad times we are living in.” Irma walked away before Peyton could gather her thoughts to respond to her.

She didn’t want to be a crybaby. Another trait she shared with her cousin, at least since Arizona. She tried to stifle the sob at the back of her throat, but it emerged despite her best effort. She reasoned that the dire situations she had witnessed the last few days were the reasons why she felt a bit sad and sorry for herself.

If experiencing these moments as Kathryn were hard for her, Peyton could only imagine how much harder they were for the woman whose clothes she wore. Kathryn was an amazing woman. She wiped at the tears threatening to spill down her cheeks at any moment. Why did life have to be so tough at times? Not always, because life was also filled with wonderful happy moments, love, and laughter as Grams often reminded her. The key was to relish those moments as they come. She could not wait to share with the people she loved the awesome events she was living through and her significant discoveries. Emily’s arrival signaled the end of another day. She stood so Emily could sit.

“Have a nice evening. Here is the list from Irma.” She reached for her purse.

“Mrs. Woodson is making a lovely dinner complete with a fresh blueberry pie for dessert. She promised to save me a piece and the homemade vanilla ice cream to go with it." She sighed. "Sounds yummy and perfect. It has been so hot today. I had better get to work. Irma will be passing this way on her way out the door."

"See you in the morning." Peyton walked out into the muggy, hot air, thankful to be out in the fresh air even if it felt stifling. What she wouldn't give for a cool evening breeze off the water in Blue Cove and a walk to the marina right now. Well, maybe not the path unless they already had the murder suspect in custody which she doubted. She held one of the keys to his identity. She still could not believe what Emily had told her. She might need to wait and see if the facts held up.

She fanned her face and began the familiar walk to the Woodson Boarding House. Peyton liked everyone living there and everyone else she had met. Dinnertime reminded her of nights at the inn. Each evening's conversation was an education in living through two major crises at once. It seemed strange how politics came into the equation. They loved the leaders, or they didn't. The war was necessary or a complete waste of lives and money. One of the boarders refused to wear a mask as mandated by Pinedale's mayor. The gentleman gave her a flier with information about a local chapter that was a part of a national movement. On the other hand, seeing all the sick folks every day kept her wearing the mask without a second thought.

Life in nineteen-eighteen might have been a slower pace, but the problems they faced were still being faced in her lifetime. Peoples' opinions and fears kept them looking for those who were different than them to blame for their troubles in life. What did that say about human nature much less about herself? She had some thinking to do about the kind of person she wanted to be.

****

The woman had slipped through the portal. He knew it with every fiber of his being. Life wasn't fair. "Damn. Damn. Damn," he muttered and hit his fist against the tree trunk. The sticky blood dripped from the scrapes and cuts when he rubbed his forehead. He should have been the one to find the portal, but he had messed up again. Where did she find it? He had been looking for the portal since his arrival through it, details of which were still a mystery to him. Did it move or remain in the same place? It had to move because he could never find the gateway. A vague memory would swish around his mind from time to time. But that's all it was—a memory refusing to show itself. To find the door back would be lifesaving. Instead, the monster inside rose again using him to attack innocent people.

Was it a monster or was it him? The line seemed to be blurred anymore. He had no idea where he ended and the other began. His mind often played tricks on him making the thoughts seem like they were his own. Were they? Is this what he had become? He slumped to the ground as heaving sobs racked his body. Death would be a release. The universe knows he tried, but he couldn't even do that right. Something in him wanted to live. The desire to survive was too powerful to let him go. Another relief he wasn't granted.

Stuck in time, he wandered between here and his lab with no place to call home, driven by a force he couldn't see or control. If he could figure out why maybe he would be free. Freedom, he dreamed of it, but he had no idea what it felt like anymore. He lived in fear of the dark moments that overtook him.

Hiding among the trees, eating what he could find, he slipped in and out of his lab trying not to be noticed. He needed the woman. She had to be his ticket out of here. Time was something he had plenty of, and he would wait until she returned. The challenge had been issued, and he knew she understood they would meet. He shuddered at the thought. Not wishing to cause her pain, he could only hope the monster would remain dormant. There was a light in her that made the darkness in him tremble. His dilemma was that there still were people who recognized his greatness. The accolades and praise he never tired of. His work continued, and discoveries were made continually. Which man was he? What was real and what wasn't? Was he a consummate liar or an upstanding man believed and loved by many? His life was amazing or a total joke. He wasn't sure at this point what was real and what was fake. Memories twisted and turned through his mind, and he had no idea what to believe of himself anymore.

****

Jaxon spent the afternoon reading his copy of the book. Matt let him use Dylan's office while he was on his honeymoon. It gave him a quiet place to read and at the same time be close to the information he needed about the case. The book had lots of pages, and he had no idea why reading it was important. Once he got past the small bit about Pinedale, the rest of the book talked mostly about the pandemic. A sad time in the nation's history. The author told the story of several families impacted by both war and the Spanish Flu. For the life of him, he couldn't figure out how the story fit into the murder case now. Peyton would understand. The pages of photos kept drawing his attention. Something important was hidden in them, and he had to figure out what. If Peyton talked tonight, he had better listen. The phone buzzed. "This is Jaxon."

"Hey, Kincaid, I'm glad you answered, or I would've had to walk back there. You saved me a trip. Jessie is on line one, and she says it's important."

"Thanks, I'll talk with her." Jaxon pushed line one.

"Jaxon, I've been talking to Reba. How far have you read in the book?"

"I have about a hundred pages left. Why?"

"I've read almost the entire book. The stories are important. Reba told me to tell you. All of life is made up of people and their stories." She paused. "Here, I'll let Reba tell you, and then I'll tell you what I'm thinking."

"Jaxon, Reba here. Every one of the stories is important. From them, you'll see the mindset and the heart of folks during the perilous times they were living in. People aren't much different now. The bottom line is that there is much more to see than what is detectable. You're seeing the visible, and Peyton is seeing the invisible, and together you will tell the story of two distinct times. This one has footprints from the one Peyton is visiting, or she wouldn't need to be there. You've seen the murder, and she is seeing where the story started. I can't wait until you both tell us what you've found."

He shook his head. "Okay, I'll try to keep that in mind."

"I know this is strange for you, but Peyton is fine.

She'll have some of the pieces to the puzzle you are looking for. Her return isn't the end. It will be just the beginning. Here's Jessie."

Reba could make his head spin. "Are you there, Jessie?"

"I am," she said. "I'm drawn to the photos. I'm glad that I scanned them. The truth is staring me in the face, but I'm not grasping it. Anyway, here's my theory so far." She went on to explain to him a few of her ideas. "I guess we'll know soon enough. Keep reading. You have a big part in this."

"That's what I'm doing now. Some of these stories are gut wrenching. They're hard to take in large doses. The one thing I know is that it's important that I read to the end."

"I'm proud of you, Jaxon, but don't tell Matt. You're catching on faster than he did."

"My lips are sealed." He chuckled. "I wouldn't want a jealous fiancé on my hands."

"There's something else—" She paused. "—I've been thinking about what Reba said a few days ago to you. Do you remember when she called this as the page turns?"

"I can't forget. It keeps me motivated to read whenever I get the chance. I keep thinking maybe this will be the page that brings her back to us."

"Well here's something else for you to think about. You both must be on the same page to turn it. At some point, you and Peyton are going to be on the same page figuratively speaking, and you'll turn the page at the same time to her return."

"How will I ever know?" Jaxon rubbed his temple. Perplexed described his thoughts with her statement.

His cop instinct didn't seem to be working at all.

"You won't, but the force that sent her there in the first place will," Jessie explained.

"Force?" Jaxon frowned.

"Force, magic, or power. Call it what you want, but when her reason for being there is finished she'll be back and you'll both be on the same page." She muttered something under her breath. "I know this sounds strange, but you have to admit nothing about the situation has been normal since the day of Katie's wedding."

"At least I can agree with you there. We will talk again. I'm sure." Jaxon hung up the phone and continued to read. With any luck, he would reach the end by tonight or tomorrow at the latest. Maybe they were almost on the same page. One could hope anyway.

Chapter 22

Another day of seeing the sad sights and emotions that came with it lay ahead of her. She walked out the door of the boarding house with her lunch wrapped in the colorful cloth Mrs. Woodson handed to her. She took good care of her and all the folks living in the house. Her kindness seemed to have no bounds. A perfect example of one who can be tough and caring at the same time. Last night's conversation still played across Peyton's mind as she walked the now familiar streets.

"If you don't mind me asking." Peyton paused giving Mrs. Woodson time to finish what she was doing. Mrs. Woodson reached into the cabinet to pull out two glasses and pour the chilled lemonade into them.

"You can ask me anything." She wiped her hands on her apron, handed Peyton a glass, and sat down to talk.

"You're not much older than I am," she began. "How did you come to run a boarding house?" Peyton watched the emotions play across the woman's lovely face.

"It wasn't my first choice of course." Her voice softened. "Life deals the cards you get to play with, and this is the result." She patted her hair. "My husband bought this home when we were first married. We lived here for a year before he went off to war. I found out right before he left that I was pregnant with our first child. Jacob couldn't have been happier." The hankie she kept in her pocket slipped out as she dabbed at the tears forming in her eyes. She stopped to gather herself. "First, I lost Jacob, and a few months later the baby. I still had to live as you know, and I had this house. The moment I felt I couldn't go on, Jacob himself told me what to do in a dream. He gave me the idea you see. Now here I am trying to make life a little better for others who are hurting too." She smiled and reached over to pat her hand. "That's why you're here too, Kathryn. All of us wounded creatures tend to need each other to get fixed. It gives our life purpose." She sniffed.

Is that why she had the gift of sight? Something more to think about.

After their conversation, she would do her best to appreciate each evening when she dragged through the door and Mrs. Woodson was there to greet her. Peyton knew in her heart that Kathryn loved those moments too. A value couldn't be put on her readiness to listen. Those conversations must have made Kathryn's wait for Stewart to come home a little more tolerable. Mrs. Woodson had every reason to be bitter in her pain, but she refused to let it encase her in sadness. Instead, she helped other wounded people.

Emily waved as Peyton approached her. "I am so tired I am almost sleepwalking. No work tomorrow for us, and it is a good thing after the week we have had." Emily stopped to talk.

"A day off is always nice. What do you plan on doing with yours?" Peyton asked.

"Sleep, eat, and sleep some more. See you at dinner. Betsy is taking my place at five." Emily waved goodbye and walked on.

Did Betsy fit into the story, or was she just someone passing through? How did Kathryn know her? "Kathryn, let me see and feel all I can from your life, please. My time here is coming to an end." She spoke the words into the air as she walked. "It has been a privilege to see a piece of your life through your eyes."

She did not want to waste a moment of this experience. Peyton understood how Kathryn, Stewart, and Evelyn fit into the picture. They were one of the reasons she had leaped through time. Kathryn held the answers to many of the questions she had asked over the past few months. What she saw in the basement aroused her sense of activism. Now all she needed to know to complete the puzzle was the little girl's story and a peek inside the locked doors of another area of the hospital that Irma said no one could go into. The mere fact she was told the space was off-limits made Peyton want to go there. Kathryn knew what was going on there. Peyton was sure of it. She picked up her pace. A brisk walk was just what she needed this morning to clear her head.

"I've been waiting for you to arrive, dear girl," Irma said when she walked in the door.

"Am I late?" she asked.

"No, you're right on time." She moved a large envelope back and forth in her hands. "I need you to run this to the south wing. You'll have to knock on the doors. Hand this to them and wait for them to give you something to bring back to me." She handed Peyton a thick envelope. "When you return, I want to talk to you about how the child is doing as I promised you I would."

Peyton's heart beat rapidly as she made her way to the locked doors and knocked. It seemed like an eternity for someone to open them. The noise and screeching when the orderly opened the doors sounded awful. What was going on in there? "Irma told me to bring this to you and wait for what you had for her."

"Wait here!" he commanded.

Standing alone in the hallway Kathryn showed her what was behind those closed doors. The longer she stood there the more Kathryn's thoughts raced through her mind. Peyton tapped her toe as she waited and waited for the man to return. *How could you have continued to work there once you knew what was going on?* Thankfully, Kathryn showed her the answer. She quit, and her stand infused Peyton with hope.

Finally, she heard the click of the lock, the door swung open, and the man shoved the envelope into her hand. He closed the doors with a slam and clicked them locked again. Happy to be leaving the hall and what she sensed was going on beyond those doors, she raced back toward her desk, where Irma waited for her and the envelope.

"Thank you," Irma said as she stood. "Please sit." She placed the envelope on the desk and rested her hand on top of it. "The girl's name is Marianna," Irma told Peyton. She explained what she had learned about the child. "She is quite sick."

"Will she make it?"

"Rest assured that the doctors are doing all they can for her. We know so little about this disease. Why does it kill some and leave others with only mild symptoms? I've never seen anything like it in my lifetime. It's all so sad." She wiped the tears streaming down her cheeks. "Time for me to get back to work." She walked away and left the envelope behind.

Peyton used the time to check the contents. She couldn't understand all of what she read but understood enough to know why Kathryn was angry and quit. She placed the envelope back where Irma had left it in the nick of time. Irma walked down the hall toward her.

"I can't believe I walked off without this." Irma clutched the envelope to her chest.

"I knew you would be back for it."

"There seems to be no easy way to tell you, Kathryn. Marianna passed away a few minutes ago." Irma stifled a sob as she told Peyton.

****

Jaxon went into the gardens after dinner. The evening air had cooled and felt good after the heat of the day. The sun would set soon, and he wanted to finish the last few pages. When he had started reading it seemed he would never get through the first couple of chapters, but the author's words pulled him into the story. Sitting on the bench, he started to read where he had left off. The stories were about real people who had lived decades ago. Yet if you changed the setting and the language, they could be stories about his neighbors or his family. The last few pages tore at his heart. He couldn't help but wonder if Peyton had seen any of the things he read about. Looking once again at the pictures, his eyes paused on the woman who looked like Peyton. He flipped through the other photos of Pinedale, the streets of the town, the shops, and a beautiful old house on one of those streets. He noticed more details the closer he looked at them. The makeshift hospital caught his attention next. He tried to picture all the patients being treated in the building. People all fighting for their lives against an invisible enemy. Some simply trying to recover from the loss of war found themselves facing another battle. The thought of Peyton being there brought tears to his eyes. Dang, he didn't cry, but he had more than once since he met her. He read the final page. Closing his eyes, he took a deep breath and spoke the words, "the end."

A hush settled over the garden with only the sound of waves lapping the shore in the distance and the rustling of the leaves in the slight evening breeze. In his head, he could hear crying. It sounded like Peyton, but he was afraid to open his eyes.

****

The weight of what Kathryn felt in that moment descended on Peyton. Fear for a fiancé she hadn't heard from in weeks, a little girl and her family that had made their way into her heart piled on top of all the strange things she saw and couldn't explain. The sadness and pain became too much to bear. A strange sensation started at her fingertips, moving through her arms, and tingled through her body. The spinning took her by surprise. She lifted above where Kathryn sat as Irma talked with her while holding the envelope. Another woman stood in the shadow, but she couldn't see her face. Peyton's tears dropped from her cheeks mingling with Kathryn's as she wept. One moment she watched the women and in the next Peyton was pushed forward through time.

Patting her side to make sure nothing was left behind Peyton arrived back in one piece. How many days had she been gone? Had it happened, or was it all in her mind? Dressed in the clothes she wore that day in the attic, had she simply dreamed it all? If it had all been a dream, then how did she end up at her favorite spot overlooking the cove? Too confusing. Yet in her heart of hearts she knew she had walked in Kathryn's life even if she didn't know how. Turning around, she knew she needed to find Jessie. Maybe she could explain what had happened to her. Walking toward the gardens, she saw him sitting there. His eyes were closed, but even from here she could see the weariness on his face. She paused and waited. He opened his eyes, and she knew the moment he saw her.

"Peyton, sweetheart, is that you? Are you real or am I hallucinating?" He rubbed his eyes.

"It's me." She took a step toward him.

"Thank God you're back." He stood reaching for her.

His words were music to her ears. It hadn't been a dream. She had lived the amazing days and couldn't wait to tell him about them. She ran toward him. "Jaxon." His name was the best she could come up with at the moment. She propelled herself into his open arms.

He wrapped her tight, swinging her feet off the ground. "We were on the same page," he spoke in her ear. "Somehow we made it to the same page at the same time. I wasn't sure I'd ever seen you again." He hugged her tight while kissing her.

"I have so much to talk to you about, but how long have I been gone?" she asked.

"A lifetime." He let her slip until her feet touched the ground.

"What were you doing?" She noticed the volume on the bench.

"Reading the book that you were sucked into on your travels through time."

"I wasn't sure if any of it was real, but it sure seemed to be." She sat on the bench.

"I have to show you something." He opened to the book and showed her the photo. "You look like her."

"There's a good reason why." She smiled at him. "I have stories to tell that you might find hard to believe. Is it all right if I tell all of you at once to make it easier?"

"Fine with me. I'm simply happy to have you back." He grabbed his phone and called Jessie. "Guess who's back," he said when she answered her phone. "She wants to talk with you." He handed the phone to Peyton.

Between the squeals and tears plans were made to invite Sadie, Reba. and Matt. They decided to meet in fifteen minutes for coffee and dessert at Patterson's. After getting her purse from the cottage, she took his hand in hers. "Let's go. I can't wait to drive my new car again."

Chapter 23

Patterson had his wait staff combine a few tables to accommodate their group in a quieter section of the restaurant. "You"—he smiled at Jessie—"and that guy I know." Patterson pointed at Matt. He whispered in Jessie's ear. "Who is the other young couple? I don't remember seeing them in here with you before."

"Maybe you weren't here at the time. Joe, I'm sorry if I haven't introduced you before." She pulled Peyton beside her. "This is my cousin Peyton and her friend Jaxon. She's staying with me for a while." Jessie smiled at him. "I'm hoping she's here to stay."

"Peyton, it's nice to meet you. I can see a bit of a family resemblance. I think you'll like our quaint town. I hope Jessie can talk you into staying. We can never have enough beautiful young women in our town. I'm sure these two would agree." He reached for the dessert menus.

"It won't take much to convince me to stay. I love it here," Peyton told him. "Everyone has made me feel welcome. And the cove is beautiful."

Patterson reached for Sadie's hand next. "You, my dear lady, have some beautiful granddaughters. I'm sure these two young fellas would have to agree with me." They both nodded, and he chuckled. "Love is wasted on the young. By the time you figure it out, you're almost too old to enjoy it. Am I not right?"

"You're right on both accounts. My granddaughters are beautiful girls inside and out. And as for love, it seems to take its own sweet time."

"Is this all of your party?" he asked.

"No, we have two more who will be joining us," Jessie told him. "Reba and Lawrence are coming, but you can seat us now if you'd like."

"Sounds good. I'll show them to your table as soon as they arrive." He snapped his fingers and motioned a waiter to their table as they sat. The server promptly began filling water glasses. "If I may suggest the fresh strawberry shortcake or our fabulous blueberry cobbler. The berries are in season and superb."

"Both sound good to me." Sadie glanced at the menu. "Reba and Lawrence are here." She waved at her friend. "What looks good to you, dear?" She glanced at Peyton. "They all look wonderful to me."

"I'm not sure I can eat anything." Peyton took a sip of water. "I'm way too excited."

"I won't hear of it. You must have something. Since we are celebrating your return to us, may I suggest something chocolate?" Sadie smiled at her. "Chocolate pairs well with coffee."

"Are you sure you're up to this? Maybe this is too soon for you to talk to us. We have no idea what you've gone through. You haven't even had the time to process it yourself." Jessie reached across the table placing her hand on Peyton's.

"Oh, Jessie, I want to tell all of you. You're each important to me and supported me through this new phase in my life. I can't wait for you to hear what I've been up to. As soon as we order I will tell you everything I can remember. At least, I'll tell you part of it now. It would take too much time to share it all. And I have piles of notes to go through. You'll be hearing about it for a long time I'm sure."

As soon as the desserts were placed in front of them several pairs of eyes turned to look at her. "We're ready, dear." Reba said what the eager faces of her friends were telling her. "I can't wait another minute to hear your story."

Peyton began, her voice steady and melodious. "The last memory I had before my jaunt back in time happened was of Jessie trying on hats and yelling at me not to open the book. Do you remember?" She glanced at her cousin. They shared a smile when she nodded.

"How can I forget? I knew something was strange when the doorknob zapped me." She laughed. "But all bets were off when the book flew off the shelf heading right for your head. I remember yelling, but the book opened anyway. All I could do was watch in horror as you were sucked into the book. I'll never forget it for as long as I live. As Matt and Jaxon can tell you I was a complete mess. I had no idea where you went or how to get you back."

"I felt the same way. I found myself wandering down a street having no idea where I was. At least I was dressed like everyone else around me. Please don't ask me how." She glanced at Jaxon. He squeezed her hand to encourage her. She described the town, the cars, and how it felt when she read the newspaper headlines and learned of the pandemic and the war. "That's when I found out I was in Pinedale in the year nineteen-eighteen."

Sadie gasped. "Oh, my."

"I had no idea where to go. I walked until I found

myself in front of what is now Pinedale Day School. Built to be an orphanage, it was being used for a hospital to hold Spanish Flu patients."

"What did you do next?" Sadie asked.

"I decided that as long as I was there I needed to find out why. Not one to be shy, I went inside. The head nurse knew who I was and put me to work. I didn't know it at the time, but my whole reason for being there was ready for me to step into and live out. They knew me as Kathryn. This is where the story gets interesting." She explained a few of the details she learned about Kathryn. "Grams, one evening Kathryn's memories played through my mind. Do you know who she was?" She looked at Sadie.

"Should I? My grandmother's name was Kathryn, but you aren't talking about her, are you?" Sadie asked shaking her head.

"Yes, I am. And I stepped into Kathryn's life. Your grandmother and our great-great grandmother's life. She married Stewart Gimble, your grandfather, a few years later. She lived at the Woodson's Boarding House." She paused for them to take it in. "I look like her."

"She really does." Jaxon turned to the page showing the photo of Kathryn and passed it around.

"My goodness." Reba took a sip of her hot tea. "You are the spitting image of her."

"Grams, I saw your mother Evelyn as a little girl. Both your mother and grandmother had the gift of sight. I know why we have it now." She pointed at Jessie. "I saw the same things that Kathryn saw. I lived as Kathryn. She wasn't married to Stewart at the time. He was overseas fighting in the war."

Sadie dabbed at her eyes with the tissue Reba handed her. “I can remember my mom telling me how her dad fought in the war.” Sadie’s eyes teared. “She told me about her mother talking about the pandemic, wearing masks, and how sad it was working with the patients at the hospital.” She shook her head. “I never knew where. I was young when I heard those stories. I wish I would have listened more carefully and asked questions.”

“When we’re young, my friend, we are seldom interested in those things. Later life keeps us too busy to think about our ancestors.” Reba handed Sadie another tissue. “How amazing it is that you get to learn more now.”

“Working at the hospital I saw many sad things through Kathryn’s eyes. I won’t share them all now. But, Grams and Jessie, I wanted you to know Kathryn was a great woman and quite the activist. She was a part of the women’s suffrage movement. No wonder we are the way that we are. We come from good stock.”

“Look at you, Peyton. You look like you could be her twin.” Sadie reached for Jessie’s hand. “You girls make me so proud.” Tears streamed down her face. “I always wondered about our ability. I knew my mom had it, and it makes sense that Grandma Kathryn did too. I wonder if she knew how to use it or if it troubled her like it did my mother.”

“Kathryn seemed to understand her gift. I only hope I can be half the woman Kathryn Gimble seemed to be. I plan to do more research on her life. From what I could see she was a loving and kind woman who helped others.”

“I will be interested to hear what you find when

you do your research." Sadie wiped her cheeks once again. "My mother was a dear sweet woman, but I never fit in her mold. I often wondered where I got my tenaciousness from."

"You'll be the first to know what I find out. I feel safe in saying that you got your feisty, fiery personality from your grandmother." She kissed Sadie's cheek.

"I have so many questions I don't know where to start. How and where did you come back to? And after you answer that one, I have many more," Jessie told her. "We'll talk later. Right now, we need to hear all about Kathryn." Jessie glanced at Sadie.

Peyton talked about her time with Mrs. Woodson at the boarding house, meeting Irma and Emily, and the little girl. "Oh, and Matt, I wish you could have seen the gorgeous Town Car I saw. You would have loved it." She went on to describe the cars she saw in detail. "I know how you love Jessie's car. I'm telling you this car had to be the envy of lots of men in its day."

"I'm going to look it up online. You've got me interested now." Matt reached for his fork as soon as the waiter placed the shortcake in front of him.

"If you had to sum up that time to us, what would your takeaway be?" Lawrence asked.

"Well, if I could only share one thing, people in general were pretty much the same. Some people played by the rules and some refused to. A lot of things have changed, and some things haven't changed at all. They had their own slang words like we do. This reminds me—I need to get a list of the slang spoken at the time. It might help me understand some of what I was told."

"I'm sure that's true." Lawrence thanked the server

for refilling his cup. “It sounds to me like you’ve had quite the adventure. I want to hear more about the headlines of the time and your days working at the hospital.”

Peyton spent the next hour sharing her adventure as her small group of friends listened with rapt attention. The entire time Jaxon rarely took his eyes off her and held tight to her hand. She found it comforting. It seemed more possible to her now than at any other time that true love could last a lifetime. She squeezed his hand wishing she could wrap her arms around him instead.

Chapter 24

Jaxon couldn't take his eyes off her. She radiated energy as she shared her experience. She had seen life through her great-great grandmother's eyes. Most people have to trace their ancestry. Not his girl. She went back and lived it. He found it fascinating, exciting, and scary all at the same time. He had never met a woman like her. But what if one day she couldn't make it back? It would only take one time. His hand tightened around hers. There was no way he would let her go, even if he had to go through the blasted portal after her.

"I have a few things to share with you later. In some way, they impact this case. I don't know how yet." She moved closer to him and touched his cheek. "I'm not going anywhere." She placed her other hand on top of his. "I think you need to know this. I missed you so much that I talked to you every night."

"How do you do that?" he asked.

"What?"

"I swear you know what I'm thinking before I do sometimes." He shook his head. "There were times in my dreams I could hear you talking to me."

"It was a lucky guess. You've been holding my hand so tight I figured you were worried I might disappear again." She grinned. "I'm not going to open the book again. Although I would like to read it if I could."

"Maybe the copied pages, but you're not getting the original book to read." He grinned at her.

Reba and Lawrence spoke softly to each other and then pushed away from the table. "I think you two kids could use some time alone." Reba smiled at Lawrence. "You remember how we were at their age."

"I sure do." He took Reba's hand. "Peyton, you're not off the hook though. This is a small reprieve. I can't wait to hear the rest of the story."

"I think they have the right idea, sweetheart." Matt said to Jessie and stood. "Let's take your grandmother home. You can stay up all night talking to your cousin later if you want."

Jaxon reached for her hand, and they walked out with their friends. Peyton hugged Sadie goodbye. He waited for her to say her goodbyes because he needed to hear it all again start to finish. She had left out some details.

Peyton handed him the keys to her car. "Your turn to drive this beauty. I'm a little tired now. If you wouldn't mind, I'd like to go to my favorite place."

"I'd be happy to take you anywhere." He opened the car door for her but hugged her tight before he let her get in.

She latched her seatbelt and laid her head back against the seat. "I missed you, Jaxon. I hope you aren't having second thoughts about me. I know I come with a lot of baggage. Seeing ghosts and time travel probably don't make me very appealing. But honestly, these have been a few life-changing days for me."

"I'm not going anywhere. I may not understand it, but the only thing I wanted the whole time you were gone was to see you again. We'll figure it out. We have time to get to know each other and get used to each other. I have some odd quirks of my own."

"I don't believe you. You're almost perfect as far as I can see." She glanced at his handsome face, trying to memorize the way he looked at this moment.

"You know better than that, sweetheart. No one is perfect. But one thing I'm sure of is I love being with you. Getting to know you has been quite an adventure." He smiled at her.

"We have a strong connection. Like you said, when we reached the same place in the story, we were able to turn the page to the end. I have a lot to tell you but not tonight if that's okay with you."

He pulled the car into a parking place at the marina. "I'm a patient man." He saw her roll her eyes. "Okay, maybe not patient exactly."

"Seems to me we had a few fights in our last case when you thought I wasn't telling you everything." She chuckled.

"I'm growing." He waggled his brow. "In this instance, I'm willing to wait until tomorrow."

"Thank you. I want to savor the look on Sadie's face when I talked about Kathryn. Memories were flooding back in her mind. I could see it in her facial expressions. You can't imagine how strange it felt to be Kathryn and to discover who she was. I learned so much in those experiences."

Jaxon's contentment grew as he listened to the melodic sound of her voice. The more she relaxed the easier it became for her to share with him. She told him about what she saw in the basement at the school. She cried one moment and laughed the next. He wanted to talk about what she had seen, but he wanted her to feel free to share without his interrupting her. She laid her head on his shoulder and continued. The emotions of the past few days spilled from her lips and eyes. He had missed hearing her voice and holding her in his arms. She snuggled closer into his side. The bucket seats and center console of her sporty car made it impossible to get close enough.

"Sweetheart, I think we need to get you home. You're tired. I can hear it in your voice."

"Thank you for holding me and letting me ramble. I'll get my thoughts together. I know there are links from the past to the present. Some of what I saw is impacting what is going on now and even may have ties to the murder that happened on the path. Besides, I took notes, and they came back with me. I was afraid maybe they wouldn't." She opened her purse and grabbed the pages waving them in the air. "We'll talk more tomorrow."

Jaxon started the car and drove back to the inn. "You can tell me when you're ready. I want to talk to you about what I've learned too. Matt has me working on the murder. I can use all the help you can give me." He glanced at her to see why she hadn't answered. She was sound asleep. Parking the car at the inn, Jaxon opened the door and helped her out. He put his arm around her waist, pulling her into his side to steady her as they walked to the cottage. At the door, he picked her up, carried her inside, and placed her on the bed. Covering her with the throw from the foot of the bed, he sat in the chair until she went back to sleep. He was on his way out when Jessie was coming in.

"How's she doing?" she asked.

"She's sleeping."

"I've seen a lot this past year, and still I'm blown away." Jessie leaned her hip against the couch.

"I hear you. That was some story, and we haven't begun to hear it all. I let her talk, and she told me a few details that have me wondering about what we are going to find out next.

****

"Good morning, sleepyhead." Jessie had her traveling mug of coffee in her hand and was ready to go out the door. "Jaxon will be here in thirty minutes to take you to breakfast. I would change and comb your hair if I were you. He's into you, but this new look you're sporting might scare him off." She laughed as she closed the door.

Peyton spent her time wisely, or at least she thought she had. She looked presentable when Jaxon knocked on the door. "Hi." She reached for her phone, shoving it in her purse.

"Where's the best place to talk?" He pulled the door shut behind her.

"That's a good question. This is tourist season. Most places will be packed. I suggest we get our food from Joe's and head to the park by the marina. It's early enough there shouldn't be a lot of activity yet. There's also Mindy's Waterfront grill. I've heard they serve a nice breakfast, but maybe Joe's would be better."

"Let's get it to go." He pulled the door shut behind her.

As they walked toward through the garden, a strange sensation began in the pit of her stomach. His threatening voice sounded in her mind, his face danced in front of her eyes, and his anger could be tangibly felt. Too near for comfort. She glanced around but didn't see anyone. She knew he watched their progress toward the car. The challenge was issued for a second time, and there wasn't a doubt in her mind that they would meet. She shivered.

"Is everything all right?" Jaxon asked. He stopped and turned her toward him.

"Let's get in the car. I'll tell you later." She pulled him and rushed toward the car.

As soon as they were in the car and he had started the engine, Jaxon asked, "Mind telling me what that was all about."

"He's near, and he issued the challenge of us meeting for the second time. The anger I could sense radiating from him is real. I can't tell you the reason for his rage, but I think we're about to find out."

"By near do you mean physically close?" Jaxon drove past the inn and out to the road into Blue Cove.

"Yes, close enough to watch us."

"Damn. I was afraid you would say that." He shook his head. "I do and I don't want him to be nearby. It's never simple."

"So it would seem." She reached over and patted his arm. "You have to admit your life hasn't been boring since you met me." She smiled at him. "Seriously, I know this must be weird for you. It is for me too. I hope I'm wrong about my gut feeling, as you would call it. I'd rather not meet the guy. I wanted to come to the cove to have a nice quiet life, but I'm thinking it's not in the cards. If I remember correctly, that's the same reason Jessie moved here too."

"Seems I remember a girl telling me she wanted a bit of excitement in her life. I think you've found it."

"I didn't have a clue." She laughed.

Jaxon pulled in front of the coffee shop. “Let’s get in and get out. I need to know what I’m facing.” He glanced at her in time to see her roll her eyes. “What?”

“I can see your patience didn’t last long. These are my friends, and if I want to linger and talk with them then you can initiate your plan to get in and out. You can go to the park by yourself.” She frowned at him and slammed the car door.

He caught up with her before she opened the door to Joe’s. “That might have come out wrong. I’m sorry for my choice of words. All I’m saying is I need to hear the rest of the story. I don’t want to be caught off guard.”

“And I’ll tell you, but I’m not going to be rude to the people who supported me through my convalescence. They are the reason that I’m sane.”

“This conversation is ridiculous. I wasn’t telling you to be rude or not to talk to your friends. You know how I get when I am on a job.”

“Yes, impatient and rude.” She pushed the door open and walked in, leaving him standing behind her with an odd expression on his face. This was the Kincaid she remembered from Phoenix.

****

Women—who could understand them? One minute you’re in a normal conversation and the next you’re wondering where you went wrong. He raked his hand through his hair. How did a simple statement get twisted into an argument? Damn. If history was any indication he was in for the silent treatment.

“Hey, Jaxon. How long are you in town for?” Molly asked.

“A couple of weeks before I have to head back to

Phoenix to pack." He could see Peyton talking to her cousin in the bookstore. "Did Peyton give you her order?"

"She said she would take the same as you and she hoped you knew what she liked." Molly chuckled. "I took from her statement and the fire in her eyes you two might have had a lover's tiff."

"I'm still not sure what I did. But I hope you can help me out with what she likes." he pleaded.

"That's easy enough. The question is what do you want?" She grinned at him.

"What would you suggest?"

"My breakfast burrito with green chili is popular." Molly pointed to the description on the menu.

"I'll take one and a coffee for me. Throw in whatever treat that she likes in the morning, would you? I'm not above bribery." He handed Molly his card and placed a tip in the jar.

"Will it be for here or to go?" Molly asked.

"Looks like we'll be eating here." He searched for a table to sit at. "I can be as stubborn as you are, sweetheart," he muttered under his breath.

"I thought you were in a big hurry?" Peyton pulled out the chair across from him.

"Not me. We can sit here all day if it makes you happy." He sipped his coffee.

"This looks good as always, Molly." She looked at the breakfast sandwich and fruit on the plate as Molly delivered their food. "You helped him, didn't you?"

"I did. I like him, and you're being a stinker. I know it because I've often done the same thing to Kenny." Molly squeezed Peyton's shoulder. "Be nice."

"And I for one appreciate the help," he told Molly.

"I was going down fast." Jaxon sat back in his chair. "Are we still at an impasse?" he asked as soon as Molly walked away.

"I guess we're okay. I don't like being told what to do. It tends to get under my skin. It makes me angry in case you don't know where I'm going with this."

"I get it. In this case, I think you might have overreacted a bit." He took a bite of his burrito.

"Do you want to go there?"

"I'm thinking I should say no to your question, bribe you with this treat instead, and give you a bite of this amazing burrito." He flashed her a smile.

She looked in the bag he handed to her and smiled. "Okay, you're forgiven." She cut off a small taste of the burrito with her fork. "Wow, this may be my new favorite."

"Peyton." His fork stopped halfway to his mouth.

"Yes." She glanced at him.

"You're forgiven too." He took another sip of his coffee and prepared to duck if needed.

Chapter 25

She knew she had shocked him, but when he was right, he was right. The look on his face had been worth her humility. "You're right, and your reverse psychology isn't lost on me." She stood and leaned across the table as close to his face as she could get. "I'm sorry." She framed his face with her hands and kissed him. She trailed her finger down his cheek as she pulled away. Yep, he was stunned. "Thank you for breakfast by the way, and for taking the time to find out what I like. Especially this." She waved the bag in front of his face. "I know a lot of guys wouldn't have bothered to find out."

"You're welcome. What's next?" He took the last bite of his burrito.

"Coffees to go, and let's get out of here." She stood and waited for him to walk with her.

"Molly, the burrito was great. It's hard to come by green chili in the east, and that's some of the best I've had anywhere."

"Thank you." She handed him two cups and lids for their coffee refill. "Have a nice morning, you two. Enjoy the beautiful day."

"We will." Peyton smiled and latched onto Jaxon's arm as they walked out the door.

Once they were on their way Jaxon asked, "Sweetheart, what was that all about this morning? I've never known you to play games. What's going on?"

"I can't stand being told what to do. I rebel against it every time. Earlier in the garden I couldn't see him, but he told me that we would meet." She pursed her lips. "He made me feel out of control. I don't like that feeling."

"And I told you to get in and get out without asking. I get it. I should have asked." Jaxon shut her door once she was in.

"I don't think you do. It wasn't what you said or even that you didn't ask. I felt helpless when I couldn't challenge him. But I could and did challenge you. It made me feel like I had control again. I know it wasn't fair to you."

"Tell me. Communicate what's bothering you. I can handle it. Look, I get the fact men have too often forced their wills on women and given them no choices. I'm not that guy. I'm not always good at how I say what I'm thinking, but I respect you and your strength. Let's try not to waste our time fighting over something we can talk about." He pulled into the town square park. "Sometimes I feel like you're testing me to see if I'll walk away."

"I don't think I'm consciously doing it. There's no doubt I find it hard to trust men. I don't see you like I see my dad, but it still impacts how I see things. That and the fact I don't want anyone pushing me around. I saw what women like Kathryn went through. That visit back in time was an eye-opening experience for me. Look at how long it took for women to get the right to vote. The idea at that time was that a woman couldn't understand the weighty matters of state. She needed to be protected from herself. It was the man's job to take care of the little woman and tell her what to think. What happened to those same women if they were left alone when their husbands died? I'll tell you. Those same men who refused to let a woman have the right to vote forgot all about them. Finding a job for a woman then wasn't easy even when the men went off to war. We've come a long way, but it still isn't where it should be after all these years, and it bothers me."

"Hell, it should bother every woman." He unlatched his seatbelt and opened the car door. "I'm ready to hear the rest of your story when you're ready to tell me." He opened the door and took her hand when she stood beside him. They went to sit on the park bench near the gazebo in the center of the park.

"I told you about what I saw in the basement. They put the poor and the minorities down there. It was a dark, damp, and musty space. The care wasn't the same. Most doctors refused to go tend them, although the nurses who worked there were compassionate and caring people. What I didn't tell you about was what I found out went on behind the locked doors in the other wing of the building." She explained when Irma sent her there with the envelope and what she read on the papers when she looked at them later. "There was something illegal and unethical going on behind those closed doors. I'm sure of it. Kathryn showed me several pictures in my mind. That's why the ghosts have gathered near the inn."

"Why the inn? Do you have any ideas?" he asked her.

"Because of the man who is there, or maybe there is something I'm not seeing. I'm not sure how it all fits together yet. But the ghosts are there for a reason. My theory is they are his accusers. I guess we'll know soon enough. There's more to the story about the man who challenged me. I want to talk to Jessie and Reba before I blurt out my idea. It's almost too much for me to believe. I might be off-base altogether."

"Fair enough. What does it have to do with you?" He turned her to look at him. "Do I need to be worried?"

"I'm sure he thinks I can show him where the portal is. The problem is the book was the method this time, but will it work again? I don't have any idea. He wouldn't be alive if he went back in time, would he? As to whether you have to worry about me, I could say no, but truthfully he will try to kill me if I can't lead him to the portal. I plan to not be taken by surprise."

"Not the answer I wanted to hear." Jaxon frowned.

"I'm not happy about it either, but it is what it is." The words no sooner left her mouth than Jaxon pushed her to the ground, the bullet narrowly missing them both.

"Stay down!" He held her face down in the grass and covered her torso with his body. He pulled his gun from its holster while searching the park. "Damn. Where are you?" Another bullet ricocheted off the bench where they had been sitting, landing not far from their heads. Too close for comfort. "We're in his crosshairs. We need backup." He called the station, which brought several officers into the park. The next shot gave them a direction, and Kip and Gary headed toward the location. Kenny and Matt fired off a couple of rounds of cover allowing Peyton and Jaxon to get out of the line of fire.

"Are you okay?" Jaxon slipped his hand under her

chin and tipped her head up to meet his gaze.

"Besides the obvious fact of bringing back memories that I would rather forget, I didn't get hit." She brushed the dried grass off her cheek.

Jaxon wiped the smudge of dirt off her forehead. "Sorry I pushed your head down so hard. I had no idea where the shooter was."

"I would rather taste dirt than being shot again." She walked into his open arms. "I have no idea who the shooter is. It doesn't feel like the guy I was telling you about."

Matt walked over to where Jaxon and Peyton stood. He had his radio on and listened to the chatter.

Kip's voice came across the line. "We found the location but no shooter. We're picking up any evidence that we've found and will be back in a few. I told Kenny to have the patrols on the lookout for a dark sedan." Kip told him the model of the car.

"Do you need gloves or evidence bags?" Matt asked.

"No, I carry one of our small kits on me in case of emergency. There's not a lot here. But we'll cover it a second time to make sure we got everything. Luckily we came around the corner in time to see the car pull away from the curb. Gary got the first two numbers on the plates too."

"Let's hope one of our officers sees the car around town. I would like to have a chat with the occupant." Matt disconnected the call. "Care to tell me what you two were up to when all this took place?"

"We were talking about experiences she didn't tell the group last night." Jaxon frowned, his fists clenched at his sides.

"In that case, I think we might need to talk. Inside, in case our shooter decides to come around looking for a second chance to finish what he started."

"You won't get an argument from me." Jaxon took Peyton's hand and followed Matt back to the station.

Sitting in Matt's office, Peyton went over everything she had told Jaxon. "I think that covers everything but who would be shooting at us."

"Are you sure it's not the guy who said you would have to deal with him?" Matt asked.

"I'm sure. I know when he's around. Besides, he wouldn't want me dead until after I show him where the portal is. That's what he wants to know."

"Have you told us everything you can remember?" Jaxon asked.

She scrunched her face in concentration. "Wait a minute. I completely forgot about this. A couple of times on my way back to the boarding house it felt like someone or something was following me. Is it possible he followed me back through the portal? No. It has to be my imagination."

"Could it had been a premonition of someone you would face? You know, like in Tucson." His thumb squeezed her hand as he talked.

"I guess it's possible. But how? I have no idea." Her lips pursed in concentration.

"Think about it. Remember, he was following Kathryn. What were you doing at the time, or better yet what were you thinking about when you felt it?" Matt asked. "Jessie might be able to help you."

"I'll stop by and talk to her. One thing I know is that someone sees me as a threat, and this is a warning shot. Everything I've experienced is connected to the murder in some way, including all the ghosts in and around the inn."

"Ghosts? What ghosts?" Matt shook his head. "Here we go again."

"It started with the murder victim." Peyton went on to tell him about the ghosts at Katie's wedding. "The murder is the starting point, but there's something more sinister going on beneath the surface. It's been going on long before the murder. It will test our ability to think differently. Pinedale School is at the heart of it, and maybe at one point in time so was the inn. Although I would never mention it to Katie until I was sure."

"It couldn't be a simple murder. That would be asking too much. And I would have to agree we only mention the inn to Katie if and when the evidence backs up what you're feeling." Matt frowned.

"I concur." She smiled at him.

Jaxon chuckled. "I guess we had better get ready to face the music. Peyton seems to be right when she sees something. If Jessie were to see it too then it'll be a matter of when and not if."

"Speaking of Jessie. I think you should stop by and have a chat with her. The sooner the better." Matt stood when Jaxon did. "Keep your eyes open, Jaxon, for a car following you."

"I will." Jaxon took Peyton's hand and helped her out of the chair. "Let's go see your cousin. Something tells me we are going to need all the help we can get."

"Okay. I could use something to drink. I still have my scone to eat, and I'd be happy to share half with you." She gave him a flirty wink.

Chapter 26

While Jaxon browsed through the books, Peyton spent the afternoon talking to her cousin and Reba, who happened to be there. Not that anything with Reba was ever happenstance. When it came to Reba as Peyton knew all too well, it was all by design. She explained to them about the events of the morning. She didn't leave out any details of the several times when she had felt someone was following her, or maybe it was Kathryn that they were following. It all seemed too confusing. Her foot tapped under the table. Glancing back and forth at their faces, she waited impatiently for the response, but silence filled the air between them. Jessie jumped up to help a customer, and Reba sipped her tea staring off into space.

"It could be they were following Kathryn and somehow were sucked forward in time with you." Jessie sat down beside her after the customer had grabbed a bookmark and went into the coffee shop. "It's possible," she said when she saw the skeptical look on Reba's face.

"You're right, it's possible. Not probable though. Where would they pick up a gun and know how to use it in this setting? Unless they are seasoned travelers through the portal. What do you think?" Reba pursed her lips.

Not one to remain silent Peyton added her two

cents. “I’ve wondered if there are others who managed to go back and forth in time. I mean, if we stumbled onto it, others before us could have. Food for thought anyway don’t you think?” Peyton noticed Jaxon had picked a book off the shelf and was reading the jacket cover.

“What do you think, Jaxon?” Jessie asked.

“Hmm. This is out of my field of expertise, but if I had to venture a guess, I would say you’re all right on some level. They might have been following Kathryn and followed Peyton back into our time. I mean the two of them do look alike. It’s true, they would’ve had to know how a modern weapon works to use it with any accuracy. And whoever shot at us this morning came darn close to hitting us. Peyton is also right. If you’ve gone through the portal, there may be others who have too. The way my mind works though I’m more likely to think it is someone worried that Peyton knows something or is getting too close to their operation.”

“What do you mean?” Peyton asked.

“Well, if I were investigating this incident, I would ask you what kind of questions the interviewer asked you during your job interview. I would want to know about any questions you asked that might trigger a red flag in their thinking. Did you see anything that seemed off when you toured the school? I’d also want to know your first and last impression of the place and the people. And did you at any time get the sense that you were being watched beyond the people you could see visibly?” He slipped the book back into the spot where it belonged.

“Whew, and here I thought you weren’t paying attention to anything we were saying.” Jessie laughed.

"Of course I am. I listen and try to feed it through my logical brain in a way I can handle it." He moved on to another bookshelf.

"I for one have to do something. I have no idea when or where another bullet might be headed my way." Peyton stood.

"What do you suggest?" he asked.

"I want to go to Pinedale and drive around the town. It's larger now, but I want to see if any of what I can remember remains."

"Not without me you aren't—" He paused. "—if you don't mind."

She laughed. "Nice save."

"I'm growing." He reached for her hand.

"One word of caution." Reba motioned to them. "Whether the person is from the past, present, or travels between them, they're dangerous. Something you've said or done has alerted them that you're a threat to their operation. I believe it's a crime that started when Kathryn was alive, and it is still going on in Pinedale today. It may be hidden from view but has hurt more lives than we'll ever know. Be careful, you two. This case will make you think things are too improbable to be real. And yet when all is said and done, justice will be served for those who have waited for generations." Reba sipped her tea demurely and patted her hair. "Go along now and have a nice drive."

Once in the car and on their way, Jaxon glanced at her. "You know the things Reba says are often unsettling. I never know how to take them. It doesn't seem to make any sense until the end. The trouble is she's always spot on, and I wish I could figure it out ahead of time."

"I know. I need to record and listen to what she says over and over until I get the nuance of her words. There must be a key to interpreting them before you're in the middle of the mess. Warnings are supposed to be helpful. Aren't they?"

"I always thought they were meant to be." He glanced in his side mirror. "Keep your eye on that red car two cars back. Let me know if it continues to follow us. Damn." He made a quick right turn into a neighborhood.

"The car turned but pulled over." She continued to watch, and when Jaxon turned again the car hung back but was still following. "It's safe to say we have a tail."

He turned back onto the highway. "Pinedale must have something of interest going on. We have no jurisdiction here, but Matt could alert them once we know what this is all about."

"More likely Tom Maxwell will need to. It must be a big crime to span a few generations." She glanced in the mirror. The car had fallen back a few spaces in line but continued to follow them.

"What makes you think Tom will be involved?" he asked her.

"Because you'll call when you find out what's going on. That's the way it works." She reached for her phone to answer as it chimed. "Hi, Jeremy. What's up? Jaxon's with me. I'll put this on speaker. I want him to hear what you say."

"Hey, Jaxon, Matt told me I should call you with some of the information I found. Are you in a place where you can talk?"

"I'm about to pull in a parking space and shake a tail." Jaxon parked between two cars, forcing the red car to move past him.

Peyton wrote down the license plate numbers she could read. "Go ahead, Jeremy, we're ready."

"How was your trip? I can't wait to hear all the details. This whole portal time travel excites me more than you'll know. I'll call you and Jessie later to hear the skinny on it. Right now there are a few things you need to know."

"Let's have it," Jaxon told him.

"I checked into the history of the Pinedale School. Upfront it looks like everything is A-Okay, but when you dig into the stats and numbers something doesn't add up. I did my thing and checked bank accounts, and I found some pretty odd facts." He went on to explain a few of his findings. "I'm sending you a few papers and a spreadsheet in your email. Let me know what you think after reading them. As I see it something is going down at the school and has been for a long time."

"Jeremy, when you get a chance, run the combinations of numbers on the plate of the car that was following us."

"Your state?"

"Yes." She told him the color and make of the car. "Hopefully, that will narrow it down a little bit."

"I have been doing a little research on Kathryn and Stewart Gimble. Your relatives were awesome. That's why you and Jessie are too. Do you want me to send you what I've found along with pictures?"

"Yes, please. I wanted to do the same but haven't had time yet. Spending a few days seeing life through her eyes taught me a lot about who she was. I didn't learn as much about Stewart. I figure if Kathryn loved him, he must have been all right."

"He was more than all right. All I can say is that you're in for a treat when you read about him. Now I know why Sadie is so cool. As soon as I hang up I'll send you everything. Matt told me you were nearly shot this morning. After you read the papers, Jaxon, maybe you'll understand what you might be dealing with. I'm sure there's more to it, and I'll keep digging."

"Thanks, Jeremy. We'll talk again soon." Peyton clicked off the phone.

Jaxon turned to look at Peyton. "Where do you want to go first?"

Following the small drawing Emily had given her, she gave him directions, and they found the Woodson Boarding House she had stayed at. It was still stately and beautiful. The plaque on the house and the sign in the yard told her the house was on the official National Register. Tours of the home were offered daily by Pinedale's Historical Society. "Do you mind if I take one of the tours?"

"No. I'm interested in seeing the house with you. Do you think it has changed much since you stayed there?"

"That question seems odd on many levels." She shook her head. "I wonder how long Mrs. Woodson ran the place before she sold it. She was a lovely woman. Not much older than Kathryn was at the time."

"It must have been hard work for such a young woman." Jaxon frowned. "As you mentioned earlier there weren't many options for women at that time."

"She told me that her husband told her in a dream to open their house to boarders. It's how she survived. Believe me, she was good at it. There was a calm and serene spirit around the woman. She made you feel instantly at home. I loved the evenings when she greeted me with a fresh glass of lemonade and a few moments of her time to chat and sort through the emotions of the day. Kindness was a part of who she was." Peyton opened the car door. "It's about time for the tour, and I'm looking forward to it."

He reached for her hand and walked to the area where the tour began. "Is this how you remember it?" he asked as they walked up to the porch.

"This porch is where Mrs. Woodson greeted the neighbors in the evening when they strolled by. Oh, and the parlor is how I remember it. I'm sure the furnishings may be different but not by much."

The big table still graced the dining room. "The residents lingered here to talk so many nights. Mrs. Woodson was an amazing cook. From the main course to the fresh pies she made, there had to be many contented people after one of her meals. I sure was." Peyton whispered so only he could hear. She ran her hand over the back of one of the chairs fondly.

"It's always interested me how people lived. History was one of my favorite subjects in school." Jaxon squeezed her hand as they started up the stairs.

"Really? It was mine too."

"Where was your room?"

"On the second floor, the third door on the right." When Peyton's foot touched the final step, pictures flashed through her mind. Disjointed images of young women and men whose faces were melting before her.

Jaxon knew that look—he had seen it on her before. He took her hand tugging her along on the tour.

The sensation of being watched overwhelmed her, and she tried to run, but something held her tight and wouldn't let her go. A dark, shadowy figure skimmed along the edges of her mind. His hideous laughing sounded nightmarish and scary along with the faces that floated before her. As quickly as they had come, they suddenly stopped. She recognized the room in which she stood. Kathryn stared at her, and Peyton understood Kathryn had seen the same faces. Her great-great-grandmother knew what had happened to those people. The ball was now in Peyton's court to finish the story and see it through to the end. She shuddered. How many people had met the same fate over the past many years? How could she ever prove it?

"Are you all right?" Jaxon whispered in her ear.

"I will be. This was my great-great-grandmother's room. I can still feel her presence here. Others may have stayed in the space after her, but something of her remains present." She glanced at him. "Her life impacted many others. Do you think that's how our legacy continues to live on? It could be said of Mrs. Woodson too. Her words and actions can be felt in every room in this house."

He squeezed her hand in his. "You ask such unusual questions. I've never thought about the possibilities of a person's essence being felt in a room or house after they're gone. I guess those who loved them could never walk into a place without a memory of that person being present in their mind. At least that's my take. Your questions and the things you sense are what I find intriguing about you, Peyton."

"We should stay up with the guide, or we can leave if you're bored." She glanced at him.

"I'd like to finish the tour. The gardens are next." He smiled at her.

"You enjoy some of the same things that I do. I find that fascinating. Most men would be waiting for me in the car." They followed the guide out the back door to the garden. Again, she took a step back in time to the moment she had first seen the Woodson garden. Her landlady had gone to collect a few tomatoes for dinner. Boy, were they ever good!

Chapter 27

Jaxon held the door open, and Peyton stepped out the door behind the tour leader. "Thank you. I enjoyed seeing the house," he told the woman.

"If you're like me, you like all things historical. I'm glad you enjoyed yourself." The woman smiled at him.

"We both love history, and my girlfriend recently learned her great-great-grandmother stayed in the house when she worked at the hospital during the Spanish Flu pandemic."

"Aren't those online ancestry searches great? I've traced my family line that way." She reached for the door handle. "No wonder you were paying attention to every part of the tour. I take it she worked at what is now the school?"

"Yes, she did," Peyton replied.

"You should take a tour of the school while you're here. They give you all the history of the place. I'm glad to have met you both. I need to make sure the house is locked up. You two have a nice evening." The woman went back inside.

Jaxon took hold of her hand and started down the porch stairs. The squeal of tires alerted him. By the time he located where the sound was coming from the red car was nearing their position with a gun already out the window. He pushed her to the ground and shielded her with his body for the second time on the same day. The car sped off. "Sorry." He noticed she groaned when he rolled to the side of her. "Damn. I feel every one of my years at this moment."

"You. How do you think I feel? Without any warning, I'm suddenly shoved to the ground, and your weight fell on top of me. Please don't take offense—as good of shape as you're in and as handsome as you are, we are talking about dead weight. Can I just say ouch?"

"I know two times in one day is a lot to ask of you. In my defense, by the time I saw the gun I didn't have any alternative action." He stood to his feet and reached his hand toward her, helping her to her feet.

"Believe me, I'm not upset with you. I'm grateful not to have the bullet touch my body in any way. Once is enough. Besides, if I have to be shoved to the ground, I'm glad it's by you."

"I guess it's one way to get to know each other. Up close and real personal." He wiggled his brows and grinned.

"Are you two all right?" The woman came running out of the house, her gray hair pulling out of the neat bun on the top of her head. "Come up on the porch and sit. I can't believe it. I simply don't understand who would do such a thing. I called the police, and they're on their way. I saw it all. We've never had anything like this happen before." Her hand shook as she talked to them. "Oh goodness. You both seem so calm. I'm not. I've never seen anyone shot at before. I'm glad you're both alive. You could have been killed." She rambled and paced. "I hope the car doesn't come back. Oh, heavens, do you think they'll return? Maybe we should go inside."

"I think we should be okay," Jaxon told her. "The police are near. I can hear the sirens." He followed Peyton onto the porch.

"There might be an ambulance. When I saw you fall on the young lady, I told the operator you might have been shot." She started to sob. "I'm sorry. I didn't know what to do."

Peyton hugged her. "You were perfect. Thank you for calling the police. Right now I'm in shock, or I would be crying along with you. Here, let's sit down together while we wait." She led the sweet woman over to chairs on the porch.

"She isn't kidding when she says she would be crying too." He smiled at them. "It's a sign of a tender and loving heart."

"That's a kind thing to say, young man. A lot of men can't bear tears." She patted Peyton's hand. "You're a lucky girl."

"Yes, I am."

They spent the next forty-five minutes answering the officers' questions. Peyton gave them the information she had on the red car that had followed them into town. After talking for a few minutes, she sat back and watched Jaxon in action. Not only handsome, he knew their lingo and how their minds worked. He also was way ahead of them. He gave them leads in how to question him.

"I imagine the guy is long gone by now," one of the officers said and then looked at Jaxon. "What do you think?"

"It's possible. But remember he followed us into town. He might be watching us now waiting to follow us home. It depends on how bold he feels. I mean he did manage to get off a few shots in a crowded neighborhood in daylight. I think this guy means business. He could have simply wanted to scare us off." Jaxon pointed toward the house. "You might want to dig that bullet out of the shutter. It might come in handy."

"Of course. I'll take care of it right away. How long are you in the area for?" the youngest of the two men asked.

"Not much longer. When you're finished with us, I think we should get on our way home. We were going to tour the school, but we might need to save it for another day."

"Sure thing, Detective Kincaid. We'll get in touch if we find the suspect or make an arrest. In the meantime, you two stay safe and have a nice evening."

Jaxon shook their hands. "Thanks. I would appreciate you letting us know if you find anything."

"It's a sad day when folks can't visit a tourist site without someone shooting at them. Pinedale is normally a friendly and safe place to live. This one is a hard one to figure. Of course, you being a big city detective I suppose this happens a lot to you."

"Not really." Jaxon thanked them again and walked Peyton to the car.

Peyton was happy to be on the road back to the cove. "This has been a strange day all the way around."

"Agreed. I can't figure out what we're up against, though. How are the two connected, if at all?" He checked his mirrors. "I don't see our tail. Since our suspect's car is obvious, he'll ditch it for another. Most likely it's a rental to begin with."

"There's one way to find out." She texted Jeremy

and asked him if he had found any information on the red car's owner. A few minutes later he confirmed Jaxon's suspicion.

They took a detour to the car rental company. When they pulled into the parking lot the red car was there. It didn't take long to get a name and a credit card number, along with an address, thanks to Jaxon's badge. They had missed the suspect by about thirty minutes give or take. He must have shot at them and rushed to ditch the car.

"Our guy made a rookie mistake by renting another car from the same company. At least we know the car he'll be driving should he come around again." Jaxon opened the car door for her.

"I doubt he thought we had a plate number or could trace it so quickly."

"His second mistake," Jaxon told her.

"Oh yeah, what was his first one?"

"Shooting at you twice. That was the biggest boner he's made in his life." Jaxon frowned and started the car.

"All I know is I'm glad you were there to throw me to the ground. I wouldn't want just anyone to." She glanced at him. He cracked a smile, but his chin still looked like it was made of granite. "Look, Kincaid, I know you're mad, but don't do anything crazy."

"You think. How can you tell?" He glared at her. "You could have been killed." His jaw twitched.

"But I wasn't, and you saved me." She squeezed his arm. "Let's go home."

"What would have happened if I hadn't been with you?" he asked.

"I might not be here, but you can't worry about it."

She flashed him a half-smile.

"The hell I can't. You of all people know how close you came to not making it the last time. I'm not willing to risk it again. The next time you might not be so lucky." He patted her hand. "You know me by now. I do everything by the book. Even if I wanted to break a few bones it's not going to happen. I want to put him behind bars. You can quit looking at me like that."

"Like what?" She gave him a sheepish look.

"You know." He checked his mirrors. "I'm good at my job, sweetheart, and you don't have to worry about me." He pulled onto the road to Blue Cove.

"Believe it or not, I don't want anything to happen to you either. I think you need to teach me how to protect myself and you if we're together. I can do well up close and personal but not against a gun."

"I remember the kick. You were awesome. A gun is a different story. I'll ask Matt for suggestions."

"I know Jessie learned, and if this keeps happening, I think I should know too." She twisted the straps of her purse.

"We'll see."

They settled into a comfortable silence as they got close to Blue Cove. Peyton couldn't believe that they were shot at twice in one day. Why? Too close for comfort, and still carrying the scars from her last run-in with a bullet, she didn't want to ever have to go through it again. Dang, she was tired of it, and this was only the beginning.

They were nowhere near understanding what this case was about. Someone thought they were getting too close, but to what? She needed to think about her time at the school. Had she said anything that might tip someone off? Or was it possible there was another traveler who had the same gift of sight and used it against people? It was something to think about.

Chapter 28

The evening had ended on a more pleasant note than the day had begun. He took Peyton out for a quiet dinner at a new restaurant on the waterfront. The food was delicious, the atmosphere conducive to intimate dining, and the owner Robert Fitzpatrick aimed to please his customers. If tonight's crowd were any indication, the Osprey would be around Blue Cove for quite a while.

After watching the sailboats coming into the cove, they retired to the cottage to watch TV which they did little of. He finally questioned her about what she had seen when they toured the Woodson house today. It opened another avenue to consider and a possible reason for someone to feel threatened by their presence. Making a mental note to call Tom Maxwell in the morning, Jaxon let his mind drift to the more pleasant aspects of the evening.

She fit in his arms perfectly, and holding her felt right to him. He could imagine many comfortable nights at home together with her. It seemed useless to think of the future and not see her in it. She made him a better man. He grinned. Tonight would be a long one. Her response to his kisses made it hard to leave. He stretched out on the bed once he got back to the inn. Damn. He took a deep breath. He needed a clear mind. Shot at twice in one day. Faces from Kathryn's time forward to recent days that had suffered in some way and were possibly linked to the school in Pinedale. What were they looking at? He needed to think through this unusual day. There had to be a clue in there somewhere. Peyton asked and he agreed with her to go back to Pinedale to tour the school. Something about the whole operation didn't add up. He opened his laptop determined to find something of interest in the spreadsheet and information that Jeremy had sent earlier.

****

Peyton took her time getting ready for bed. Jaxon made her feel like anything was possible. He never berated her when she told him about one of her premonitions or the ghosts that she saw. She couldn't imagine having any of these conversations with any other man. At least after walking a few days in Kathryn's shoes she knew where this strange ability came from and how it could fit into normal life without making a big deal about it. She didn't need to be psychic. All she had to be was herself.

With that settled, she could think more clearly about their night together. She hadn't wanted him to leave. Feeling safe was the descriptive word that came to mind whenever he was near. She hadn't felt safe most of her life. His kisses left her breathless and fanning her face. The mere thought of his arms wrapped around her made her feel both hot and content at the same time. All she knew was that it wasn't something she had expected to ever experience.

If her past taught her one thing it was to be cautious. She wouldn't jump into anything too quickly, which included a job or a new place to live. As for

Jaxon, as much as she loved being with him, she worried he could suffocate her and keep her from her dreams. Not likely, but she wouldn't chance it. He told her he felt like she was testing him. Maybe on some level she was. Growth, change, and becoming all that she could be were top on her list, and she didn't want to be stifled.

"Hey, cousin, are you still awake?" Jessie called out as she came into the cottage.

"I'll be out in a minute." Peyton threw on a robe and walked out into the living room. "What's up?"

"Matt told me there was another shooting incident. I want all the details of your day. You know men—they never remember the small things. Matt's eyes glaze over when I ask him certain questions."

"Like?" Peyton asked.

"How do you feel? Feelings stump him every time. As much as I love my hunky cop, he's not what you'd call a great conversationalist." Jessie laughed. "He does have some amazing talents though." She smiled batting her lashes. "He's a great kisser."

"I was thinking about Jaxon's great talent in that exact area right before you walked in." Peyton playfully fanned her face. "It could make holding out for marriage a bit harder."

"Heavens no. Who knows how much they'll kiss you after they say I do? You know the whole thrill of the chase thing. I'm thinking I might stretch this out for a while. If you know what I mean."

"I'm in no hurry myself, but I don't want to run him off either."

"We'll have to be wise, won't we? Okay, I've goofed around long enough. I want to hear everything you can remember. Our guys need a bit of help with this situation." Jessie tucked her legs under and watched Peyton.

"It all started when Jaxon noticed a car following us on our way to Pinedale." Peyton explained all the events of the afternoon including the trip to the rental company.

"What was it like seeing the vision in the room where Kathryn stayed?"

"It reminded me once again where our sight comes from. She managed to live a normal life. She married, had children and grandchildren, and we should be able to do the same."

"I need to hold on to that. Sometimes I worry Matt will wake up one day and wonder what he got himself into. I would hate for him to have regrets. It would be devastating if he ever walked away."

"I think about the same things, and we're not even engaged yet. One thing I know for sure is that I need to concentrate on what's going on. Bullets twice in one day is not a good thing. Someone is serious about killing me or at least scaring me. They're doing a good job on the second part."

"I know it's hard to think about, but if we've gone through the portal others may have too. Someone might have followed you back both ways or one." Jessie repositioned the pillow behind her on the chair. "I'm glad no one can hear us right now. Our conversations would sound weird to a casual observer."

"I know." Peyton closed her eyes. "It doesn't help that I sense something is taking place at the school besides learning. I'm sure it was there in the time of Kathryn too. I have no idea what. I wonder if it is the same person. How crazy is that?"

"Nothing, and I do mean nothing, seems beyond the realm of possibility to me anymore. I still can't believe you saw our great-great-grandmother. Tell me all about her."

"I can do one better. Jeremy did some research on her and the school and sent us what he found. I was getting ready to dig into them. We may as well do it together." Peyton reached for her laptop.

"Count me in. I'll be right back. Set your computer on my desk next to mine and pull up a chair. It will take both sets of eyes poring over the info." Jessie rushed into her room and closed the door.

Peyton couldn't hide her amusement. Her cousin never walked anywhere. She placed her computer on the desk, plugged it into the power strip, and turned it on. Heading to the kitchen she grabbed one of the chairs and plunked it down beside Jessie's desk chair. She opened her emails and downloaded the attachments from Jeremy. She forwarded the information to Jessie. Her cousin was right—it would take them both going over all the pages. There seemed to be a lot of information to work their way through.

"I'm back." Jessie turned on her laptop and plopped down in her chair. "Where should we start?"

"I forwarded Jeremy's email to you because you're better at reading those bank numbers than I am. Why don't you start with the spreadsheets? I will read over the pages on the school. I may have to rethink taking the teaching position they've offered me."

Peyton couldn't believe what she read on the pages. All the strange sensations she had standing outside the doors in the locked area in the other wing of the building rushed back through her. Goosebumps started at her neck and raced down her back. Kathryn knew something bad was happening behind those locked doors. During her daughter's generation, the orphanage in Pinedale became an insane asylum and was eventually shut down because of abuse complaints that could never be proven. There were stories of mass graves and illegal experiments on patients. Was it possible for Radar, the FBI search dog, to find something if there were still bodies buried on the property somewhere? "Jess, do you think Radar could find a body buried years ago?"

"I suppose it would depend on how long ago you're talking about. Radar found the twins, and they were murdered in the sixties. I would think anything is possible, but I'll ask Frank. If you want to know what his dog can do, it's best to go to the source. I'll call him tomorrow." Jessie glanced back at the computer screen. "I guess I should ask why?"

"It's a hunch after what I read. That and something I experienced as Kathryn working at the hospital. A possible angle to look at which might not amount to anything, but I think I should pursue it." Peyton stretched her arms behind her back. "Did anything stand out to you in all those numbers?"

"Let me say someone is doing some fancy bookwork There is no way a school can make this kind of money. Trust me. Their operational expenses should be higher. Simply put, the figures don't add up. I want an expert to look at these documents. Do you mind? Besides, my eyes are starting to glaze over. I have a busy day tomorrow and need to get some sleep." Jessie printed the spreadsheets.

"Of course. I would appreciate any help we can get. If you get a chance to read the other pages, please do. You'll love what you read about our great-great-grandmother. It will make you proud to be one of her descendants. I have more questions than ever, but I'm too tired to think about them now." Peyton turned off her computer. "Sweet dreams, cous. See you in the morning." With papers in hand, she walked into her room. *Kathryn, I would appreciate any help you can give us.*

Chapter 29

As soon as she stretched out on the bed the vision began. The faces of children rolled through her mind. Happy children at play, carefree, and without concern as the storm clouds built in the sky around them. The wind blew, lashing against them as they played on. A dark, foreboding creature rose behind their happy faces. Peyton tried to warn them, but they couldn't hear her voice above the roaring of the beast. He swooped down, consuming them in his embrace until she could see them no more. Suddenly the scene changed, and she saw them once again in hospital beds within the walls of the school. Nurses, doctors, and parents all looked on hoping for one good sign. Their masked faces couldn't hide the fear that she saw in their eyes. "The doctor said it is the Spanish Flu." One nurse said, her voice filled with dread. "The numbers of deaths are rising rapidly, and he doesn't know what more can be done." The same whispers rose from lips in a steady crescendo in every room she could see. The darkness like a mist rolled through the halls of the building, creeping from room to room and bed to bed with its claw-like fingers reaching out to touch anyone in its path. Kathryn's impressions continued to play in her mind. She knew what was going on behind the closed doors. Locked away from public view. Kathryn waited outside the doors, but this time Peyton could see what took place behind those doors. She understood the screeches and the cries, and the madman had to be stopped.

She awakened in a puddle of sweat with the sheet tied in a knot around her. Jessie stared at her from the foot of the bed. "Are you all right? I heard you calling out and ran in here. You were thrashing about, and I didn't want to awaken you for fear you were seeing something important."

Peyton struggled to sit up. "Kathryn showed me what an awful time she lived through and how heartbreaking the images she had witnessed were. The pandemic was bad enough but not as bad as what she knew was going on behind locked doors. How do I prove it? They couldn't stop it from happening then. What can we do?" She told Jessie about the dream and what she saw.

"All I know is that you were taken back in time for a reason. It must be time for all of this to stop. The ghost activity in the garden says they're here to seek justice, and it's past time for it to be served. The proof will come with the help of Jaxon and Matt. That's what they do. All we can do is see what we see. But if our great-great-grandmother saw it in her day I can only imagine how many lives have been impacted over the past decades. I like to believe you get what you give. If you give love eventually you reap it back, but the flip side to it is if you are mean to others you will suffer the same fate." Jessie sat on the edge of the bed.

"Karma, fate, or justice or whatever words you want to use to describe it, I believe it's real. At least what I've seen so far tells me it is." Peyton pushed her hair out of her eyes. "Would you look at us?" She pointed at her cousin with a grin. "We're a couple of freaking philosophers." Beyond tired, she dissolved into giggles soon joined by Jessie.

"What's next?" Jessie asked when she stopped laughing.

"Jaxon didn't want me to take the job at Pinedale. I guess I need to find out why. Something is going on there. Still, I wonder how it's possible for a person in Kathryn's time to be involved in any of this now. I get the idea of finding the portal, but he wouldn't be an immortal."

"Remember what I told you about Skylar, and how he jumped between dimensions?" Peyton nodded. "He also controlled the actions of Garrett Massey and a few others. Through mind control, he manipulated them to do what he wanted. I don't know how, but I don't discount anything anymore. You won't find any of the information in a police report, but Matt can tell you how real it was nonetheless. If it's true he took your friend's husband and found a way through the portal, he could still be manipulating someone else that he has jumped into. He may still be continuing his experiments like a mad scientist in our era." Jessie shuddered. "It gives me the creeps thinking about it. Skylar controlled peoples' actions. Who knows what this guy has been up to for the past one hundred years?"

"I can't imagine. That's a loaded question. I guess it's time to find out who John worked with at the hospital and if they went missing at the same time. I hope they kept good records back in the day." Peyton tried to free the sheet wrapped around her legs.

"If anyone can find it Jeremy can." Jessie jumped up. "In the meantime, we need to find out what is going on at that school. There seems to have been a problem there for several years. Changing the function of the building hasn't seemed to fix the problem."

"You're right." Peyton yawned. "But first we need to try and get some sleep and look at this with fresh eyes in the morning." She laid her head back on her pillow. "Nighty, night, cous."

"Goodnight." Peyton shut off the light as Jessie left the room.

Her body wanted to sleep but her mind wouldn't let her. All the jumbled pieces of information kept surfacing in her thoughts until she started to place them in the puzzle of the events since Katie's wedding. Working through each fragment of information, she placed them in an order in which they started to make sense. Too tired to turn on the light, she hoped she could remember the same order in the morning. The famous last words of every writer before drifting off to sleep, she mused.

****

After he left Peyton for the night, Jaxon put in a call to Tom Maxwell. He needed to run some items by him while the events were still fresh in his mind. The fact that Maxwell had worked with Matt and Jessie on several occasions made it easier for him to tell him some of the stranger pieces of the case to date.

He explained about Peyton's journey back in time and what he had learned about the school so far. "After being shot at twice on the same day and the information Jeremy sent us, I'm sure the school is involved. I'm forwarding some copies for you to look at. This might require the Agency's involvement and not just local police. I think that brings you up to speed with what's going on. We still don't have a suspect in the original murder case yet." Jaxon sat on the edge of the bed.

"It sounds like Peyton is right up there with her cousin. Two in one family—there's a head-scratcher. What are the odds of something like that happening?" Tom asked.

"I'm not sure about the odds, but considering their great-great grandmother's ability at least they know where they get it. Sadie, her mother, and her grandmother all had the gift of sight, and it showed up in both of Sadie's granddaughters. Who knows if Peyton's sister Madison will display the gift at some point." Jaxon leaned forward in his chair.

"I look over your email. Keep me in the loop, if for no other reason than this has all the earmarks of being an interesting case. Matt hasn't had any exciting cases lately, and I'm thinking he's about due. I wonder why he wanted your help with this one."

"With Dylan gone on his honeymoon, I think the department is a bit shorthanded. It's Peyton getting the premonitions and not Jessie. Jessie may have caught a break. Katie kept her busy the last several months with her wedding plans. Still, the ladies are both working on this case." Jaxon rubbed his forehead.

"A high-powered team if you ask me. I'm sure the case will be solved soon," Tom said.

"Let's hope so. I have to leave soon to head back to Phoenix and close out the case there. I'd like to see how this one ends. I admit I'm hooked. I think you'll be too once you get a chance to read over the papers I sent you." Jaxon stood, kicking off his shoes. "Call me if you have any questions."

"I will. Talk to you soon, Kincaid."

"Sounds good." Jaxon propped himself up against

the headboard, stretching his legs out on the bed. He grabbed the remote and turned to the sports channel. He needed a break from ghosts, time travel, and shooters. If he needed a break, he could only imagine what Peyton must be feeling. He glanced at the clock. With any luck, she was sound asleep and not thinking at all. After the day she had rest was what she needed most. “Sweet dreams, sweetheart. I hope you dream of me.”

Chapter 30

The sunlight spilling through the small opening in the curtain hit her squarely in the eyes. Rubbing her eyes, Peyton stretched before sitting up. Somehow after her odd dream, when she finally went back to sleep again she dreamed of Jaxon, a far more pleasant subject. Scooting to the edge of the bed she slipped her feet into her slippers. It was surprising how rested she felt all things considered.

Turning on the shower, she stepped into the warm water mist and let her body enjoy the refreshing moment. The new soap Jessie had bought her smelled like roses. An hour later she walked out of her room ready to take on the day. That is, after a cup of her favorite tea and a scone from Java Joe's. Her cousin always kept a fresh supply of mini scones on hand, one of the many perks of working close to Java Joe's. Looking in the bag on the counter had her clapping her hands. Blueberry was the flavor of the day, and she couldn't be happier. Jessie introduced her to the blueberry scone with a light lemon icing drizzle on top. Maybe she would have coffee instead. The pot was ready. All she had to do was pour it into her cup.

"I see you found the coffee." Jessie raced into the kitchen. "Mine will have to be on the go this morning." She pulled her travel mug out of the cupboard and filled just enough to leave room for the cream.

“Don’t forget your scone. They are extra good today,” Peyton reminded her.

“Never!” Jessie grabbed two mini scones and wrapped them in a napkin. “Jaxon called. He said he tried to reach you. Call him back so the man doesn’t worry that you’re off on another trip. I tried to reassure him you were in the shower, but I’m not sure he believed me.” She laughed as she rushed out of the kitchen. “See you later. For heaven’s sake call the man.” The front door slammed on her way out.

Taking another bite of her scone, she licked the icing off her lips and reached for her phone. “Good morning. Jessie said you called.”

“I did. Do you still want to go tour the school in Pinedale this morning?” he asked.

“If you’re coming with me, of course, I would love to.”

“As if I’d let you go without me. We’re in this together. I’ll walk down to the cottage to get you in thirty minutes if that works for you.”

“I can meet you at the inn if you want. I walk there all the time. I’m a big girl.” She smiled and waited for his reaction.

“I know you are quite capable of taking care of yourself. But you know me. It’s all about not wanting to disappoint my mother. She’d slap me upside my head if I didn’t pick you up at your door and escort you to the car. Where it’s a must that I hold the door open for you. Humor me this once, please.” She could hear the laughter in his voice.

“Seems to me I’ve heard this story before. I may have to talk to your mother about making you work so hard for a friend.”

"It won't do any good to argue with her. Believe me, I know. She always wins."

"Well since you said please, I'll be waiting for you. It's the right thing to do. Besides, I need to make a good impression when I meet your mother." She popped the last piece of scone into her mouth as soon as she disconnected the call. With a final sip of her coffee, she placed the empty mug in the dishwasher and headed for her room.

A quick glance in the mirror, a touch of her favorite perfume, and her preferred shade of lip gloss, and she was ready to spend the day with the man of her dreams. He had been in her dreams a great deal last night. The moment she started seeing Jaxon differently, she told her cousin, was when she saw him as a hunky cowboy on the streets of Tombstone. She smiled at her reflection. The truth was Kincaid had proven to be a good man and not at all like her dad. She found herself willing to get to know him better. At least, that's the story she told herself when she tried to put the brakes on her growing crush. He made her stomach flutter whenever he got near her. Jaxon Kincaid was far too handsome for her own good.

"Peyton," Jaxon called out. "The damn door should be locked," he mumbled under his breath.

"I'll be right there. I didn't hear you knock." She walked out of the room.

"I did. And if the door was locked as it should be with a suspect at large, I wouldn't be able to walk in your house to get your attention." He frowned.

"Is that your attempt at a lecture?" She frowned right back at him with her hands on her hips.

"Not a lecture. Let's call it a friendly reminder.

And while you're being reminded, you might also want to tell your cousin the same thing."

"I find the whole idea of locking a door almost useless when a couple of strong kicks could break it open." His grim expression made her rethink her statement. "But at least then I would hear the door being kicked in, and I guess that's the whole point isn't it." She took a step toward him. "You can stop frowning. Your point is taken."

****

The drive to Pinedale kept Jaxon on edge. Not far as miles were concerned, but there were plenty of spots to conceal a shooter from view. He breathed a sigh of relief and the tension left his shoulders when they drove into the town limits without incident. No tails or bullets. *It might turn out to be a good day after all.* With that thought came the realization that he had heard little of what Peyton talked about on the ride over.

"I hope you weren't telling me anything important." He glanced at her.

"Nope, not a word. I could see you were watching for trouble. I tend to talk nonstop when I get nervous. It doesn't matter what I say so long as there is no space of silence. I do have something I need to talk to you about though. It can wait until after the tour at the school."

He turned into the parking area at the school. "Stay alert. I want to hear about any impressions you have or any premonitions." He reached for her hand.

"You know I will," she told him.

Jaxon listened to the guide as she talked about the history of the building. He could picture Peyton walking through the halls during the pandemic as Kathryn. He couldn't wait to hear what she thought about the tour. After they finished walking through the main section of the building and reception area, they went down the stairs to the basement. Peyton's rapidly changing facial expression told him she was reliving something. He held tightly to her hand as the guide openly talked about the problems of the day and admitted that this dark damp area was where the indigent and people of color were treated. She finished by saying it was one of the sadder statements of the times. Peyton's grip on his hand grew tighter as they made their way to the other side of the building.

****

Kathryn's memories flooded through her mind as soon as her foot touched the bottom step, bringing to her mind the suffering and the cries of people. This was the last place that many of them ever saw. A depressing way for a life filled with promise to end. Were their families ever able to find them or were they buried in a mass grave? The longer Peyton stood there the more she became aware of a darkness that seemed to envelop the space. But as they turned to walk up the stairs, she was faced with the truth it wasn't the basement that was dark. Something or someone watched them. She held tight to Jaxon's hand as the desire to run grew stronger. Her eyes began to search for possible exits out of the building. The sensation grew stronger the closer they came to the other wing of the building.

"We can't go through these doors. This is where our full-time folks live, and so it's off-limits for tours. There is also a research lab in a section of this wing. It's dedicated and funded by the orphanage's founders." The lady talked about the students who lived there and why.

The more she talked the harder it became for Peyton to breathe. She needed air, she struggled to free her hand, but he held tight. “Please,” she whispered. “Let’s get out of here.”

“A few minutes more. The tour is almost over,” Jaxon whispered. He held tight to her hand as they walked with the group back to the main section of the building.

The sensation never left her until she gulped in the fresh air outside. It wasn’t physical, and yet it felt like she was fighting for each breath.

“Are you okay, sweetheart?”

She inhaled deeply. “I will be.” She took another deep breath and exhaled it. The light turned on in her mind. She knew exactly what she had experienced but not why. Fear. Paralyzing, debilitating, and suffocating fear had gripped her.

“Do you mind telling me what that was all about?” Jaxon asked as soon as he got in the car.

“I wished I knew how to explain it.” She glanced at him. “Can we leave this area?” She shuddered.

“Where do you want to go?” He turned the key in the ignition.

“Anywhere but in Pinedale.” The engine’s whir gave her comfort. Right now she wanted to be away from this town. The farther the better. Which didn’t make sense, but neither did what had happened to her in that building.

As soon as the car left the town limits Peyton’s breathing returned to normal. The suffocating sensation lifted. Plain and simple something bad had gone on in that building, and if she had to guess it still was.

“Better now?” His glance her way spoke volumes

to her.

"Much, thank you." The closer they got to Blue Cove the more relaxed she became. "I'll be ready to talk about it soon, but I doubt you'll believe me. I'm having a hard time with it myself."

Jaxon parked in front of Joe's. "Wait here." He came out a few minutes later with a bag. "Lunch." He grinned at her. "How does a picnic at your favorite place sound?"

"Perfect."

Chapter 31

Jaxon determined to let her eat in peace. But waiting to let her talk until she was ready wouldn't come easily for him. An impatient kind of guy when it came to an investigation, he had to clamp his mouth shut to refrain from asking questions. He knew whatever had happened in Pinedale earlier was a big deal. Her body had trembled, and her hand in his had grown clammy. He could sense a change in the atmosphere around them, which was saying something. More often than not he was dense when it came to feelings, emotions, and details. But even he couldn't deny the building had a bad vibe. At least now he understood why he didn't want her to work there.

Peyton folded her hands on her lap. "Are you waiting for me to start?" she asked.

"Whenever you're ready," he encouraged.

She proceeded to tell him about her vision last night. "Kathryn was trying to tell me something. After today I might have to say she was warning me. There is something pure evil about what has happened within those walls."

At times when she spoke he had to lean forward to hear what she was saying. "You know me. When it comes to seeing ghosts it's probably never going to happen. I don't want to. But even I could tell there was a bad atmosphere in that building. For me to be aware of it says a lot." He unpacked the bag with their lunch in it. "Let's eat. You can tell me as little or much as you want. Maybe there are no words, and that'll be okay too." He handed her a napkin and plasticware. "The chicken salad comes highly recommended by your cousin, by the way."

Peyton took a bite. "A good choice, and she's right."

"What happened in the basement? That's where I started to sense you began to struggle. Am I right?" He took a drink of his iced tea.

"Yes. It started with Kathryn's memories. I thought of the people who died there and began to wonder about what happened to them. It quickly changed to something dark and sinister. The walls seemed to close in on me and got worse as we went up the hall near the living quarters. Not all those people died from the Spanish Flu."

"How did they die?" His forehead furrowed.

"It scares me to even think about it. The fear was suffocating to me. All I can think is some of them died in fear. It makes no sense to me."

"Here's a theory. What if there was a doctor who used them as test specimens? You know, like you read about in the death camps during WWII."

"The thought crossed my mind. But it seems so improbable, and yet maybe it isn't. All I know is those people knew fear. It paralyzed them and eventually killed some of them. That's what seems scary to me now. There was nothing humane about what was going on." She stretched her legs out in front of her.

"If you've ever read the real stories of survivors of torture, you will see how diabolical a human can be when he is given over to his baser instincts. Believe me, normal people can sometimes do some awful things if they let their hate or delusions of grandeur motivate their actions." Jaxon reached for one of the gooey brownies in the bag. "Sorry, I couldn't pass these up."

"I know all about Molly's treats. Matt is a big fan of Molly's brownies." She broke off a small piece and popped it in her mouth. "I wonder if…" She licked the chocolate frosting off her lip.

"If what?" he asked. Her tongue dancing across her lips reaching for the small dab of chocolate fascinated him. Quite frankly it was a bit of a turn on. Concentrate, man.

"I wonder if during other awful times, like WWII for example, if there were folks who could see what was taking place out of sight. Were there any people like my great-great-grandmother?"

"I'm no expert on the matter, but it would seem to me if there was a Kathryn, a Sadie, along with you and Jessie, there could have been more of you folks. It's entirely possible." He took another bite of the brownie. "Man are these good."

She nodded with a knowing smile. "I guess if you can imagine it, chances are that it is doable in some form." She wrapped up what was left of her sandwich. "You're welcome to this if you'd like. I did touch this half."

"I'd be happy to finish it for you." Jaxon took it from her hand. "I take it we agree with the assessment that if you have the gift of sight in your family line, there may be others that do too. In the same vein, we need to consider the possibility of others coming through the portal the same way you did."

"Let's use that as our starting point and work our way out from there. Is it probable that there are many more weapons than we realize in the battle of good over evil? It's an old, familiar story but one we need to consider. The biggest war we face as humans is often within ourselves over what is good and what is bad. At the end of the day, we live with ourselves." Peyton told him about the vision her cousin had in one of their cases of the dragon and creatures of light fighting in the stormy night sky. "Jessie saw it as the battle over the victim's own life to do what was right. It was like a battle for her soul or who she was meant to be." Peyton gestured with her hand. "I think you know what I mean. Does this go on more often than we know? Maybe not with such dramatic flair but with the voice inside us that lets us know we are headed the wrong way."

"I think that is a safe premise. We might use different terminology to describe what you're saying, but that's not important here. Occasionally someone comes along who breaks all the norms. They not only cross the line but obliterate it and can't turn back."

"Exactly, and that's what we're looking at now. Someone who no longer has a conscience or is moved by the suffering he is causing. He feels no remorse at all. Rather he sees himself as a hero, a messiah of sorts to help mankind with his findings at the expense of destroying what he sees as the expendables." She reached for his hand. "This is scary to me. It's not only bad but immoral."

"Tell me in the simplest form what you're thinking." He smiled at her. "I want to understand what you're telling me."

"I'm working on a theory." She went on to explain

her ideas that had been rolling around her mind. “I don’t know if it’s him. I have Jeremy researching that now, but someone has come through the portal and is still doing awful things today.”

“Damn. I was afraid you would say that. How do you logically fight a time traveler?”

“The same way you fight any criminal. With proof and truth. We will take him or his host down and send him back to his fate.” She scrunched her face.

“What?” he asked.

“Jessie said Garett Massey disappeared when they wrestled him to the ground. Edwards from the Arizona case was there, but his cap was gone. It makes me wonder if they were merely a host. I have no idea how this works. I guess we’ll find out soon enough. None of it might be real.”

“Your track record speaks differently. What’s the next step? For now, I hope you’ve given up on the idea of working at that school. It would make me feel a whole lot better if you weren’t there.” His hand fisted and his shoulders tensed anticipating her reply.

“Of course not. Unless I could be the bait to bring the monster out.” She glanced away from his face.

“Not going to happen. Don’t even go there.” He lifted her chin to see her eyes. “We will come up with a plan. You’re already enough of a target without being at the school. Promise me you’ll consider what I’m saying.” His hand gently caressed her cheek.

“I will. As a cop, you also need to think about it too. It might be the only option we will have to get this guy so he can’t move on somewhere else.”

“At least for now he seems to operate in the same space. The school building has been his primary domain. And for some reason around the inn as well. He's committed similar crimes in towns a few miles either way from Pinedale. I'm not sure how that fits in."

"It could be something like what Jessie experienced. He has found his way into two dimensions at the same time. Possibly three."

"Why not?" He rubbed his temple. "It makes about as much sense as you being sucked through a book into another time."

"Sorry. I know I have complicated your life a bit." Peyton hung her head.

"I'm not complaining, especially about you. Your premonitions present a bit of a challenge to my logical brain. But hey, challenges help me keep my edge." He stroked her hand. "I am still amazed you walked into my life, and there's no way that I'm going to ruin this opportunity. I'll just have to learn to fight crime on a new level. I'm okay with it as long as I don't get sucked through the portal without you." He winked at her.

She stood brushing the grass off her slacks. "I don't want to think about it anymore. It's too draining. Let's walk." She reached for his hand and tugged on it.

"Sounds good to me." He picked up their trash and threw it away. While they walked Jaxon formulated his plan for a romantic night out. He would make one rule apply—that they couldn't talk about the case at all. She had dark smudges under her eyes. What she needed after this strange week was a break.

****

The man watched them for the longest time. An odd sense of contentment filled him for a moment. Creeping closer to where the couple sat, the man lifted his binoculars to get a better view of their faces.

Strange, but this was the longest he had stayed still in one place without torment. The glances that passed between them as they ate their lunch and the way he caressed her cheek brought tears to his eyes. A new phenomenon for him. Up to this point, he only cried after murdering someone or when he experienced regret. With each tender look the man gave the woman, the wall his heart was encased in cracked a little more letting in an emotion that he had no words to describe. And with the small crack came sweet memories that had been sheathed in darkness mingled with the hate at the recesses of his mind. At peace, for the moment he relaxed against the tree beside him. He sighed. Rare were the moments like this one when he could almost remember the sound of a voice and being enveloped in a warm embrace. Almost. But then darkness would push the memory back as quickly as another would surface. He never knew when the monster would rise and force him to act upon some dark urge being fostered within him. The quest to change the world was in the driver's seat catapulting him toward his own personal hell. Where could a man like him find peace? He longed for silence, but it seemed to be far out of his reach no matter how hard he searched for it. They had found harmony. Why not him? The hate surged within him. Jealousy took over his moment of peace, and he slunk back into the shadow where he belonged.

Chapter 32

Peyton's phone rang. She glanced at the caller ID before answering it. "That was quick. It's Jeremy. I think I should take it."

"Absolutely." He pointed to the bench that was near them.

"Hi, Jeremy. What's up? I have you on speaker because Jaxon is here with me."

"You'll never believe what I've found. It seems your hunch was spot on. It will take too long to tell you everything. I've already emailed both of you what I found. I sent a copy to Matt and Jessie too. Read it slow and easy. When you've had a chance to absorb the info you can call me. I will be interested to hear your observations. I'm going on the record as saying it blew my mind. I've known Jessie from her days in New York and watched her evolve to this point. I've researched a few crazy things for her, but this is the strangest by far. I've read novels based on what I found. The adage about truth being stranger than fiction fits this scenario to a T. You can't make this stuff up, or then again maybe you can." He chuckled.

"You've piqued my interest." Jaxon slipped his arm around Peyton's shoulders.

"If you don't mind me asking, how'd you find the information?" Peyton laid her head against Jaxon's arm.

Jeremy replied, "A trip through the records

department and labor department of Pinedale. It's amazing what you can find in the records department. It helped that you gave me a couple of suggestions on where to start. I think you'll especially find the part about how the doctor came to work at the hospital overflow and the statistics of the people he treated. It's a bit of a wild read."

"Thank you for all your work. We'll get back to you after we've had a chance to go over your email."

"Is there anything else you want me to check?"

"Jessie is having the spreadsheets looked at by a pro. We might have more questions about them. I also want to know more about the history of that building. Something isn't kosher," Peyton said.

"I'll see what I can find. In the meantime, you kids stay safe. This is some crazy stuff you're looking at. We'll talk later."

"Okay." Peyton disconnected the call. She turned to Jaxon. "Looks like we have some interesting homework to do. Your place, mine, or neutral ground."

"How about yours, and the pizza is on me."

"Perfect. We can stop at the bookstore on the way home and see if Jessie and Matt can be there. Otherwise, it's just you and me, handsome." She took his hand and walked toward the car.

"Either way works for me. You won't hear me complain if it's only the two of us though. We work well together." He opened the car door for her when she handed him the keys. "Tomorrow I'm going to work at the station with Matt. The survivor is working with their sketch artist. We hope to have a likeness of the suspect by then. At which point, my dear, you will need to come in and see if you recognize the guy." He started the engine and pulled out of the parking lot of the marina.

"I will be happy to. I have a feeling he might be a familiar face." She clutched her purse in her lap. "As odd as this past week has been, I know there are important reasons for every part of what I've lived through. Each one holds a piece to our puzzle that must be inserted for it to be solved. That's where you come in." She glanced at him. "You're the logical thinker between the two of us, and your approach to this will be crucial."

"You flatter me." He smiled at her. "I like to believe I can analyze the situation and solve the crime. But this one has me scratching my head with too many elements outside of my wheelhouse. As I said earlier, we make a good team, and I'm going to need your help with this one." He parked in front of the bookstore.

"Hey, guys, what brings you here?" Jessie rushed up to them as soon as they walked in the door.

Peyton talked to Jessie, and Jaxon looked at books. She approached him and said, "It looks like it's the two of us for dinner. They will stop by later. Matt is going help Jessie here tonight. The store is open later."

"Sounds good." He turned the book over to read the back.

"What are you looking at?"

He showed her the title. "This book caught my attention. It says it's about the weird, bizarre, and unusual. Sounds like it might be right up our alley." He took it to the counter to pay for it.

"I just got that book in. I was thinking of buying it myself." Jessie took his money and put the book in a bag. "Let me know what you think. I haven't had time to read over the papers Jeremy sent yet. I wonder if anything in this book will live up to the hype after what you've already lived through." She handed him the bag. "See you later." Jessie waved as they walked out the door.

Peyton pulled the book out of the bag as soon as she got in the car and began to flip through the pages. A few of the chapter titles caught her eye. "You'll never guess the name of one of the chapters."

"I'm sure I won't, but I know you want to tell me. It's hard for you to keep a secret." He grinned at her before he checked his mirror and pulled away from the curb.

"Hey, that's not fair. I can keep a secret. See if I tell you now." She kept flipping through the pages, laughing at the titles. The sudden abrupt motion of the car sent the book flying out of her hand.

"Hold on." Jaxon suddenly turned around in the middle of the street, picking up speed while heading in the opposite direction. He made a quick left turn on Blue Cove Drive and headed toward the police station.

"Hey, be careful this is a new car…" She stopped when she saw the car coming up on their tail. "Hurry, he's gaining ground." She held on to the strap on the passenger door.

With another quick right, they pulled into the police station. "Did you see any numbers or letters on the plate?" He watched the car circle back around and drive off down the road.

"It happened too fast. I couldn't catch anything. Not even the make of the car." She shook her head. "How did you know we were being followed?"

"The guy came up fast behind us. He must have

been waiting for me to pull out. I didn't mean to scare you. I knew I needed to get us here to have a chance to get him to back off. I think he would have rammed your new car at the very least. These guys are serious. I think it's time to have a chat with Matt, don't you?"

Their conversation accomplished what Jaxon had hoped. Matt decided for around-the-clock protection for Peyton and Jessie. That decision was made thirty minutes later when Jessie called the station after a car driving by and shot at her store breaking her main window. The other decision made was that Peyton's car would be put in Matt's garage for the time being and Jaxon would drive a patrol car. Whoever was following them knew her car, and it made her an instant target.

"Jess and I will be over later, and we'll talk a whole lot more. I'm anxious to read what Jeremy sent in his emails. Something tells me it's explosive. Someone is trying hard to keep their secret operation from coming out." Matt handed Jaxon the keys to the squad car. "I'll need Peyton's too."

Jaxon placed them on his desk. "Are you going by the bookstore or do you want me to?"

"Let's both go. I'll show you the car you can drive. Peyton can get her items out of the car. Besides, with both of you with me, Jessie won't get mad when I tell her you girls will have around-the-clock protection." Matt chuckled. "She's had her life upended one time too many. I don't think she'll be happy. I'd appreciate any support you can give me."

Peyton said, "Good idea. I'm not happy about it, and I'm sure my cousin won't be either. We've spent most of our adult lives fighting against the weaker woman image."

Matt smirked. "I didn't say weaker, did you, Jaxon?"

"Not me. I wouldn't be that dumb. Remember I've seen you and Jessie in action, Peyton. The only reason for protection is for the other guy. I wouldn't want you girls to hurt a suspect that we might need to question."

"Ha, ha. Is that supposed to be funny?" Peyton poked Jaxon in the ribs.

"I thought so. Didn't you, Matt?" Jaxon playfully slapped at her hand.

"I might have chuckled. I was visualizing us having to rescue the guy from you two." Matt smiled at Peyton and patted the top of her head. "We're teasing. Although, that kick of yours is lethal. I wouldn't want you to use it on me." They walked down the hall together. "I forgot to ask what make of car are we looking at?"

****

Jaxon answered Matt while Peyton got the book Jaxon bought out of the car. No longer laughing or enjoying the carefree lunch they had shared, the weight of the case crashed into her life once again. Jessie expressed the same emotions as she had. At least Matt took charge and promised to have her window repaired before closing time. Peyton was sure it was his way of making up for the fact she was about to be put out once again. Frustrating was the word that came to mind.

Jaxon, on the other hand, seemed relieved to have someone to help watch over her. Maybe she needed to have a serious chat with him about how her being shot had affected him. Having someone care about her brought a smile to her face. One side of her loved it while the other side didn't want to get accustomed to it.

Who knew how long the sentiment would last?

Chapter 33

Once the pizza arrived, Jaxon and Peyton got down to work reading the information that Jeremy had emailed them. Content to be next to her every chance he got, Jaxon took advantage of the time. He found himself stealing glances at her whenever he could. Hopefully she didn't catch him in the act. Her focus on the paper she was reading was written on the lines of her face. He, on the other hand, could hardly concentrate while she was near him. He admired her work ethic and tenacity. Once on a trail, she kept digging until she could make sense of the situation. He usually did too, but her proximity and the smell of her perfume made it hard to center himself. Exhorting himself to focus on the task at hand, he took a bite of his pizza.

"Hits the spot." He smiled at her. "You should try a piece before it's cold."

She took a bite. "Angelo's is always good." She started reading again.

"Why don't you eat and then we can work? The pages won't go anywhere."

"I guess you're right. Once I get hold of something I find it hard to let go of the idea." She took a drink of her iced tea.

"I'm the same way. I do stop to eat, though." He reached for another slice of pizza. "You know what else

I enjoy?"

"What?" She wiped her mouth with a napkin.

"Being with you. I love the expressions you make when you're excited about something. Your eyes light up, your cheeks get a rosy blush, and your dimples… Well, I don't need to tell you how much I love seeing them. I enjoy being with you any chance I get." He ran the back of his hand gently down her cheek. "Which brings me to something I need to tell you."

"Is it good or bad?" she asked with a worried look on her face.

"I guess it depends on how you look at it. It's likely to bring up some tough memories. But it can't be helped."

"I'm not sure I like the sound of that. Tell me straight out, and I'll tell you how I feel about it." She frowned.

"I got a call yesterday from Captain Stolberg, and it looks like you'll be needed back in Phoenix at the end of September to testify against your shooter. Are you okay with that?"

"Of course. I want to see him in prison. I'll be fine. I still have time to gear up for the trial. I hope this murder case will be solved before then." She finished her slice of pizza.

"I'd like to fly back here the week before the trial and take you to meet my family. I thought we could travel together to Phoenix if that works for you."

"Perfect. I'd like that. I don't enjoy flying alone, although I've done it often enough." She straightened the pages she had printed earlier and changed the subject. "I prefer to read from paper. I'm used to it."

"I get it. I like using this." He pointed at his tablet.

"I don't have to worry about losing a page." He brought the subject back around. "I'm happy you're down with my idea. I would like your suggestions for a place to live in the area."

"I would love to help in any way." Her eyes lit up.

"After the main part of the trial is over, my time in Arizona will be done. It's time to think about where I want to call home. I may have to fly back a few times to testify, but not many." He reached for the third piece of pizza and took a swig of his beer, smiling to himself. *One step at a time*. "One more thing before we start reading. I would like to take you out Friday night if you want to go."

"Where?" she asked.

"I'd like to surprise you. You've had a rough few days. I think you could use a small break."

"I'd like that." She smiled at him. "Thanks for thinking of me."

Damn, he was happy. "Okay, let's get busy." He scrolled through the pages on his tablet, and she read through her paper pages. She used a yellow highlighter. He noticed her marking several passages. Before long they migrated into the living room to be more comfortable. Jaxon found it hard to believe what he read. How long had this been going on? When he read the last of the pages in the email, he shook his head. Stunned wouldn't begin to cover his emotions. Had he been living with his head in the sand?

****

Peyton checked him out when she thought he wasn't watching. Handsome for sure but more than that Jaxon was thoughtful. A man like him didn't come along every day. Engrossed in reading, a myriad of expressions crossed his face, which kept her guessing every time she looked at him. She wondered what he was reading at that moment that caused him to frown or smile.

Shocked might be a good description of how she related to what she read. She had traveled through time, lived in her great-great-grandmother's head, and experienced enough to understand at least some of what she read. Jaxon, on the other hand, his world must be spinning around and turning upside down after what he read. How could she logically explain any of this? Impossible! She glanced at the clock. Matt and Jessie would be here soon. It would take all of them putting their heads together on this one.

"How is this possible?" Jaxon stretched his arms over his head. "It's like reading a sci-fi book. It's unbelievably believable in a strange kind of way."

"I've been asking myself the same thing. Speculating about it is one thing, but to read that someone else is researching the possibilities is mind blowing." She flipped through her pages. "Look at all these yellow marks. All of them are paragraphs that gave me something to think about or research. I wonder if any of this challenged Jeremy to keep searching for connections. I thought I might have a few questions, but I've marked almost every paragraph. I agree this reads like a novel. I have no idea how to process what I've read. I hope Jessie and Matt might have some ideas."

"Let's go paragraph by paragraph, and they can put their two cents in when they arrive."

In each paragraph they read they bounced ideas off each other, writing each question that came to mind and trying to look for any answers they could find. They pored over her notes from Pinedale and considered any premonition or vision she had seen that might help. When Matt and Jessie arrived, they added to the conversation.

"I told you your head would spin the way these cases can unfold, didn't I?" Matt clapped Jaxon on the back "If anyone could hear this conversation, they would think we've all lost our minds."

"I have no words. How do you fight this?" Jaxon asked.

"Glad you asked," Jessie told him. She shared with him about their case with Garrett Massey and Skylar. "Skylar took over Massey's body, but that wasn't the only thing. The mind control was unreal. I've seen the same thing in two cases. In the end, Matt arrested the people he could and stopped them from doing more damage. I'm not sure you can do much about the people who travel through the portal. I've had no experience with that aspect to relate to. But you can stop the host, who would die without the traveler."

"In other words, we do what we can right here and right now." Matt reached for a piece of leftover pizza. "Do you mind if I heat this and eat it?"

"Knock yourself out." Peyton smiled at Matt.

****

"Who is on duty watching over these two tonight?" Jaxon walked into the kitchen with Matt.

"I am tonight, and you'll be on tomorrow. I also have a patrol officer watching the house." He lowered his voice so the girls wouldn't hear. "Truth is I don't want any other guy in this house with my girl."

"Works for me." Jaxon grinned. "I like how your mind works."

"A man has to protect what's his." Matt put a finger to his lips. "Don't quote me. Jessie would not appreciate the sentiment. She belongs only to herself, and I'm sure Peyton feels the same way. They are both like Sadie in that regard." He took the pizza out of the microwave and started eating it.

"My lips are sealed. I'm still trying to build trust with Peyton. I have no plans to ruin the work I've done by saying anything that might blow it up." Jaxon reached for a glass and filled it with water. He gulped it down and placed the glass in the dishwasher. "I say enough stupid things without repeating anyone else's. No offense, man."

"None taken." Matt took the last bite of his pizza.

Jaxon leaned over the desk when they walked back into the other room. "I need to leave, sweetheart."

"I'll walk you out." Peyton followed him to the door. "What do you think?" she asked when they were outside.

"It's going to take me a while to think about what I heard tonight. If I even can find a logical thread in there anywhere."

"I'm sorry. I know it opens up a whole strange world." She latched onto his arm.

"No apology necessary. The night wasn't a total bust. You were there, and anywhere you are makes it a good night for me." He pulled her close, hugging her tight. "I'll get used to the unusual sooner or later." He pulled his head back and gazed into her eyes. With a slow and deliberate goal in mind, he bent his head and kissed her. Her response made it hard to walk away. "Sweet dreams, sweetheart." Releasing her, he smiled at the bemused look on her face. "I doubt either of us will sleep well tonight," he muttered under his breath. He waited until she went back inside and started toward the inn.

The moon slightly obscured by a cloud moved out from hiding, lighting the night sky. He hadn't told Peyton what Maxwell had told him earlier. The Agency wanted to open a new field office, and they were searching for office space near or in Blue Cove. When he had confirmation and could talk about it, she would be the first one he'd tell. Maybe things did have a way of working out if you had the patience to let them. If that kiss were an indicator, their relationship could be headed somewhere good.

Chapter 34

The minute Peyton closed the door Jessie asked her, "Is Jaxon still close? Hurry and check."

Peyton looked out the door. "I don't see him."

"He needs to hear what Jeremy just told me. Call him and put him on speaker." Peyton reached for her phone and called.

"You miss me already?" he asked when he answered the phone.

"Are you back at the inn or still roaming around the garden?"

"I'm sitting on the bench outside listening to the ocean and thinking about that kiss. Why?" He stood. "What's going on?"

"Jessie has some new information she thinks you need to hear. I can put you on speaker if you want."

"I'm already on my way. It must be important. Between you and me I wouldn't mind telling you goodbye a second time." He knocked and walked in the door. "Let's hear what you've got."

"Remember I told you Jessie took the spreadsheets to a pro who checked them out? He did, and I'll let her tell you what he found," Peyton told him.

Jessie sat close to Matt on the sofa. "Like Jeremy, he found a lot of money changing hands. No surprise there. He also told me they had cleverly hidden what they were doing in some fancy backdoor maneuvers.

He showed me a few ways to move around them so I could see what they were doing."

"What did you see?" Matt asked.

"It's like there are two sets of books, one hanging out there to be seen and one that is encrypted and coded for those who know what they're looking for. I just got off the phone with Jeremy, and he has continued to follow the money trail. He said his research has led him to some major surprises. He refused to tell me over his phone, but he will call us on a secure line. One that can't be traced."

"That sounds serious." Jaxon leaned forward in the chair. "I wonder what he found."

"I had three takeaways from our conversation. Whatever he found shook him to the core. It might take more than us to sort through all the corruption involving a list of high-powered people. And as odd as this may sound, he's traced a link between a few of those on the list and the school at Pinedale. Believe me, it's not like Jeremy to be concerned. He goes where most folks wouldn't dare to go. Even in our cases he never seemed concerned about telling me over the phone or in email. This tells me this time is different, and I can't imagine why."

"I wonder if he's worried someone is on to him. He's a researcher and not a cop. His life could be in jeopardy." Jaxon moved to the arm of the chair where Peyton sat.

"I'd hate to think what he is doing for us could hurt him some way." Peyton struggled with the idea.

Jessie looked at an incoming text from her friend. "Oh, my goodness. I think I have the answer. My friend who looked at those pages told me not to open them.

They have a tracer attached to them."

"I'm sure Jeremy knows that and can disable it. I think it's the information and the people who had him shook." Matt reached for Jessie's hand and held it tight.

"All I know is that this case is getting stranger by the minute. It seems to span from your great-great-grandmother to the present. How is that even possible?" Jaxon rubbed Peyton's back as he talked.

Those words hung over the two couples. While they discussed all the possibilities, Jeremy called back confirming what Jessie's friend had told her. Thankfully, he had escaped detection and found a few more details that popped up in the process. "I'll stay in touch, and you guys watch your backs. There's some high-powered names on that list." Jeremy hung up.

"I keep coming back to what Kathryn had seen. I'm not sure how to explain it other than to say people were and are being used as guinea pigs in some kind of controlled experiments that started under the guise of helping people. I think now it is more sinister." Peyton shivered.

"I don't know about you. I'm going back to my room and read the email from Jeremy again. I'll be up for a while. You can call or text me if you see something." Jaxon walked to the door with Peyton right behind him.

"You are free to stay here if you want." She stood at the open door.

"I would, but I get distracted when you're near me." He reached for her hand.

"I'll try not to bother you."

"Honey, you don't have to do anything but simply be in the room. I like looking at you. One thought leads to another. What can I say? You're my weakness." He tugged her out the door into his waiting arms.

She liked being held in the circle of his strong arms. "Thank you," she whispered before she kissed him.

"For what?" He pulled his head back to gaze at her.

"For being you." She pulled his head down and kissed him again. "Call me if you see anything new. I know it's right in front of us if only we see the clues."

"See you in the morning. I would say sweet dreams, but sometimes those dreams are exactly what we need, and they're not always sweet." He turned to leave.

When he was no longer in view her sense of security disappeared with him. She quickly went inside and locked the door.

****

Jaxon had read over the pages several times. Glancing at the clock, he noted it was after one when he pulled out his notes on Peyton's dreams and premonitions. He made a chart listing the various key points. He tried to figure out how each one fit together with the new information they were learning and speculating about.

What Peyton mentioned as a possibility earlier didn't sound that farfetched when he looked at the chart. It would make more sense if they could learn more information about the original doctor who was alive in Kathryn's time. The pandemic was burning out of control and taking many lives. The doctor's cause may have begun in earnest with him wanting to save lives. At what point did it change? Did someone else take his findings and push them to another level? He shook his head and scratched through a couple of ideas he wrote down.

Who came through the portal? He wrote his thoughts by the question on the chart. Next to Peyton's notations, he noted the word "experiments" and several possible ideas in answer to the question. He thought about who might be living today who would benefit from any discoveries. As names came to mind, he jotted them down. Satisfied, at least he had the beginning of a working theory. It didn't matter if it panned out, only that he had something to work from. He stretched on the bed. Bone weary, the last few days had taken their toll on him.

Jaxon had a hard time believing how fast and hard he fell for Peyton. This wasn't a high school crush or even a case of lust. She filled the corners of his mind. He wanted to be with her and protect her, something she wouldn't appreciate hearing. She needed stability in her life which she never had as a child. With this new phenomenon, she had to deal with the needed security even more. He wanted to be that and more for her. What he would like now besides answers was sleep.

Sleep, now there's a novel idea. If only he could forget a beautiful pair of hazel green eyes gazing into his in such an inviting way. Never had he been so unsure of the next move to make. It all seemed like a test he could fail with one wrong action. The pressure wasn't coming from her. At least, he didn't think it was. He put unnecessary stress on himself, not wanting to mess up a relationship he found himself tiptoeing around her. Damn, he needed to get it together. He closed his eyes. His last thoughts were plans for a romantic evening away from the case.

****

The wrestling within the watcher grew stronger. He wiped the sweat running down his face with the back of his hand. The night was warm, yet his body shivered with the chills threatening to overtake him Attuned to the moment, he knew what it meant. He had lived through the scenario often enough. The monster inside, no longer content to sit idly by, was beginning to rear his head. Soon the non-stop thoughts would start as mere whispers until they became shouting commands. Ones he could no longer ignore or fight. How he hated these moments as the urges began to awaken inside him again. He was filled with desperation to stop them before he was forced to hunt and kill again. Where was that damn portal? It was his only way to be free. Free. The mere thought of the word "freedom" heightened every emotion in his body. He jumped to his feet, filled with energy, wanting nothing more than to run shouting through the woods. Breathing deeply, stilling himself, he whistled and chanted the word freedom repeatedly, willing it to be true.

Chapter 35

Peyton couldn't sleep. Her mind went over the conversations of the evening. There had to be some simple clue she was missing. Turning on the light, she sat up, resting her back against the headboard. Reaching for her computer on the nightstand, she placed it on her lap. With a push of the button, the screen lit up, and she was ready to start her search. She wanted to search the name Jeremy gave her in the email and any experiments he was working on at the time. Narrowing it down might be hard to do. She could only hope they kept good records.

At least it would make a good starting point to jump off onto any trail that presented itself. If she found evidence, she hoped to make some "necessary trouble" for some folks who might be causing problems right now. Knowing who stood to benefit from what was going on and the money trail would help. Money was Jeremy's department. She had a picture of the doctor in her mind thanks to Kathryn. One could hope his record would have a photo attached. She also knew what the murder suspect looked like and who he possibly was. She moved around the internet searching.

One trail led to another, and before long she was reading about medical experiments gone wrong. Peyton was stunned as she read about some of the horrifying trials over the years. The poor, minorities, and children were often at the center of decent intentions gone awry. After them came the military and prisoners. How could anyone feel justified in hurting soldiers serving their own country? Had she always been this naïve? Some of those trials couldn't even disguise themselves as having been started with any moral purpose. It shook her. This seemed to be the one area of life she never thought to question. She understood there were people capable of doing bad things.

Living in New York she heard about crime every day. But unprincipled research practiced in such a diabolical way was never in her wheelhouse. WorldStar Drug Company in Arizona and their illicit drug trade seemed bad enough. The idea of hurting people in the name of research was taking bad to a whole new level. This guy practiced his unsanctioned, amoral biomedical experiments up close and personal with the people he was supposed to be helping. She shuddered at the thought. Kathryn saw what was happening when she was alive. Peyton could only imagine what was taking place. Add in the money that could be made behind the scenes, and the case continued to grow.

She followed one story to another. Harvesting organs, mustard gas testing on the military, and using prison inmates as test subjects were only some of the things she read about in her search. Electroshock treatment on children, the youngest being only three, all because someone thought they had social issues. From mind control to injecting mentally disabled children with hepatitis to try and find a cure were each bad enough. Most troubling to her was the monster experiment on twenty-two orphans that followed the kids for the rest of their lives. The cruelty people could imagine and inflict in the name of research seemed limitless. After reading a few Holocaust stories, her eyes were filled with tears, and she couldn't read anymore. It came down to the fact that there have always been people capable of doing the unimaginable to others they considered weaker without feelings of remorse. *Enough is enough.* She closed her computer and reached for a tissue to dry her eyes. She wanted to believe that most people were good, but she could only shake her head at the ones who made life miserable for others. How do you deal with a person who has no empathy for people? When you view yourself as superior, doesn't that make someone else inferior and expendable?

"Kathryn Gimble, as you know I'm your great-great-granddaughter. I need your help with this one. I'm not as brave as you were, but I want to be. I'm counting on you to show me what to do next," she whispered into the darkness. "I'll accept help from anyone who has suffered and is searching for justice. At this point, I won't be picky," she added, shaping her pillows behind her head. She rolled onto her side. They had to find their suspect. She knew he had answers. They might need extra help to stop what was going on at the school. Too many lives had been harmed already, and it was crucial to stop it now. She closed her eyes, and before long the sleep that eluded her earlier finally caught up to her. With tears still wet on her cheeks, she slept.

****

After breakfast, Jaxon went outside to finish his coffee. Another picture-perfect morning. He took a deep breath. The sun rising over the cove and a bench to watch it from—what more could a man ask for? Except for someone to share it with possibly. He watched a yacht make its way out of the harbor into open waters. Sipping his coffee, he thought about the price tag on a luxury boat. Thoughts of the dollar signs brought a whistle from his lips. Not on his salary. What he could afford and needed to do was work a trip to the gym into his schedule today. Working out was how he dealt with stress, and this week had dished out plenty of pressure to go around.

Through the dark tint of his shades, he viewed the sun as it made its grand entrance into the morning sky while its reflection danced in the movement of the water. Beautiful. Always an earlier riser, he liked the mornings to contemplate and sort through his thoughts about a case. A new day often brought a fresh new perspective with it. That's what he had needed last night when he sent all the information he had to Tom Maxwell in an email. He figured Tom would get back to him if he had questions or any information pertinent to the case.

He enjoyed working with Matt at the station. Matt's work ethic could be seen in the respect his officers had for him. He ran a tight ship and seemed willing to do anything he asked his officers to do. Tom Maxwell thought highly of the Blue Cove PD. The sketch artist and the victim were meeting this morning, and hopefully the suspect's likeness would show up in one of their mug books or online. It would make it easier if he had a record and a booking photo. Jaxon doubted it would be that easy. With all the strange elements already surrounding the case, he couldn't see it suddenly becoming normal. What did normal even look like?

What he wanted at this point was a break. Something to wrap his logical mind around and find justice for a murder victim. He still hadn't figured out why Matt Parker had put him on this case. Because of Peyton, he was glad that he had. As he sorted through the events of the past few days, he could only shake his head. Leave it to him to be attracted to a woman who could see spirits and travel in time. As a kid, he would have thought of it as cool. Now it stressed him out. What if she went and never returned? He could be married with kids, and his wife could suddenly be gone. He knew what his mom would say. She would tell him nothing in life is without risk. Life is filled with peril, but it's also filled with possibility. It's worth taking a chance at happiness. He had already jumped off that cliff, but he still needed a bit of normal to hang onto for his sanity's sake. The notice of a text sounded on his phone. Pulling it from his pocket he read:

—If you're awake, we need to talk. Call me. Tom.—

"Hey, Tom. What's up?" Jaxon asked. In the next thirty minutes, he got an unexpected answer to the question. By the time they hung up, he had learned more than he wanted to know about what was happening.

Chapter 36

Peyton overslept, and now she needed to hurry and get ready. Jaxon was working at the station, and she had promised to help Jessie for a while at the store. She enjoyed working there. The bookstore seemed like the perfect spot to meet people. She couldn't spend every waking moment thinking about crime and mayhem or she would curl up in a ball and never go out again. She rushed through her morning routine and ran out of the house remembering as she got to where her car should be that it wasn't there. She checked her phone for any messages and read one from Jessie.

—Jaxon left the keys to his rental car for you to drive. I put the keys in your purse. See you soon, cous.—

At least she didn't have to go back and get the keys. She got into the car, adjusting the seat and mirrors. Latching her seatbelt, she backed the car out of the space and was on her way. A brief respite seemed perfect to her way of thinking. This had been one crazy mixed-up week so far. Dylan and Katie should be back in a few days. It might be fun to tell Katie about the books in her attic and the trip she had taken while they were gone. Fun, if she didn't mind Katie going ballistic. Peyton parked the car at the back of the store next to Jessie's and entered the store through the rear door. "Do you want me to lock this?" she asked.

"Yes, please. I don't like to leave it unlocked." Jessie walked into the back room. "Matt wanted me to remind you they'll bring by the suspect composite once it's finished for you to look at."

"Jaxon reminded me last night." Peyton followed Jessie into the front of the store. "Put me to work. My brain needs a break. I spent a good portion of the night researching things that still horrify me. If you don't mind, I want to get a coffee and something to eat. I overslept this morning." Peyton slipped the keys inside her purse and pulled her wallet out.

"I know a great place." Jessie laughed. "Go ahead." She motioned with her hands. "As you can see the store is quiet right now."

"Do you want anything?" Peyton asked. "Before you shake your head no it's not nice for me to eat in front of you. I'm buying you a coffee for sure. Don't worry. I know how you like your coffee, and Molly does too." She walked through the open doors into the coffee shop. "I'll surprise you."

The minute she walked into Joe's she had the strange sensation of someone watching her. She refused to look around not wanting to tip off whoever it was. Doing her best Peyton went into an animated overdrive trying to appear natural. "Hey, Molly, I'll take two coffees, one for me and one ah la Jessie. I know you understand.

Molly laughed. "I sure do." She poured two cups of coffee, one of them decaf with lots of milk. "I just took out these yummy peach scones from the oven. Does that sound good to you?"

"Perfect, I'll take two." She handed Molly the money. She put a few dollars in the tip jar.

"Have a nice day." She carried her goodies into the bookstore. "Come and get it."

"Thanks." Jessie walked over to the counter. "I have a question." Jessie leaned close to her and softened her voice. "Do you get the feeling someone is watching us?"

Peyton nodded and handed Jessie a coffee. "This is yours. Just like you like it." She handed her one of the scones. "Peach."

"Yum. I'm going to the back room and call Matt. Keep acting like you're unaware and going about your natural routine. It's probably something we can handle between us. But Matt gets upset and tends to lecture me if I don't let him in on what's going on."

"Sounds good. I have no idea who I'm looking for, but I suppose I'll know it when I land on the right person." Peyton went to work cleaning the counter and straightening the bookmark basket. From that position, she could almost see everyone in the coffee shop. The only person who seemed to stand out to her was a woman with dark hair. She sat with her back against the wall. Her long hair was pulled back tight off her face, and as strange as it seemed to Peyton the woman seemed vaguely familiar. Where had she seen her before? She racked her brain searching for the memory. Had she seen the woman in her visit to the past or at the school in Pinedale?

The woman pretended to read a magazine in front of her on the table but spent more time looking inside the bookstore. She wasn't hiding anything, which didn't seem right to Peyton.

Two things happened simultaneously. Matt and Jaxon came through the door grabbing her attention, and she realized where she had seen the woman before. When she glanced back in the store the woman was gone. She rushed past the two men out onto the sidewalk in front of the store.

"Whoa, where are you off to?" Jaxon followed her out the door.

"I missed her." She frowned, looking up and down the street. The woman had simply disappeared. "Of course, she did." Peyton shook her head and frowned.

"Who did what?" Jaxon stood beside her. "Did I miss something?"

She told him about the woman watching the store from Joe's. "I've seen her before, and it took me a while to figure out where. I wanted to talk with her. I have no idea where she went or if I'll ever see her again."

"I take it you want to see her again and our entrance might have messed up the opportunity. Is that why you're frowning at me?" Jaxon asked.

"I'm not frowning at you. I got distracted for a moment, and she left. It's uncanny how she simply disappeared. How could she move that fast?" Peyton shook her head.

"I don't know. Was she human or otherworldly?" He grinned at her.

"I thought she was human, but she did look a lot like someone I've seen before—it couldn't possibly be her—unless it's her twin." She paced in front of the store.

Jaxon grabbed her arm to make her stop. "Okay, not an answer I was expecting. Would you care to explain?"

She did, and even as the words came out of her

mouth it made little sense to her. "Never mind. I need to think about it some more." She walked back into the store, and he followed her. "Why are you here?"

"Jessie called about the person watching you, and we were on our way here to show you the composite drawing." He placed two sketches on the counter for her to look at.

"Is that the man you saw in the garden challenging you?" Jessie asked.

"Yes." Peyton picked the sketch up and examined it closely.

"Who is he?" Jaxon's hand fisted at his side.

"You know how you felt a minute ago when you said you didn't expect the answer I gave you? Hold on to the counter because this one will blow you away. He's your suspect all right, but he has come from a different time, or he's the spitting image of someone who lived in Kathryn's time." She plopped down in the chair shaking her head. "He's either the one or a look-alike relative."

"You look like Kathryn, don't forget," Jessie reminded her. "What do you think?"

"I think he came through the portal, and he needs me to get back through it again. Hence the challenge he issued me." She held up her hand to stop any questions from them. "It's only a theory."

"We may as well get lunch before we head back to the station. It's hard to concentrate on any crazy theories on an empty stomach." Matt kissed Jessie on the cheek and walked into Joe's.

Jaxon frowned. "And I thought this case couldn't get any stranger. Something tells me this is the tip of the iceberg when it comes to uncharted territory.

Nothing should surprise me anymore. Who am I kidding?" Jaxon turned to follow Matt. "Lunch it is." He followed Parker's lead but kissed Peyton on the lips.

"Sorry. The unusual seems to walk hand in hand with me lately." She patted his hand and turned away when the bell above the door rang signaling a customer. Jaxon might not be surprised anymore by the case, but she was flabbergasted. And if the look on Jessie's face was any indication her cousin was too.

Chapter 37

Kathryn's ghost floated around them, which by itself was an astonishing event. The fact that both she and Jessie could see her at the same time took the whole Reynolds' connection to a different level. The only possible thing stranger would be if Sadie could see her too. She didn't want to test the theory. At this point, the two of them watching the spirit of their great-great-grandmother was more than enough to digest. Why was she here?

"You do know who she is, don't you?" Peyton moved close to Jessie and whispered.

"Kathryn, right?" Jessie leaned her hip against the counter. "The question is what is she doing in my store?"

"Is it possible she's here to find closure? After all, she is the family member who revealed what she saw to me. Or maybe she's come to help us get on the same page. Right now, we have a scattered approach. Speculation at best, with no real idea of what we're looking for. She would know. Wouldn't she?" Peyton followed Kathryn's movement around the store. "Besides, I asked for her help."

"I guess we'll find out soon. In the meantime, we'll have to go about our work and wait to see what she does." Jessie shook her head. "I'm speechless, which doesn't happen often."

They got busy helping customers, but Peyton was constantly aware of Kathryn's presence. She found herself following her movement around the store. She sat in the chair, flittered around the store and the customers when they came in. Kathryn seemed to be checking out book titles and observing the people coming in and out of the coffee shop. The mere thought of her in the store much less observing them made Peyton smile. A secret, knowing smile infused with how bizarre the moment had turned. It would be next to impossible to explain. She might need to be analyzed after this case concluded.

At one point, Kathryn seemed to be looking at the books on the front table. She couldn't help herself. Peyton rushed to the front of the store to stand beside her. Her ghostlike finger pointed at a word on one of the books' covers. Murder stood out in bold red letters. A knife dripped with blood. Her finger then moved onto another book and pointed to the word death. The excitement built in Peyton. They were communicating. Another point in time to tuck away and ponder about later. A few more words pointed to several more books, and the message became clearer. The murder and stabbing in the park and the horrific experiments locked in her memory were one and the same. Kathryn moved from the new books to an old classic where she pointed to a book title. The light turned on in Peyton's mind, and she understood that she needed to read that book. She had read it many years ago and could remember the gist of the story but not the details. Those details could be important to the case.

Thank you. I understand. She hoped Kathryn could hear her thoughts. Her spirit danced and floated around her. Then it became Kathryn's thoughts filling her mind with words and pictures.

"Peyton, are you, all right?" Jessie shook her gently.

"Oh my gosh," she muttered. Her eyes opened wide and her hands flew to her face. "I can't believe it…"

"What? Don't leave me hanging, cousin." Jessie sat on the arm of the chair to get a closer look at Peyton. "Tell me."

Before she could answer several people came into the store, and the conversation had to be abandoned.

****

Jaxon knew the expression on her face. He pulled up a chair and sat down beside her. He had told Matt to leave if he needed to. Peyton was caught up in some event that he couldn't see. He understood it might take time before she could explain it to him or anyone. He could be patient when he needed to be. Holding her hand, he observed the activity in the store. Nothing seemed unusual, and yet his gut told him something unusual was going on around them. She recognized the photo, which added another strange twist to the story. Was it possible that the past and the present collided, forming an ongoing crime?

There would have been a time he would say no way. But having seen Peyton in action, he couldn't rule anything out at this point. He hated to think of the possibility of an unseen criminal world when the one right in front of them seemed overwhelming most days.

"How is she doing?" Jessie asked after the last customer she waited on left.

"I'm waiting for her to come around, which could

be at any moment." He smiled at her.

"I should have known." Jessie slapped her forehead with her hand. "Here comes Reba. She's always right on time. She'll have something to say about this whole situation." She waved at her when she walked in the door.

"Hi, dear girl." She stopped the moment the door shut behind her. "Goodness, what is going on in here? Something told me I needed to stop by today, and now I understand why. Tell me what's going on, besides the fact that you have a supernatural visitor. I'm sure you're already aware of that."

"I am. The crazy thing is Peyton and I both saw our great-great-grandmother come in. I had customers, but Peyton had an experience that still has her rattled."

"We'll have to see about this." Reba patted her hair and made her way to where Peyton sat. "How's our girl doing?" She sat in the chair Jaxon vacated for her.

"I'm fine. Kathryn spoke to me. Maybe that's the wrong word. She did communicate with me, and I understand this case a bit better now." She explained how Kathryn had talked to her. Peyton held up the book she had taken off the shelf. "This book was first published in 1886. I read it in my high school lit class. It's the story of a man who shifts between two personas and the attempt to try to separate good from evil."

"I remember reading it too. In the beginning, he thought he could manage the dual personalities with potions that he made. In the end, he found out he couldn't halt the process."

"Right, he became the evil he could no longer manage. Are you saying that we're dealing with a similar situation?" Jaxon squeezed Peyton's shoulders gently.

"In a way, I believe we are. That's the suspect we are looking for. He came through the portal."

Reba took Peyton's hand. "You've had an eventful morning, dear. I have something to add. The one you are looking for is from the past, and he has unleashed many in the present to do his bidding. It's a crowded field that is benefiting from the evil this man has created. It will take some clear thinking on your part, young man." She glanced at Jaxon. "But you'll solve the crime, and we'll all sleep better after the sordid story is told."

"You've managed to do it again, Reba dear." Jessie smiled at her. All three of the ladies began talking at once.

He needed time to digest all that he had heard. "I'm going back to the station. I'll take the car and pick you up when you're done here. Do you mind if I take this with me?" He grabbed the book off her lap. "Jessie, I'll pay you later for this later."

Peyton went behind the counter. "You'll need these." She handed him the keys. "I'll pay for the book since it was my idea." She pushed his hair off his forehead. "Thank you for trying to understand this weird side to me. I'll see you later." She brushed her lips across his in a whisper of a kiss.

Jaxon slipped out the back door while the three women continued their discussion. His brain could not wrap itself around what Peyton had told them. Frankly, he needed a breather to think. He clutched the book in his hand. *I hope, my little friend, you hold a key for me. Reading you will be a part of my work this afternoon.* He had read the story in school too and even saw the movie version, but the details were sketchy at best. It would take hard evidence and not supernatural conjecture to solve the case in the here and now. Evidence was what he needed now and a trail to follow.

The one element of the story he did remember was that it revealed the tension between reason, science, and the supernatural world. His teacher had told them that logic was limited in its ability to cope and understand the phenomena of the supernatural. He smiled remembering the words of his lit teacher. The fact that he could remember anything he had read in high school or something a teacher said was a miracle. The fact the book was suggested by a ghost was out of his wheelhouse, but help was help even if it wasn't logical. Right now, they needed it, and he would take it.

His mind raced through the details of the investigation. From the moment Peyton was sucked through the portal nothing had been normal. But according to Reba, there were people involved now who were normal in the sense they weren't ghosts or time travelers. He shook his head. Maybe this was a new crime-fighting normal. No way!

Chapter 38

She hadn't helped Jessie much during the day. Other than to wait on a customer occasionally while her cousin was busy, she spent most of the day hanging out in the chair. After Reba left to go home the book club showed up. She immediately grabbed another copy of the book off the shelf and started reading. She read a chapter every chance she got.

If she had to classify the book's genre it would be a psychological horror story. No, it wasn't filled with blood and gore, but there were enough twists and turns built into the bizarre scary premise of the story to last her a lifetime. A close reminder of the day she had experienced so far. Wow, her life could read like a horror novel, which wasn't a comforting thought.

She steered clear of those books and movies growing up because she could never understand the thrill of being scared senseless, although her friend Destiny loved them. The more she screamed the better. Peyton would close her eyes and plug her ears during the scary scenes. Thankfully, the music alerted her when something terrifying was about to happen. After reading parts of the book, she could understand why Kathryn had pointed it out to her. The story jived with her theory of the suspect. And it made the notion seem somewhat possible even if a bit out there.

Their suspect appeared to be a man with a dual and

complex personality. Good and evil were at war within him. Like most people, only on steroids. He might appear normal to anyone who saw him but then could display supernatural feats of strength like carrying a victim who was twice his size into the woods. Which is exactly how several victims had described the suspect in their police reports. All important details they couldn't forget in their rush to solve the crime.

Locked in Kathryn's memories was such a man. Kind, unassuming, and cable of great compassion, but then something happened. She heard rumors but wasn't sure of what caused the transformation. The woman in the coffee shop earlier knew. If only she could have caught up with her. They had to meet again.

"You're quiet." Jessie plopped down in the chair beside her as soon as the book club ladies left the store.

"Thinking. You know how that goes." She glanced at Jessie and held up a copy of the book. "Do you remember the storyline?"

"Vaguely, but enough to recall it seemed scary to me at the time that I read it," Jessie told her.

"It is. What makes it scary is the possibility it could happen. It's not farfetched, like I used to think portals and alternate dimensions sounded. And just look at us—we've both been there and done that." Peyton shook her head, handing the book to Jessie to read the blurb on the back. "A book way ahead of its time."

"The story, yes. It was published when Kathryn was a child, and the man might have been a teen. Who knows? Maybe he read the book, and it formulated the idea inside of him." Jessie flipped the book over in her hand.

"Stranger things have happened, I guess. As a point

of discussion, let's say he did. While we are at it, let's consider the idea that he experimented on himself with personality-altering effects over time. It's a possible theory of how he could do what he's done. Now all we have to do is take him from the year nineteen-eighteen and bring him into our time. Or did he go first to another time before coming here?" Peyton pushed her hair out of her face.

"Interesting idea. Truthfully, I'm still blown away by both of us seeing our great-great-grandmother in my store. Don't you find that completely fascinating?" Jessie handed her back the book. "I can't believe I had this on the shelf. Two copies no less. I'm reading it when you're done." She stood when the bell rang. "Mind blowing, I tell you. And freaking awesome. Wait until Sadie hears about this."

"Yes, Jess, it's awesome and way cool." She started reading where she left off.

****

Besides reading Jaxon spent a good portion of the afternoon scouring over composites of suspects wanted in towns in the vicinity and with similar crimes. It didn't take long for him to find their suspect wanted in several towns close by. The MO in each of the case profiles seemed too similar not to be their guy. He talked to the officers in charge of a few of the open investigations and came away knowing the guy was active in the area and had been for some time. One of the murders had taken place over a year ago. The first murder was done with medical precision. It seemed to him after reading the files the different departments emailed him that the suspect was growing more frenzied and careless with each murder or slashing.

Jaxon wondered if their guy was losing control. Case in point, this was the first time the person he abducted made it out alive. He gave them a firsthand account of being carried into the woods and the man's actions afterward. He had pretended to be unconscious but was fully aware of the war raging in the man. The one fact that concerned Jaxon was that the man seemed desperate to find the portal. Both Peyton and Jessie were targets as long as the guy thought they could help him find a way back.

It would be his turn to stay at the cottage with the girls tonight. The knock at the door of Dylan's office pulled him out of his thoughts.

"Have you found any new evidence?" Matt walked in and sat in the chair in front of the desk.

Jaxon explained what he had read from the files. "Our suspect is not only getting reckless but frantic and becoming more dangerous. He's acting on impulse and no longer controlling what's happening within him."

"News I didn't want to hear. Tell me about what happened earlier in the bookstore. How does it tie into what you've just told me?" Matt inched forward in the chair.

Jaxon told him about the message from Kathryn's ghost and the book she had pointed out. "Reba came in with one of her messages that messes with your mind. I have no idea how Peyton or Jessie can deal with it. They manage, but I find myself on the sidelines scratching my head. The only thought that comes to mind is what the hell."

"I get it, man. I've wrestled more than once about my relationship with Jessie over it. Life is crazy with her, but I couldn't imagine life without her. That, my friend, is what love does to you. The question is if this guy wants access to the portal, how are we going to keep him from them? I mean he picked up our victim and ran with him like he was a toy doll into the woods. That's not normal. There's only one way this guy can be stopped, but it's too risky to think about." Matt frowned.

"How? We need to discuss every possibility. He has murdered before, and he'll do it again." Jaxon wanted to cover every scenario. Evidence told him their guy was close to spinning out of control and he didn't care who he took out with him.

"He has to feel boxed in. Cornered with no way out. Without hope, the dark side of his character is controlling more of his life. In the end, the good can overtake the bad if the right factors are in play. Take our case where Skylar was controlling people to do his dirty work. An upstanding doctor in the community tried to kill us more than once. Jessie talked him down. Don't ask me how. It's another one of those 'I don't get it' items. But it worked." Matt talked about it, explaining the details he remembered.

"Are you saying we should let Jessie or Peyton be the bait to draw the guy out? I don't like the sounds of it." Jaxon raked his hand through his hair.

"As you said earlier, they already are. He needs them to access the portal. As Jessie has told me more than once, if you have the plan you're the one in control."

"It sounds too risky to me." Jaxon's mouth twitched.

"No doubt there's risk involved. But to wait until he takes charge with the element of surprise on his side is equally dangerous. Hell, we're cops, and the job comes with a certain amount of hazard."

"Yeah, but they're not." Jaxon tapped his pencil on his desk.

"They date us. That's risky if you ask me."

"Okay, for the sake of discussion only, let's say Peyton agrees to this idea. Tell me a plan that makes sense. I might consider it as a possibility, but I won't speak for her." Jaxon shook his head. He couldn't believe Matt would even suggest something so crazy, much less develop a plan to put in place.

The rest of the afternoon they went back forth trying to come up with a workable plan. Nothing was without risk. Of course, it would take one of the ladies signing up for the gig. Only time and serious discussion would prove whether Peyton or Jessie would do it. Jaxon was sure it would be Peyton. He was just as sure that she would think the idea had merit. She had told him on more than one occasion that she and the murderer were destined to meet. She might jump at the chance or even at this moment be designing a plan of her own.

"What time is it anyway?" Matt asked.

Jaxon glanced at his watch. "Damn. I was supposed to pick her up fifteen minutes ago." He raced out of the office listening to Matt chuckling in the background.

Chapter 39

Peyton had settled a lot in her mind after the events of the day. She understood one side of the case but not how Pinedale School or the list of people fit into it. One thing she knew for sure since seeing the woman at Joe's earlier was that the case was now on a fast-track. How many people had been impacted by the experiments over the years? Would they ever know for sure? And it all began with one man and his delusion. All the souls were gathering because his reckoning was coming. It was time.

"Hey, cous, the good detective soon to be FBI man is here." Jessie motioned to her. "How do you like him best?"

She grabbed her purse from under the counter. "I'm partial to the hunky sheriff. He's the man in my fantasy." She laughed and met Jaxon at the door. She walked into his open arms. "Did you miss me?" She brushed the piece of hair that fell across his forehead back with her hand. "I missed you."

He smiled. "Is that so?" He tightened his hold on her.

Oh, how she loved his lopsided grin. "Yes. Do you have plans for the evening? I wouldn't mind spending it with you if it works for you." She waved at Jessie as she went out the door that he held open.

"Being with you works for me. The more time the

better. Remember, I have the task of convincing you I'm a man who can be trusted." He pulled her into his arms. "By the way, I've been wondering how I'm doing."

"Well now, I might have to think about it for a moment." She tugged his head down and gazed into his eyes. "You're doing well. Very well, indeed." She fluttered her lashes at him playfully.

He grinned right before he kissed her. One long, hot kiss and she melted against him. "I'm happy to hear it. I'll keep working hard to convince you, sweetheart, especially if I can collect a reward now and then for a job well done."

"I think I can manage to reward you sufficiently." She jumped when a car driving by honked.

He reached around her and opened the car door. "Nice to hear. I feel incentivized." He pounded his chest. "Prepare yourself to reward me often. I'm highly motivated."

"I studied all about how to motivate students who do a good job." She glanced at him when he got in the car. "I know a gold star student when I see one. You're not a bad detective either." She turned her head away from him and whispered, "And one hunky cowboy."

They went to dinner at Donovan's and Connor's place. A nice Rueben sandwich sounded good to her. During the summer months, they had live music. Blue Cove almost doubled in size this time of year. Businesses made a good portion of their yearly budget during the tourist season.

Liam greeted them when they walked in the door and led them to a more secluded table where the music wasn't quite so loud. The group playing sounded great.

Music and dancing were a perfect way to end the bizarre day she had. She would take any chance at normal she could get. Dinner, dancing, and yes, even flirting with her handsome guy didn't take much effort on her part. It made her life seem more like everyone else's, except for one small detail she tried hard to forget. Someone had followed them, and she could tell they were being watched.

****

She surprised him again tonight which concerned him. Whenever she had a premonition or something troubling her, it was as if she worked twice as hard at having a good time. The night she was shot came to mind. For now, he would play along, but he would get answers before the evening was out. Following her lead had its perks though. He held her close for a slow dance. Her head rested on his shoulder, and her hand toyed with the hair at the nape of his neck. Her feather-light touch seared his skin making him feel hot all over. She didn't have to do much to entice him. He loved everything about her.

"Did I mention to you before how perfect you fit in my arms?" He tightened his hold on her.

"I'm sure you might have told me once or twice." She sighed. "But this girl doesn't mind hearing you say it more than once." She pulled her head back far enough to see his face. "Now don't you agree this is a perfect ending to an unusual day? I couldn't have planned it any better if I had tried."

"Speaking of your day, did it improve after I left?" He tested the waters to gauge her reaction.

"It didn't get any worse if that's what you mean. I don't want to talk about it. I'd rather simply enjoy being here with you."

"I can live with that." Yep, something was up all right. Getting her to tell him might be difficult, but he had to try. He didn't want to be taken by surprise, and she didn't need to be shot again.

The music changed. "Do you mind if we sit this one out?" She grabbed his hand, tugging him off the dance floor and back to their table.

"I'm game. You know me. I like the slow dances best of all. I get to hold you close." He grinned at her. Jaxon knew if he waited long enough, she would tell him some of what was going on in her head. He chilled, danced, and let her talk through the things that were troubling her. The evening was nothing if not eye-opening. Peyton was one strong woman. This case had lots of moving pieces and insufficient evidence.

"Did you get a chance to read any of the book today?" She thanked the waiter who topped off her iced tea.

"I did. It brought back memories of my lit class in high school. Not one of my favorite classes in my senior year. I also saw the movie. The story made me think. Is this what you tried to explain to me earlier at the store? The dual aspect of his personality is an interesting take. Where I struggle is when I think about our suspect coming from the past. I'm a logical thinker, and the conjecture doesn't fit with my line of thinking."

"I understand, nor mine for that matter. But finding myself walking in Kathryn's shoes kind of messed with the idea that this was an ordinary case. I saw someone this morning in Joe's, which might shake it up even more." She sipped her iced tea and explained another part of her premise. "You can see why it's important for me to find her. She may be able to help the suspect find peace."

"Wow! Every new piece of information messes with my head more. Is there anything normal about this case?" He frowned.

"Yes, it's a combination. The list Jeremy gave us has real people alive and well now. Something is going on behind closed doors at Pinedale that involves these folks in some way. That area needs your expertise. Frank can bring Radar whenever we get to the place where we have a search warrant for the property." Her fingers tapped on the table. "I have a strong sense someone from that group sent the shooter and is not afraid to send them again because we are getting close to figuring this all out. Although I'm not sure they understand who the doctor is."

"It's hard to see since we aren't any closer to solving the case. We're speculating at best."

"I beg your pardon." She shook her head and then proceeded to lay it all out as she saw it.

She was feisty when trying to get her point across. Her face lit with the passion of her ideas. He didn't have the heart to tell her that all she said wasn't evidence acceptable to today's standard of burden of proof. Still, he smiled and listened to every word. Until he heard her say she could be used as bait. Matt and he had talked about it earlier, and he liked it less when it came out of her. "Excuse me, but I don't think so."

"Although I appreciate your concern, if you would think like a cop for a moment, you'd know that I'm right." She reached for his hand. "I've told you from the day of the murder he challenged me that we would meet again. Right now, I hold a key that may change the whole situation." She quickly changed the subject. "Aren't you the one staying at the cottage tonight?"

"I am." His thumb stroked the palm of her hand.

"We should probably get home. I don't want Jessie to be there alone." She pulled her hand away and stood. Thanking Liam for the great evening they walked out the door into the warm summer night.

Jaxon had closed the car door when he noticed the car idling near the front of the parking exit. "We might have company. I may be wrong, but I doubt it." He called the station requesting backup. A quick plan was put into action. Jaxon was told where to turn so the other squad cars could help in the pursuit. If they timed this right, they might be able to take someone into custody for questioning. He glanced at her. "I'm waiting for a text that our help is in place. When I tell you to duck you need to do it." He turned the key in the ignition and waited.

"Is this good or bad?" Her hand tightened around the seatbelt.

"A bit of both if they have a gun." His phone alerted him to a text. "It's showtime. You may as well duck down now."

She placed her hand over his hand on the wheel. "One question. Who is looking out for you?"

"Hopefully I won't need it." He backed out of the parking space and first went the opposite direction away from the idling car. When he got halfway up the row, he stopped and checked the parking lot for pedestrians or moving vehicles. All clear. "Duck!" He pushed the gas pedal down, propelling the car forward and squealing out of the parking lot onto the street. The other car pulled out in pursuit. Jaxon saw the gun come out of the passenger window. “Gun, stay down,” he shouted. After a couple of rapid shots, a bullet came through the rear passenger window, piercing the glass and embedding it in the headliner.

Peyton covered her ears and screamed. “Are you okay?” Her voice trembled.

“I’m good. Hang on.” He turned the corner quickly when their suspects followed. Before the shooter could get off another round, they were met by three patrol cars. One pulled in behind the suspect vehicle and two came at them from the side street. Their car’s momentum was stopped. It worked the way he had hoped. Pulling his gun from its holster Jaxon joined the other officers with guns drawn surrounding the car.

The standoff was joined by two more patrol cars. On command, the passenger suspect opened the door and placed his gun on the ground, kicking it toward the officers. The driver followed suit. The two men were handcuffed and placed in the back of Kip’s patrol car. Jaxon went through the car with a couple of the officers before the tow truck arrived to take the car to the impound lot.

“Are you okay?” he asked when he got in the car.

“Yeah, but it brought back some memories I would rather forget.” She toyed with her purse strap. She took the tissue he handed her and dabbed at the tears already forming in her eyes.

“Do you mind spending some time at the station? I want to question these guys, and I don’t want you at home. They’re getting bold, and I want to know who’s paying.” He started the car.

“I don’t mind, but what about Jessie?”

“Matt is bringing her to the station too. You can

hang out together."

"Okay, that works." She fiddled with her seatbelt.

Jaxon pulled into the station and parked the car. Adrenaline pumping and seeing her tears didn't help. He was angry. He'd like to do more than talk to the two of them. He wouldn't go near them until he calmed down or Matt got there. This could be the break he was hoping for, and he didn't want to screw it up.

Chapter 40

Peyton went into the lunchroom to wait for Jessie to arrive and happy to be all in one piece. She hated feeling so vulnerable. In one swift moment the memory of that night in Arizona came crashing in on her, and the fear rose like bile in her throat. Clammy and sweaty at the same time, she took a deep breath to calm herself. Would she ever be free or be forced to carry the memories locked in her mind like the scars she now had on her body? She shivered. The memory of the searing pain, the sounds and smells of that night still had the power to paralyze her. She survived the bullet wounds, but her mind still dredged up and struggled with the trauma. No, it wasn't all the time, but the sound of gunfire or even a car backfiring brought the ordeal front and center. Head down in the racing car tonight left her reliving it once again.

Hopefully their arrest would produce helpful information. Ready to move on, she didn't want to live in fear. If the experiences of the past few days taught her anything, this was her new normal. She wanted to learn to use a gun. A scary thought. Add to it Jaxon's life being at risk, and she needed to do something to feel more in control.

"Hey, cous, are you okay?" Jessie sat in the chair across the table from her. "From what I've heard so far it's just another crazy night in the lives of the Reynolds girls. It makes you wonder if we'll ever have a normal life. Doesn't it?"

"I was thinking those same thoughts before you arrived." Peyton pushed her hair behind her ears. "When I heard the gunshots tonight, I'm ashamed to admit I relived the night I was shot like it was yesterday." She hung her head. "If I'm going to have these premonitions and work with Jaxon or anyone for that matter, I need to be able to take care of myself."

"I understand, believe me, I do. Don't be so hard on yourself. I still know fear. Matt told me once you have to have a healthy respect for the risk and not get complacent or you lose your edge."

"It's safe to say complacency is not a problem yet but fear is." She swiped at the tears forming in her eyes. "I'd do anything to be strong like you."

"Whoa, hold on there." Jessie handed her a tissue. "I remember when I came to the realization that I had better learn to use a gun. I've never liked them or wanted to own one. Hanging with Matt taught me quickly you can grow and still be who you are." She patted her cousin's hand. "I went to class and learned to shoot. Do I like carrying a gun? No, and I rarely do. But I like the fact I can use it if I need to. And I've had to use it a few times." Jessie told her about shooting Stuart, the stalker from her past. "I only wounded him. Billy took him down with his slingshot."

"At least you're strong enough to use one." She shook her head. "I'm not sure I could ever shoot one."

"You'd be surprised what you can do if you have to. In the meantime, lighten up on yourself. The scars are fresh, and you're new to this crazy world in which we find ourselves."

"I'll try." She sounded pitiful to her own ears. "I wonder how it's going in there." Peyton pointed down the hall.

"We'll know soon enough." Jessie picked up her phone and began to search through email messages.

****

After questioning their suspects and getting nowhere, Jaxon needed a break. It was either that or knock some heads together. "I'll be back." He stood and headed to the door.

"Wait a minute." Matt followed him. "Tell Jessie and Peyton to go into the observation room. I want them to watch. Maybe they can see something we're not. Tell Jessie to think about our last case. She'll understand."

Jaxon found them in the lunchroom. He told Jessie what Matt had asked of her. "Matt said you'd understand." Jaxon grabbed a bottle of water from the fridge. Unscrewing the lid, he took a drink.

"I do. I'll fill you both in as we walk." They followed Jaxon down the hall. Jessie told them what she remembered about the interview with the doctor who was under the mind control of Skylar. "Don't worry, I know what we're looking for, but you'll have to be the one who does it, cous. This case is yours. We could be talking about ESP, telepathy, or hypnosis." She glanced at Peyton. "Look, if your theory is true, the guy has been around long enough to perfect the art."

"What do I do?" Peyton asked.

"Reba told me once that I was the gatekeeper of my mind. I could keep out what I didn't want to let in. I remember saying that a few times and singing a song I learned as a kid. I'm not joking. You do what you can.

With the doctor, I touched him and commanded his attention. I have no idea why it worked. You'll figure it out. You're the one in charge." They walked in the door Jaxon held open.

"Okay, ladies, do your thing. I'll check in later." Jaxon closed the door when he left. He nodded at Matt when he returned to the interview room.

"Kip, read them their rights while I fill out the arrest charges. Shooting at the FBI carries some serious time." Matt stood.

"Look, mister, you can do your worst. Lock me up, please. I'm more afraid of the man I'm working for. If he wants to, he could kill me right now. I'm not talking."

The other man nodded. "Me either."

"How could he kill you? We're here, and you're protected." Kip stood leaning over the table as he spoke. "He can't get to you in here.

"You don't get it. He doesn't need to be near us to kill us. I've seen him do it."

"Lock them up." Matt opened the door. "Get them out of my sight."

Jaxon followed Matt into the observation room. "Did you watch?" he asked Jessie and Peyton.

"Yes. They're scared. Their reactions are similar to those of the people at the crime scene the other day. The unexplainable is always scarier. Jail seems a blessing at this point. I get it." Peyton tapped her fingers on her arm, her foot shaking under the chair. "I've seen the conflict in the man who is at the epicenter, and he isn't at peace with himself either. He fears the other person living within him too. That could be our opening," Peyton said.

****

Once again, they had failed him. He had half a mind to kill them where they sat in their cell. What a lark. The police would find them and have no idea how they died, with no marks to be found on their body to tell the story. He knew enough about the dark arts. Years of learning from the best minds had taught him enough to do what he needed to do. Control was the easy part. People were rarely attuned to the unseen world around them. But stupid he couldn't fix. He could outsmart them all. Blood dripped from his hand where he pounded it against the tree. Seething and furious, he hated the voice of reason who kept him penned in. *Hire some goons to scare them you told him.* "I'm the only one who could control them. They'd never talk."

"They'll talk. Can't you tell something is wrong? Our strength is waning. We need to leave before they find out about us," he said to the monster raging within him.

"No!" The word vibrated from deep with him as he continued to pound his hand. His voice took on the rhythm of each causing more blood to flow. "I'm in control, not you. You're nothing without me!" he shouted. "They still think I'm wonderful." He chuckled while wiping his blood on his pants.

"They'll see. There are people already asking questions. Don't you get it? We are fracturing apart. We must leave." The man warred with himself.

"Not yet! You can't reveal us yet. I've almost won. They believe in me. I'm their hero. Keep hiding. You've got to stay in the darkness with me," he muttered to himself.

As quickly as it came the voice quieted within him. Shame filled him as he stared at his hand and the blood smears on his pants. The bouts were getting worse. He found it harder to fight the beast. Soon he would cease to exist. He would be lost to himself forever. Maybe it didn't matter anymore. The losses were stacking up against him, and the bad outweighed the good. Life no longer seemed worth living. The only consolation he had was the rare happy memories that teased his mind about simpler times. If only he could find his way back. His weeping stirred the restless spirits to race about the woods around him filling the night with wails. The monster inside of him was growing stronger, and it wouldn't be long before it no longer needed him. Someone new would take his place. At least he would be free. The torment would cease, and he would be at peace. Only a dream at that point. He would always live or die with the knowledge of all the terrible things he had done through the evil within him. It wouldn't matter in the end. He could never change what he had become.

Chapter 41

After Jessie's pep talk Peyton went into the interview room. She went to the open chair between Jaxon and Matt. Once the suspects were brought back in, they sat directly across from their interrogators. The youngest of the two slumped in his chair with his hands covering his face while the other stared off into space. Defiant best described him. On the other man, she saw fear. She would start with him. Her soothing voice drew his attention.

"I heard you when you spoke a while ago." She looked at the man who had said he was afraid. "Can you tell me why you're afraid of the man who hired you?"

"I'm not afraid of him. It's the other one. He's always in my head. Since the first day I interviewed for a job and he came to meet me. I can hear him in my head. It never lets up. I have no power to stop him, and he's driving me crazy." He gulped.

"Tell me, did he ever touch you."

"Yes, once when I had a migraine. He did something that made it go away." He explained the procedure.

"It sounds like hypnosis with a dark side," she whispered to Jaxon. She watched the man while trying to figure out what to do next. "You have the power to stop his constant noise. You are the one in control of your thoughts." She reached across the table and touched his arm gently. "Look at me," she told him and snapped her fingers.

He began to cry when he looked into her eyes. "I never wanted to shoot at anyone, but I found myself doing it all the same. I don't know how to stop him. Even now he could choke the life out of me if he wanted to. He almost killed me before when I refused to do what he asked."

She squeezed his arm. "You're free from him. He has no power over you. The fear he holds over you no longer has any power to harm you. After all, he is only a man. His own life is shattering as we speak. He's losing his ability, trust me." She removed her hand from his arm. "Tell me what you hear."

"Nothing. My head is quiet, it's quiet." His hands covered his face.

"Don't believe her, man. What kind of hocus pocus are you up to? He'll kill us. You know he will, Carl," the defiant man shouted at him.

"Carl, you know I'm right. You can tell the difference." She saw him nod. "The doctor hypnotized you to control your mind, a game he's been playing to hurt a lot of people. His time of control is ending. And anyone helping him will go down with him. If I were you, I would get out while I could. He's unraveling."

"I won't talk." The other man folded his arms and stared at her. "Carl, keep your mouth shut."

"You don't have to talk to me." Her face softened. "While you are here you are free from his games."

"Kip, take him back to his cell." Jaxon stood to stretch his legs.

"Carl, are you ready to talk?" Matt asked.

"Keep your mouth shut or I'll kill you myself," the man yelled as he left the interview room.

"Yes. I'm ashamed of what I've done. If I can help stop this guy, I'm ready." He looked at Peyton and mouthed the words, thank you.

"You're welcome." She started to stand.

"Peyton, I think you need to stay and hear this. Feel free to ask any questions that come to mind." Matt pulled a small recorder out of his pocket. "If you're ready we'll begin." He turned on the recorder.

"Let the record show that Carl Baker waived his right to an attorney present at this interview."

Over the next hour, Carl gave them plenty of information, much of which confirmed what they had theorized about the case so far. He gave them enough info about what he knew was going on in the Pinedale facility to warrant getting the FBI involved. Frank and Radar would need to be called in as well. What started out looking like a crazed drug-induced murder now had all the earmarks of a high-level conspiracy with a strange supernatural twist. On some level, Peyton knew all murders had an evil element to them, but rarely would an investigator think of a crime in this context. The ghosts changed all that for her.

When she had talked to Carl earlier, she knew the moment he was no longer influenced by their suspect. The man's eyes cleared, his appearance and demeanor changed. How she knew he had been hypnotized was a mystery to her. Maybe it was the odd look in his eyes. It was only a matter of time before Carl's sidekick, Dominic, would realize he was free in his mind too. What he did with the freedom was yet to be determined. Freedom didn't mean they could get out of jail as Matt had reminded her. Prison time was in both of their futures for attempted murder and assault with a deadly weapon.

How odd life seemed at times. She realized how easily humans could be manipulated, especially when money was involved—and there was plenty of money changing hands. Only after all these years could she now see how the words she heard every day growing up kept her from being who she knew in her heart she could be. It became an excuse when she didn't want to try and a battle cry when she tried to break free of the chains the words had built around her. The saddest thing about seeing crime from this side was how quickly people could lose sight of their values and convictions.

"You're quiet. Is everything okay?" Jaxon leaned close to her when Kip escorted Carl back to his cell.

"Thinking." She smiled at him.

"I'll ask you about what later. Right now, I want to know what happened with Carl. What did you do to cause his sudden desire to talk?"

"You heard what I said. There wasn't any magic. It's about the control that our suspect had over him." She explained about Matt and Jessie's case in Palm Springs. In that case, the suspect controlled people using curses and voodoo. "Control and domination take many forms but always seem to be packaged in fear."

"I honestly thought it was a joke until I touched the fetishes he had placed on one of his small altars around the ladies' suite at the resort. I ended up picking myself up off the ground. There is a dark side to crime." Matt chimed in with his memories of the time and Jessie did the same when she walked in the room.

"Things started to change when a bit of light was added to the subject. I sang an old Sunday school song. It's strange what you do when faced with a new challenge. That case still holds some of the most unusual elements that we've faced to date." Jessie laughed. "Believe me we've faced a lot that has made us have to rethink things more than once."

****

Jaxon's head was spinning after they had wrapped things up at the station for the night. He glanced at his watch. It was after midnight. Grabbing her hand, he walked with Peyton out to the car. What a night. One minute they were enjoying music and the next they were dodging bullets. Followed by what had to be one of the strangest interviews with a suspect and a bizarre conversation with friends. He didn't like where this case seemed to point. On a scale of one to ten, this ranked number ten on his meter of the unusual, although some of what Jessie and Matt talked about seemed odd too.

After he closed the door and got in the car he glanced at Peyton before he put the key in the ignition. Her head leaned against the headrest with her eyes closed. She looked peaceful and beautiful.

"I'm not sleeping." She opened her eyes and smiled at him. "I am tired though. What time is it anyway?"

"It's after midnight, and you've had a long, eventful day. I don't mind if you close your eyes." He started the car. "Let's get you home. I'm staying with you and Jessie tonight. It's my turn."

"That's nice." She sighed.

"Does it bother you?" He backed out of the parking

space and started for the cottage.

"Does what bother me?" she asked.

"You know, like tonight. Hearing what Matt and Jessie talk about. And the whole Carl and Dominic thing. You know, seeing ghosts and all that goes with it. How do you feel about it?"

"If you're wanting to know if I'd rather be normal, the answer is an unequivocal yes. I guess I don't have a choice in the matter. Who knows, maybe it will go away as suddenly as it came." She laid her hand on his arm. "As neat as it was to see my great-great-grandmother up close and personal I could live with normal. At least now I understand how I've come by it and possibly the good that can come from it. How about you, are you okay with me being like this, or is it too much for you? I would understand if it is."

He patted her hand. "I'm not saying I'm leaving. I can't imagine what you're dealing with. I wish there were some way I could make it easier for you. Peyton, in case you haven't noticed I'm crazy about you. You intrigue me more each time we're together. I have no idea what the future holds for us as many times as we have been shot at lately, but I do know I want you in any future I have." He turned onto the road leading back to the inn.

"Thank you. I wouldn't mind having you there either."

He parked and went around and opened her door. "I'm curious. What is the evidence we have so far saying to you?"

As they walked hand in hand toward the cottage, she sensed the eyes watching their every step and proceeded to tell him her ideas about the case. "There will be hard days ahead for us, but at the end of this case, many folks will be able to finally rest in peace. They've all gathered here to see justice for the crimes committed against them. We will stop this man. As life goes, in time there will probably be another to take his place. At least maybe he won't be on our watch."

Chapter 42

Jaxon stretched out on the couch positioning the pillow under his head. Finally Peyton and Jessie were settled in the rooms for the night. God willing, Peyton wouldn't come out of her room again to add to his heightened discomfort. Knowing she was in the next room made lying on the couch and trying to sleep an impossible task. How did Matt do it when he watched over Jessie while all alone with her? A question he needed to put to him. "I'm on the job," would be his answer, which at the moment seemed stretching it a bit to him. At least Jessie being close in the other room kept him in place. What exactly had started this line of thinking was when Peyton walked by him in her nightshirt. A vision with long legs, she made it hard for him to remain on the couch. *Hell, stop thinking about it, man.* He hit his pillow again. At this rate, he'd never get any sleep.

"Matt's a better man than I am." He closed his eyes, but her image followed behind their shield. Dreaming isn't illegal. He grinned and let his mind drift. He could only hope she thought of him with the same degree of wanting.

****

Something had happened. The scowl deepened the creases on his face. His connection to Carl and Dominic no longer existed. How was it possible? He paced, tearing a small branch from the tree and stripping the leaves from it. Someone was on to him. His laughter cut through the silence of the night. While they slept, he prowled. He devised, roamed, and sought another victim to practice on. Practice made perfect, he snickered. It was time. All the years, the people he had fooled, and the test subjects had brought him to this moment. He stopped and raised his closed fist into the air. No one could foil his plan. Who's delusional now? He wouldn't go down easily, and the end had already been written by him. He clutched the small black bag to his chest. His master plan—only he knew of its existence, and those wanting to buy his genius. A secret weapon with the potential to do great harm. His ride might be coming to an end, but he would take a lot of people with him. His place in history would be written. No one could take it from him.

The beast in him was stirring. His laughter vibrated through the man's body. The man could only imagine the evil being conceived. He had to stop him, but how? Only a short window in time remained, and he had to make the most of it. Once the monster set his plan in action there would be no recourse and no way of stopping its progress. Sitting down under the starry sky, he waited, hoping the beast within him would settle again. He knew what he had to do. Humming a song that came to his mind, he found peace for a moment once again.

****

Peyton tossed and turned, her dreams filled with terrifying images of people dying one right after the other for no apparent reason. Suddenly he was there in her dreams, his face altering from calm to contorted with rage. His hand clutched a bag, and his mouth spewed vile threats. His form changed to a rising dragon from the fires to unleash his plague upon the earth and unsuspecting people. The dragon reverted into the shadows when a light came from a star in the heavens. The calm face returned in front of her. There was only a small window of time to defeat his plan. His voice melodically spoke to her. Her mind was filled with images from different eras of time. People who were destroyed by one experiment after another came before her. Back and forth it went through her dreams. Light pushed against the darkness to defeat it only for the dragon to rise again, coming from his hiding place to destroy the lives of many. All the while the man's face alternated with the personas that warred within him. The man issued warnings and pleaded with her to help and stop the monster, and then he became quiet.

A faded image in his mind of a woman appeared in her dreams. Peyton knew the woman. She had seen her earlier at Joe's. That woman could change the course of what was about to happen. Her eyes opened. At least she had an idea of what she needed to do. Both faces belonged to one man. When rational, he controlled the darkness within himself. His ability to constrain the dark side seemed to be slipping with time. The man begged for her help, and she had to try.

She turned on the light. Slipping out of bed, she pulled on her robe and tied the belt tight around her waist. Opening the door, she walked into the living room. "Jaxon, are you awake?"

"I haven't got to sleep yet. What's up?"

"I had a dream. You know, one of those vision-like dreams. I think you need to hear it while it's fresh in my mind."

He sat up. "Fire away."

She explained the vivid imagery she had seen. And about the two sides of the man. "I know what he has in the bag and what he plans to do with it." She explained her theory to him.

"Damn." He raked his hands through his hair. "How do you stop a madman bent on killing people? What is even more disgusting are those who are financing it and looking to turn a profit on the suffering of others."

"You'll take care of that end I know. The man has asked for my help. One of the memories I saw in his thoughts was of a woman. I met that woman in Pinedale in 1918, and I saw her at Joe's. I need to find her. She is a key to stopping him along with locating the portal to the past." She laughed at his puzzled expression. "You do your part, and I'll take care of my end. Together we will solve this case." She stroked his face with her hand. She leaned close and kissed his forehead. "Night, night." She walked back into her room and closed the door with a smile on her face.

****

Jaxon heard the ladies rousing. He sat and lifted his arms over his head, trying hard to stretch the kinks out his back and neck. It was one thing to nap on a sofa but another thing entirely to toss and turn the night away on one. After Peyton shared her vision, his mind wouldn't stop long enough for him to sleep. He spent the night planning his next move. First on the agenda would be Parker and Maxwell on a conference call. Both needed to hear this. The next course of action at the top of the list had to be the contents of the black bag. The sooner the better. He sent off a text to Tom and Matt about a possible time for a call. He folded the sheet and placed it on top of the pillow. He turned when he heard the door open.

“Morning, Jessie.” He grabbed his briefcase. “Tell Peyton I’ll check in with her later.” He rushed out the door.

A quick shower and change of clothes later, Jaxon was in his car headed for the station with a quick stop at Joe’s for a breakfast sandwich. It seemed more important than ever to him that they get this suspect along with those who enabled him. He wasn’t keen on Peyton taking on this guy or having to deal with him at all. But as he was learning firsthand, he might not have any say in the matter. Like she had told him last night, there were civil and moral issues along with legal aspects to this case. Each of them had the area they needed to look after. When it came to dragons and the other supernatural stuff, that was her area. The law was his.

Jaxon arrived at the station and quickly filled Matt in on what he knew so far. “Peyton is concerned that our suspect has used himself in his experiments and is slowly losing his sense of reality. He’s about to do something that could kill many and infect countless others.”

“What about these folks?” Matt held up the spreadsheets with the list of names on them.

“They’ve enabled him by thinking of the profits which they’ve made. I checked. It’s being marketed as the next line of defense in biological warfare. What it is according to Peyton is a highly toxic microorganism to be used as a weapon of war. Its release could infect people instantly. Others could be infected through transmission."

"What does it sound like?" Matt frowned.

"According to one of Peyton's theories, the man started with the intention of finding a vaccine during the Spanish Flu. He tested the experimental drugs on people during his time. He found the portal and moved forward and continued to find victims to further his experiments."

A knock at the door stopped their conversation. "Hey, sir, Tom Maxwell is on line one."

"Thanks, Kenny." Matt picked up the phone, pushed line one, and turned on the speaker. "Hey, Tom. I hope you're wide awake."

"Something tells me I'm not going to like what I hear. Is Kincaid with you?" Tom asked.

"I'm here, sir."

"Let's hear what you've got."

They talked for the next thirty minutes. They agreed that Peyton was on to something, but they would have to have more physical evidence to get a search warrant. The two people in jail could help in that regard. New questions were devised for another interview. Tom would investigate the marketing of the drug and the company along with the people who stood to profit from it. The list of people loomed large along with the Pinedale location, considering the history of the place. They all agreed it seemed to be the logical location for the experiments because it was familiar to the doctor. All three of them agreed to keep certain aspects of the case quiet and let Peyton deal with it. They would help her as they could. In the meantime, Matt needed to line up Frank and his dogs. Tom would work on the search warrants.

****

Peyton followed Jessie out of the cottage into a gorgeous day. She would have loved to spend the morning with a good book and a cup of tea in the garden, but time wasn't on her side. Her part of the case waited for her, and she had no doubt it was only a matter of time before she would come face to face with the doctor. For now, she would call him Mr. Smith.

The ghostly activity around the inn made her wonder. Why were they all gathered here? To her, it seemed more likely that they would be in Pinedale near the school. Another mystery for her to think about. Working at Jessie's store today would be good for her. Maybe Reba knew something about the history of Blue Cove or the inn that would shed light on why ghosts seemed to congregate in the area. Maybe it was as simple as the suspect being nearby, but something told her it wasn't that simple. It could be the fact that she and Jessie lived here, but that didn't seem like a plausible reason. If you want to know the story of an area, ask the people who have lived there the longest. But if you want to know all things supernatural, ask Reba.

Chapter 43

Working side by side with Jessie she got the store ready to open. With two topics in her head, Peyton dusted the counter and straightened the bookmarks in the basket. She wanted to see Reba and a friend from the past today. Both held a key to bringing this case to an end without seeing anyone else hurt. She waved at Molly when she opened the doors into the coffee shop.

"I've been thinking about what you told me on the ride over, and I think you need to carry this book with you. Don't ask me why. It would seem to me this book brought light to the case, and it will be part of the closure." Jessie handed Peyton the book that Jaxon had given back to her. "Whatever you do, don't open it until you feel like you need to. Remember what happened the last time you did."

"I won't. As weird as it all seems, I have to admit it was also amazing. I wonder if we'll ever see Kathryn again, or is her job done? I would like her to know when the case is solved. It really is hers." Peyton slipped the book into her purse.

"I'm sure she'll know." Jessie unlocked the front door and turned the sign around to open. "Peyton, hurry. Come look at this." She stood at the front window pointing across the street.

"Wow!" The spirit activity in the cemetery by the church seemed over the top. It brought up the question she had thought about earlier. Why Blue Cove, and why now? Peyton opened the door and rushed out. "I'll be right back." She ran across the street and tapped the young woman who stood near the gate at the front of the cemetery on the shoulder. "I was hoping I'd see you again. May we talk?"

"Please, I need to talk to someone." The woman followed Peyton through the gate.

"This is a perfect spot. We shouldn't be disturbed here." The bench was across from Pastor Gina's grave and under a beautiful old shade tree. Jessie had told her all about how Gina's spirit appeared to her when she first moved to the cove. Because of Gina, Jessie met Matt, and the rest of the story was still being written. It seemed befitting to be in this spot at this moment. "You're Emily Smith, aren't you?"

"Yes." She hung her head.

"You were the woman in the shadow that day." Peyton jumped up when the memory rushed back into her mind. "How did you get here?"

"I wanted to know what happened to my husband. I came back to work that day in hopes I could continue my search. I saw Irma leave the envelope on your desk and your reaction to what you had read. I wanted to know what was in it. I waited and listened for a clue." She sobbed. "I have no idea how I got here. I only know I watched you lift out of Kathryn. Frozen with fear, I couldn't move. Strange waves of energy shot out from you as you began spinning. When I could no longer see you, I got caught in the final wave. Here I am, but I don't belong here. When I saw you the other day it gave me hope I could go back."

"I suppose everything happens for a reason. Your

husband is somewhere in the area."

"He can't be. We both should be dead."

Peyton explained to her the theory about her husband, what he had been doing since traveling through the portal. "Before he disappeared had you noticed any changes in his personality?"

"The pandemic changed him. His work with Dr. Heisenberg went from fascinating to a place of deep concern. He brooded several days before he decided to quit. The last day I saw him after he kissed me goodbye, he said he was going to stop working there. He told me we had enough money to see us through the next few weeks until he found another job. Those were his last words to me." Emily's hands covered her face as she cried.

"Come with me." Peyton frowned. Darkness filled the cemetery even though the sun still shone through the trees. A dark shadow loomed large around them. She reached for Emily's hand. "Hurry, we need to hurry." Peyton pulled her as fast as she could across the street. Jessie held the door open, closing and locking it behind them.

"You feel it too, don't you?" Peyton asked her cousin.

"Yes. Who is she?" Jessie handed the crying woman a tissue.

"Kathryn worked with her. They shared the reception duties and lived in the same boarding house." Peyton leaned close to her cousin. "She is the wife of the suspect. He disappeared one day."

"How did she get here?" Jessie asked.

Peyton relayed to her cousin what Emily had told her. "We now have a name to get Jeremy looking into."

Remembering a detail from a conversation she had with Emily in the past, she walked over to where she sat. "Emily, you told me that wasn't your real name. What is your name?"

"A name I have missed being called for a long time. My name is Mary Ballard. Mary was a really popular name back in the day." She sniffed. "John was too. I still miss him. If what you say is true, I doubt that I would know him now. None of this makes any sense to me. I only want to go back where I should be even if that is dead."

The one thing Peyton knew for sure was that the battle raging within John Ballard with Dr. Heisenberg was growing exponentially. Did Heisenberg take over John or the other way around? Was John a host for the doctor, whose experiments had gone horribly wrong? She wanted answers, and if the dark shadow growing over the area was any indication the answer would come sooner rather than later. John knew his wife was here, and the doctor did also. One side of the puzzle seemed to be coming together.

Reba got out of her car and rushed through the door Jessie held open for her. Jessie was on the phone with Matt. "They're coming," she mouthed.

It would take more than a gun to fight against what was happening outside. Peyton had an idea that might work. It would take a lot of luck and wouldn't come without risk.

****

Jaxon glanced at the open door when he heard the knock. "What's up?"

"Let's go. I'll fill you in on the way. Jessie called, and she described a strange situation at the store."

Jaxon listened to Matt's explanation on their way to Jessie's store. "Does she know who the woman is?" Instinct told him the case was about to break wide open. Between the two sitting in jail who were talking more each time they were interviewed and whatever Peyton found herself in the middle of they were on a fast-track.

Jaxon opened the car door as soon as Matt stopped. Once inside Jessie's store, Jaxon didn't know where to look first. Reba was talking non-stop, and no one was listening. Peyton was on the computer and was trying to console a woman he had never seen before, and Jessie seemed to be running back and forth between them talking on the phone.

Peyton smiled when she saw him and motioned him to where she stood behind the counter. "I'm glad you're here." She reached for his hand. "As I'm sure you can tell things are a bit chaotic at the moment."

"I noticed." He glanced around the room. Matt walked in the door, and like Jessie he was on the phone. Hopefully they weren't talking to each other.

"You're going to find what I'm about to tell you on the strange side. I thought I should warn you before I tell you. I'll wait until Matt and Jessie get off the phone. I only want to do this once."

"Jaxon." Matt walked over to him. "Maxwell got the search warrant based on the lists Jeremy sent us. Frank will be here tomorrow to search the premises in Pinedale." He stopped, taking in the store. "What the hell is going on in here?"

"My thought exactly. Peyton was about to tell us all about it, weren't you, sweetheart."

"Jeremy is going to research the name you gave me. He'll get back to us as soon as he has something."

Jessie joined the group.

"Finally, it's quiet enough for one of you to answer me. What is going on, girls?" Reba took a deep breath and plopped down in the nearest chair. "I'm quite worn out trying to get your attention."

"Sorry, Reba. You arrived on time as usual but right in the middle of something out of my control. I believe Peyton is about to explain who this young woman is to all of us," Jessie answered.

Jaxon held Peyton's hand when she introduced them to Mary Ballard and told them how she knew her. "Kathryn worked with Mary, and they lived in Mrs. Woodson's boarding house at the same time. I met her when I traveled back in time. When I came back, she got sucked through the portal with me on a weird time delay. I saw her for the first time the other day. Thankfully, we saw each other again today."

"There's more to this story isn't there, Peyton dear? What you have left to tell us is the reason why there's a strange presence hanging over the church and cemetery. Am I right?" Reba fanned her face with her hand. "It's most distressing out there."

"Our murder suspect was her husband who disappeared in nineteen-eighteen. I believe John Ballard is aware that she is in the area and so is the beast inside of him, Dr. Heisenberg."

"Okay, that explains a lot," Reba said.

"Dr. Heisenberg is a new name, isn't he?" Jaxon asked.

"So is John Ballard. When I met Mary, she called herself Emily Smith. I think she should stay with us tonight if that is okay with you, Jessie. Our suspect has a war waging inside of him, and when they search

Pinedale School tomorrow, I think it will send him over the edge."

"There will be trouble." Reba frowned. "Let me suggest if I may a different scenario. I think Mary should stay with me for the night. John has a vague memory of his wife at the edge of his mind. Right now his interest is in you, dear Peyton, and the portal. He wants to be free. The dark side fights to keep him under his control. If she is with me and Lawrence, she will be safe. Both you and Mary will be the bait that finally draws them both out if there are really two." She patted Mary's hand. "Don't worry, dear, you will be back where you belong soon."

Reba's words hung in the air. Jaxon knew she was right. Mary should stay with her and Lawrence, especially with the search happening tomorrow. He had no idea what would happen when the noose tightened around the Pinedale school. He had no idea of the number of lives that had been impacted over the years. He did know the men who were profiting now and the dark purpose for which the drug had been created. It was Matt's turn to stay at the cottage tonight, but they agreed to shake it up for the night. All of them would stay at Matt's. Jaxon didn't like surprises. With a morning search in Pinedale, he didn't want to be worried about Peyton's safety all night.

Chapter 44

Matt's house was beautiful. Peyton would rather be at the cottage, but if it took the pressure off the guys for one night she could live with it. After she placed her overnight case in the guest room, she went in search of the perfect spot to work. The kitchen island called to her. She glanced around the space as she set up her laptop. The kitchen looked like a magazine photo. From this spot, she could still hear the others talking in the living room which made it seem less alone. Plus, the pop of aqua amid the polished stainless-steel appliances and gorgeous granite countertops made the room visually appealing. A win, win as far as she was concerned. Jessie had told her on more than one occasion about Matt's remodeling skills. She had seen it on a small scale at Liam's and Connor's place, but this house showed his ability off to perfection.

Sitting on one of the padded counter stools, she started to build her working theory of the case line by line in her mind. She worked one piece into the equation until it fit and then went in search of another fact among her thoughts or notes, building out from there until the puzzle took shape in her mind to form a complete picture. One of their suspects fought to take himself back to the past where he could end it all. The other one fought to remain here and to build his rule of self-importance until he could move forward in time.

Delusional, he believed himself to be a savior of mankind in his twisted mind. The doctor was willing to destroy lives to prove his worth supported and funded by some famous people. Their sponsorship gave him an excuse to rationalize his actions.

Peyton had a small idea of who she was dealing with. Whether they were two men in the same body or one man with two personalities she wasn't sure yet. That's where more research should help to set the record straight. With a few name searches and the click of the mouse, she hoped to know more. A photo would make it even better. Please. She crossed her fingers and got to work.

She typed Dr. Heisenberg's name into the search box with a year by his name and she was off. One link led to another. She read the bio-information of Dr. Heisenberg who worked in the Pinedale hospital during the time of the Spanish Flu pandemic. She couldn't believe what she read. Wow.

"I wondered where you had gotten off to" Jaxon's voice startled her. "What are you doing? You didn't even hear me when I walked in the room."

"Sorry." She turned to look at him. "You've got to read this." She pointed to the article.

He sat beside her, leaned close, and started to read. "Damn, that gives a clear picture of the doctor. He disappeared at about the same time that Mary said her husband John did." As he scrolled down through the article, he lighted on a photo of the hospital staff. "Look—there's Kathryn." He pointed her out.

"And this is John Ballard. Mary showed me his picture in the locket she wore at the time. He's also the man I saw outside the window on the day of Katie's wedding." Her finger touched his face in the photo. "Do you see what I see?"

"Yes, I do. I'd say you're on to something. Kathryn knew exactly what she wanted you to see the other day in the store. Another disquieting moment for me." Jaxon shook his head.

"Look—this photo is of a doctor during WWII. Now read his bio." She squeezed his hand resting next to hers.

"Hell, how can you explain this to anyone with a rational mind? I'm looking at it, and I can hardly believe it." He frowned.

"I've found photos like this in the Gulf War and the Iraq War." She opened a tab on her computer to show him.

"Damn. I hope tomorrow is filled with some high doses of logically explainable facts and evidence. I'm going to need it after this." He studied the photo she pointed out to him.

"I'm sure there will be enough evidence for you to build a case and send some bad guys to jail. I can only imagine the copious notes he's kept. He would want to document every detail for posterity."

"One can hope," Jaxon told her.

"I'm positive. His ego demands that every detail be known." She stretched her neck from side to side. "Now all we have to do is figure out what to do with our dual man. Tomorrow night Mary must stay with us." She turned in the chair to get his attention. "This is important. I'm convinced John can't be sent back in time. At first, I thought it might be the answer, but it's not."

"Why? It seems like a logical solution to me,"

Jaxon told her.

"We can't tamper with history. It's happened already. We need to stop him here even if it means to kill him. These events have taken place already, and he has interacted with too many people—maybe Mary can but not him."

"I never thought about changing the events of history. Heck, I've never thought of any of this unless I was reading a sci-fi novel." He paused. "John or the doctor will come after you and his wife. Depending on who is the stronger of the two, he will try to take his wife back through the portal or he'll try to kill you both. We can't let him near you or the book portal."

"I would prefer not to ever see him, but I can't see how else we'll stop him. I don't want Reba put in harm's way though. I've known this moment would come since he challenged me the day of the murder. I had no idea then what we were dealing with other than a man filled with rage." She noticed his clenched fist and grim look. "We'll get through this, and after tomorrow we'll know how far he's gotten with this deadly pathogen."

"I'll trust you because I have no idea how to move forward or how to deal with a madman from another time." Jaxon squeezed her hand in his.

"Maybe some of the stories you read as a kid can give you some ideas. We are going to have to think outside the box on this. Nothing about this case is normal except for the murder at the beginning, but the details of that weren't normal either."

"You call Reba, and I'll tell Matt. Between all of us, we might come up with a plan." Jaxon walked into the living room.

Peyton picked up her phone and dialed. Reba answered immediately. “Peyton dear, I knew you’d be calling. She’s safe enough for tonight and sound asleep. Mary has no idea about the changes that have occurred in her husband. For her, he simply disappeared one day. But you aren’t calling me about that but rather to tell me she must stay with you tomorrow. I wholeheartedly agree. This is coming to an end soon, and he knows you know where the portal is. For the first time, I’m stumped by how this will end. I know he won’t go down without a fight. Whether that war is within himself or with you I’m not sure. I do know he’s wrestled with the darkness only to have it overpower him many times. He won’t fight fairly, but light trumps darkness every time. And it only takes a little light to dispel it. Remember that, dear girl.”

“I will. He can’t go back in time.” Peyton was emphatic.

“Why is that, dear?” Reba asked.

Peyton explained her theory. “We have to stop him. We can’t let him find the book portal.”

“Of course, you’re right. I never thought about tampering with what has already taken place. You’ll think of a way to stop him because you have to.”

“We’re going to try.” Peyton stood and stretched her legs.

“I will bring Mary to the store. I can’t wait to see how this will end. Hopefully we will learn why there are so many agitated spirits around. I also would like to know why that portal was found at the inn,” Reba told her.

“You and me both. I’m not sure this case will answer that question. It might be for another time.”

Peyton frowned shaking her head.

After she disconnected the call, Peyton walked into the living room. She sat on the couch next to her cousin. Jeremy was on the speaker so everyone could hear him. “Hi, Jeremy, Peyton is here.”

“Did they fill you in with what I’ve found so far?” Peyton asked.

“Hi back at you. Yes, they did. Pretty crazy isn’t it?”

“More than you know.” Peyton reached for Jaxon’s hand.

“Here’s the deal,” Jeremy said. “I have something more to add to what you have. First, the same doctor was involved in medical experiments for more years than you can count. Same name and the same photo, only now it’s in living color.”

“I know. I found several of those photos.” Peyton leaned closer to her cousin, who was holding the phone.

“His interest started in the field when he wanted to find a cure for the Spanish Flu pandemic and to end the war quickly. Over time it digressed to awful experiments on the poor and the disabled. He’s come full circle to developing a biological weapon with an untraceable pathogen. It isn’t perfected yet or at least at the time of the last article I read it wasn’t. It is being touted as a painless weapon of war. At the time of the article, the conclusion was that the formula wasn’t stable enough to weaponize yet. But its use has killed, disfigured, and maimed many in the past decades. His investors are pressing him hard because time means money. Over the years he was one of his own test subjects. I’m sure it messed him up mentally and physically.”

"How can we stop him?" Jaxon asked.

"That's Jessie's and Peyton's department," Jeremy replied. "I only do research. I'll send you the case study that I've put together when I hang up. I'm convinced this has to be fought on a different level. Peyton, what do you think? This guy isn't normal."

"I agree. I'm still thinking about the situation. I do know we can't let him go back through the portal. He must be stopped here and now. If the good inside of him can overcome the evil, maybe we can take him without killing him. I'm not counting on it though. History has already felt his impact so there's no way it can be rewritten."

"Sounds reasonable." Matt shook his head mouthing the words, "Not really."

"About as reasonable as traveling back in time through the pages of a book." Jaxon frowned. "What I know for sure is Peyton will be vulnerable, and I don't know how I feel about that."

Jeremy replied, "Let me put it this way. If this guy gets spooked and releases this unstable chemical into the air, none of you will be alive to tell the story. No matter what it takes, you must stop him and get your hands on his notes and files. In the wrong hands, this could be the death of many. I'll get back to you if I get more."

"No pressure." Jessie glanced at her cousin. "All you have to do is stop a madman and save the world while no one has clue what you're doing. If you fail, a lot of people could die. Are you kidding me! This is insanity." Jessie jumped up, and Matt pulled her back into his lap.

Peyton agreed. "Let's not talk about it anymore. I

could use a break and something to eat. Popcorn and a movie anyone?"

****

Jaxon sat next to Peyton on the couch with his arm around her. A large popcorn bowl on the coffee table and a movie on TV kept their thoughts somewhat quiet for a bit. Her survival mechanism was to shut down and his was to rev up. Jaxon's mind was never quiet when the stress of an investigation kicked in, but Peyton seemed to be relaxed. How she dealt with each of her supernatural episodes he would never know. No wonder there were times when she would put off talking about them. He had seen plenty in his years as a cop. Nothing compared to what she had seen in a few short months. He couldn't handle half of what she had recently. He honestly didn't know what to say that might help or encourage her. The only thing he wanted to do for her he wasn't sure if he could. "Keep her safe" were the words that resonated through him. He wouldn't go down without fighting for her life.

He had no idea what they would find tomorrow, but he had enough warnings from Jeremy, Peyton, and Jessie to know it wouldn't be good. Agent Maxwell had told him the Pinedale Police weren't thrilled about them or their warrant but would work with them in serving it. Working with the local authorities was paramount to solving cases. He could understand their view because no one wants to believe crime is happening right under their noses. It had a way of making their whole department look bad. Most cops were honest, hardworking men and women who loved their community. No doubt these folks were too. Their world was about to be shaken and turned upside down.

"You're quiet." Peyton glanced at him. "Is the movie boring for you?"

"No, I'm thinking too much. Sometimes it's hard for me to shut my mind off." He squeezed her shoulder. "Having you beside me is nice though."

"And I love being here. Are you worried about tomorrow?" she asked.

"We've had enough warning about what we are likely to find. Not to be concerned would be foolish. Maxwell told me the local authorities aren't happy about the warrant. Which can mean only a couple of things—they've had a bad experience with the FBI, or someone may be complicit in what is going on there."

"Is that likely?" she asked.

"When it comes to a criminal conspiracy you never know who is involved. Jeremy's list makes that clear."

"I guess you're right." She yawned. "To tell you the truth this movie is boring. I'm tired. I think I'll turn in." She stood.

"I'll walk you to your door." Jaxon noted her lips turned up at the corners. "A guy has to walk his girl home for the night even if it's only down the hall." He leaned close so only she could hear. "You can't fault me for wanting a goodnight kiss."

"You'll get no argument from me." She smiled.

Once outside the guestroom door he stopped and pulled her into his arms. She laid her head against his chest. His chin rested on the top of her head while he spoke. "I missed you while you were gone. It left a hole in my heart that only you could fill. I'm not about to waste time worrying about if it'll happen again that you get sucked through a portal. I'll take any moment I get with you, any day." She lifted her head and gazed into his eyes. Never taking his eyes off her, he lowered his head and kissed her. Her reaction told him all he needed to know. She had missed him too. “Sleep well, sweetheart.”

Chapter 45

Jaxon and Matt left early the next morning to meet the FBI agents in Pinedale. The ride was quiet as Matt drove. Jaxon had too much on his mind. He hated leaving Peyton in Blue Cove knowing that their suspect would be enraged before the day was over. Sipping his to-go coffee, he thought about the several conversations they had with Carl and Dominic in the last few days. The two men talked more freely in each interview after Peyton had talked with Carl. They agreed to turn state's evidence and cooperate with the authorities in exchange for a reduced sentence. Carl gave them several names he had heard mentioned by the doctor. He had also identified a few of them from the photos that Kip showed them. Dominic, after realizing he was free from the voice in his head, recalled conversations he had overheard while waiting for their marching orders from their boss. Both men were low-level thugs, but people hadn't been careful of what they said when the two were nearby.

Taking a deep breath, Jaxon knew this was the peace before the storm. Everything about this case boggled his mind. From the suspect to Peyton's time travel and Kathryn's ghost visiting the store he had no logical explanation for any of the strange occurrences. And here he was returning to the place where he first understood that things weren't as they should be. It was time to find how well his instincts were working. He tapped his hand on the armrest.

"It's the next left," Jaxon told Matt.

"Whoa. That building lives up to its reputation." Matt turned into the school parking lot and parked the car. "The perfect haunted house, complete with ghosts and a mad scientist. As a kid what more could you ask for to scare you on a dark Halloween night?"

"I thought something similar when Peyton brought me here the first time. The inside feels about the same as the outside looks." Jaxon got out of the car and walked over to where Tom Maxwell stood.

"Good morning." Tom shook Jaxon's hand.

"Hey, Tom." Matt slapped Maxwell on the back. "You ready to get to work?"

"We're ready to serve the warrant. I thought you guys might like to be here." He shook Jaxon's hand. "By the way thanks for all the information you emailed me last night. I can't pretend to understand how any of it is possible, but I followed your links and photos, and they panned out. Agents are stationed around the premises to make sure no one leaves or comes in. Frank is here with his dogs. His drug dog will search the building with us, and the bloodhound will search the property after we're done here. Let's get it done." Tom walked into the building. "Jaxon, this is your case. I want to see you in action." He handed him the warrant.

Jaxon approached the receptionist desk. "May I help you?" She glanced at him and smiled.

He showed her his badge. "We have a warrant to search the premises inside and out." He handed her the warrant signed by the judge.

"Why, for heaven's sake? We're a school." She

looked over her glasses at him and frowned.

"We have received a credible complaint about criminal activity taking place on the premises. Including the west wing and basement area. You'll need to remain at your desk for questions. Is the west wing open?"

"I highly doubt it. The doors are always locked. With the children, we have to keep certain areas of the building off-limits."

"Do you have keys to the doors?"

"Not that I know of." She became agitated and rummaged through her desk drawers. "I have no idea which key it might be."

"Don't worry about it. We can get in without a key." He motioned to one of the men. "This is Agent Jackson. He needs to ask you some questions. Don't get flustered. If you don't know the answer, just be truthful." He thanked her and left Jackson to do his job.

Several agents fanned out over the building, some standing guard in front of the classrooms where the children were until arrangements were made to transport them to a safer location. Once the children were removed, they approached the west wing of the building.

Jaxon would never forget what they found when the locks expert in the group opened the door. Stunned wasn't a strong enough word. One section was a lab complete with lab techs and a few doctors to monitor patients. Putting on protective covering, Jaxon and the agents began their round of questions and arrests. In the next section of the wing they discovered people strapped to their beds in various stages of consciousness. The fear on some of their faces was palpable. One of the younger patients reached for his gloved hand and wouldn't let go. Jaxon's emotions threatened to get the best of him. He thought of his niece Emmie and what this young man had suffered. He was determined to stop the suspect once and for all. They couldn't let him escape to do this somewhere in another place or time. He held the young man's hand until the medics dressed in hazmat suits arrived and ambulances transported the six patients to the hospital to be placed in isolation until they could be checked thoroughly.

Peyton had been right. The good doctor had documented every experiment and trial on each of his many victims over the years. Mounds of files and photos existed both in filing cabinets and on the computer sitting at his desk. A hazmat crew had to be brought in to carefully transport the Petri dishes and vials in the lab area because they had no idea of the pathogens they were looking at. Nothing could be left to chance. Some would be sent to CDC to see if there was a lab-created virus capable of killing people.

Jaxon stood next to Matt and looked at Dr. Heisenberg's picture surrounded by a group of men. Jaxon recognized many of them from the photos Jeremy had sent. Files were boxed and carted out as more agents were called to the site.

"I can't imagine what's in those vials. What the hell was this guy up to?" Maxwell rested his hip against the door frame.

"I wonder what numbers we're looking at. There has to be a special place to send people capable of torturing the disabled and indigent people." Jaxon's fist clenched. "I wonder how many he's buried over the years without anyone knowing."

"That's a scary thought. I guess we're about to find out if any of them are buried on the property."

"You ready, Frank?" Matt asked.

"I am. I've seen some bad things in my time, but this has to be right at the top. I'm glad Peyton and Jessie aren't here to witness the carnage."

Jaxon agreed. "We should have the air quality of this building tested. It may need to be shut down considering what we've found in this lab."

The day went from bad to worse for them when Radar indicated on several areas of the property after scenting off decomp. They would have to bring in a crew to carefully unearth any bodies buried on the premises.

"I can't believe this has operated here all this time and no one knew it. How many times has the building changed hands over the years? Has this lab always been a tenant? Did anyone ever check out who they were renting to?" Tom shook his head.

"When I questioned the receptionist, she mentioned that this wing in the building was donated to Ballard and Heisenberg Research for perpetuity as long as the building stood." Jackson went on to explain what else she told him about the "twin brothers." "Of course, she thought they were the original doctor's descendants. She said one was always so nice, but the other brother was moody. She would try to never get in his way. She rarely saw them and never together," Agent Jackson told them.

"Twins, so that's how he managed. That answers a few questions for me. I hope those poor folks will be okay. I wonder if he ever came up with an antidote to his lab-created pathogen. Why would anyone want to create something that could harm many? Including himself." Matt frowned as more boxes were carried out in front of him. "This is in your hands now, Maxwell. Jaxon still has to deal with the man who started this and killed someone in Blue Cove."

"It's a hell of a way to welcome someone to a new job. I have one question for you both. Are there any more Reynolds women with this crazy gift? The FBI could sure use one. I can't imagine how big this case will be. Although in the end this will probably be top secret and not hit the news, other than arrests for insider trading. It'll be filed away in the unknown category. Like UFOs." Maxwell picked up a file from the desk dated this week. "These are his last entries. I want to check them out."

"Sir, could you send me a copy of those? Peyton is invested in this in many ways, and I want her to see some of what we found today," Jaxon asked.

"That's Tom to you. I'd be happy to send you one. Be sure to tell me when you get this guy. From what I've seen so far, there won't be anything normal about that either. We'll see you in a couple of weeks if not before, Jaxon." Tom shook his hand.

"You'll be the first one I call." Jaxon followed Matt out to the car.

"I'm glad it's their case from here on. They have a lot of material to comb through. Only God knows all the crimes our twins committed in the name of medical science. I need to wash the filth of this day off me." Matt started the car.

"I hear you. I'm glad Peyton didn't have to see this. Although in some ways I know she already did."

****

Peyton was happy to see him alive and well. It was late when Jaxon and Matt dragged into the house. Kip had spent the day at the store watching over herself and Jessie in what thankfully turned out to be an uneventful day. Reba brought Mary to the store like she had promised and issued one of her strange warnings that left her shaken. Seeing Jaxon in one piece relieved her for a moment. He shared some of the rest of the day with her.

"I don't want to work in Pinedale anymore. I'm taking that school off my list. It must have been hard for you when you saw that young boy. I get mad just hearing you talk about it." Peyton sat beside him on the couch.

"Smart decision." He grinned. "Honestly, Peyton, I'm glad I didn't see Ballard at that moment. Mary needs to know what her husband has become. The unvarnished truth. She'll need it to be free of him once and for all."

"It might take her seeing for herself what he's become. Jessie and I told her the truth leaving out no details, but she is having a hard time believing he is capable of the atrocities. But before she went to bed, she remembered several times that made her question. She knew John was changing. But she chalked it up to the stress he had on the job." Peyton leaned her head against Jaxon's shoulder. "Kathryn will be free too once Ballard is stopped." She lifted her head and gazed into his eyes. She brushed her hand against his cheek. "Thank you for believing me. Not many men would." She brushed her lips across his. "I will always remember this moment." Peyton kissed him with all the emotion that ran through her. Jaxon was a wonderful man.

Later when she had time alone with her thoughts, she knew she could love Jaxon. Anyone else would have written her off as a crackpot, but he had stayed. In her book that was worth everything. And the looks he gave her set the butterflies in her stomach fluttering. Maybe she could simply trust him and quit testing the poor man. Her nature seemed to be to hope for the best but expect the worst. She needed to work on that a bit.

The day had brought many surprises, but she wasn't shocked by any of the news he had told her. She already knew that the doctor had kept meticulous notes. It had upset her more than she let on to hear the experiments were still going on and that several lab techs and a couple of doctors were part of the scheme. All those people would pay the price for John's action. It was ironic that the receptionist thought of them as twins. But she would ask Mary in the morning to rule out the possibility. The names Ballard and Heisenberg Research were the icing on the cake or the ultimate con depending on how you looked at it.

The one thing Mary had told her was that she wanted to go back to her own time. Peyton had been so sure that she could. She no longer saw it as a possible option. Going back to see something and return was one thing. But coming forward and trying to return to what was no longer there didn't seem feasible to her anymore. Mary might need to pick up the pieces of her life and finish what was left here and now. How did this whole time travel idea work anyway? She was not an expert, that's for sure. Was it possible that Mary was stuck in two dimensions as Jessie had been? The problem with that theory applied to this situation was that Mary would be dead in one. She would have been dead in this time if Peyton dragged her through the portal if she did not leave her body behind, as did her cousin Jessie when she went through the mirror. Crazy. She slapped her hand to her forehead. Jessie was alive in both. *Stop it, Peyton, you're giving yourself a major headache*. It was okay not to know the answer. It was doubtful anyone knew. Only time would answer the question if Mary would go or stay. They were destined to find out at the same time.

Chapter 46

Jaxon spent the next morning asking Mary questions about John. He hoped something would stir a memory. Armed with more information that he received from Maxwell in his email, he dropped a few names from the handwritten notes in the years they were married. By the time morning was over, they found out John didn't have a twin brother but was an only child. His mother had smothered him with affection. Mary at least could admit the possibility of him attempting medical experiments to find a cure for the flu.

"Good morning." Peyton placed her notes and the book she was reading on the table and went to pour herself a cup of coffee.

Jaxon noticed Mary staring at the cover of the book. "Is everything all right, Mary?" he asked.

She picked up the book, turning the cover over. "John loved this book. He read it over and over. He thought the author was a genius. When he heard they might make a movie from it John couldn't contain his excitement. Especially when it was rumored that the studio wanted to cast John Barrymore in the lead role. Barrymore was one of his favorite actors." She placed the book back where Peyton had set it. "You don't suppose this story became his in some way. Maybe he tried to emulate it by experimenting on himself?"

"It's a possible theory that we are considering."

Jaxon could see the light turn on in the expression on her face. He let her speak her thoughts aloud without interruption. Each statement she made enlightened them both at the same time. By the time they were ready to leave, he agreed with Mary, John had become lost in a fictional character that he wanted to become. Scrolling through his emails from Tom backed that conclusion. Ballard ceased to know where reality ended for him and fantasy had begun. The problem seemed to be his fantasy destroyed the lives of real people. He chose to live it in real time. One big question he still had when he drove them to the store might remain unanswered unless Peyton could get John to talk. Only time would tell.

****

Most of the night Ballard waited for the opportunity that never came. The police presence continued around the clock. When one group left the next had already arrived. Not able to get any closer he hid in the trees and watched unobserved. His mind couldn't accept what he saw. How did they find his secret place? How—how? He slumped to the ground and wept. All the years of his precious research were lost to an uncaring world. They didn't get it then, and they never would. His was a labor of love. They would never understand the wealth they held in their hands. He covered his face with his hand as the tears rolled down his cheeks. They could never comprehend his masterful mind or appreciate the sacrifices he had been willing to make. All the times he had tested on himself would mean nothing to them. Nor would they ever get the honor of reading his works and benefiting from the great wealth of his knowledge. He had men willing to pay for the privilege. They could steal his ideas and never pay a penny for them.

He had spent years perfecting and refining his discovery until it was ready to be shown to the investors. The cry of denial began deep within him, and he couldn't seem to control the shattering. Anger, rage, and frustration vibrated through him, followed by sorrow, only to be replaced by the cycle all over again. Anger built in intensity as he paced, hitting his head with his fist. Had he escaped death only to die at this moment? Could it be this was his end?

He had watched as they carefully began digging up the grounds. The police would find the people buried there. Each one was a privileged sacrifice needed for the greater good. Mankind couldn't see its folly or how they were headed toward total annihilation. His discovery might kill many, but it would save enough to begin again. A new world, a better one. He turned and walked away. If this was the end, he would go out in a way that only his brilliance deserved. Portal, who needed it? He would go out leaving his mark on this generation.

As soon as the words left him contentment filled him. John awakened after a long, dark night of his soul for a moment while the war within him ceased and thoughts once again cleared. He knew Mary was nearby. How was it possible? He needed one last look at her. One side of him didn't want her to see the man he had become, but the other man's pride wanted her to see what a great man he turned out to be.

The time had come to take his place in the annals of history.

****

Peyton had finished reading a story to the kids at the store when she became aware of a shift in the atmosphere around her. She rubbed her arms trying to ward off the chills running up and down her arms. Ballard had made his decision. She could sense his rage. It was only a matter of time until he would confront her.

"Kathryn, I know you orchestrated this moment, but I have no idea what to do. How can I fight a person who should have died many years ago?" she whispered. Putting words to her thoughts and speaking them out loud brought a measure of comfort to her. "Jess, I'm going to get an iced tea. Do you want anything?"

"No, I'm good. Take a break. You've earned it." Jessie waved at Peyton while she went to help a customer.

After Peyton ordered, she found an open table to sit at. Molly had become one of the many new friends she had made since staying at the cove. The town had grown on her, and she couldn't imagine not living near these wonderful people. Plans were in the works for her to move here, and she couldn't wait. When it came to Molly's baked goods, she couldn't come to the coffee shop without buying one. *You're weak.* She shook her head. Still, she enjoyed the first bite of the fresh blueberry scone. No recriminations. She took another bite and smiled.

Peyton knew that for now Mary was safe. She had gone to the station with Jaxon and Matt earlier, and Peyton hadn't heard how it was going yet. They had more that they wanted to talk to her about. Peyton couldn't wait to hear what else they were learning from all the files. One thing she knew for sure: their dual man was not a happy camper. As soon as she thought the words, she braced herself for what would happen next. She placed the scone back in the bag to finish later and asked Molly for a to-go cup for her iced tea. The minute she walked back into the store she couldn't believe what she saw. Jessie was helping a customer and was surrounded by spirits flittering around the store. Her cousin looked at her, shrugged her shoulders, and rushed over to her as soon as the customer went into the coffee shop and said she would be back.

"What is going on? They're everyplace." Jessie pointed in all directions around her. "You've got to see this. Come here and look across the street at the cemetery. There seems to be a gathering of sorts." Jessie motioned for her to follow.

"I wonder…" Peyton glanced at her cousin. "They are recovering the bodies buried at the Pinedale property. If they're victims of the doctor they are anticipating justice at last."

"This is my opinion because I have no idea. I believe they are here to help. We will need all the help we can get." Jessie paused. She went on to explain all that had happened in their case when a serial killer came to town and his victims had gathered. They ended up saving her life. "They saved me from him."

"Wow, that's quite a story. Someday, cousin, you and I are going to have a long talk. I hear something new every time you speak about one of your cases. I told Jaxon he might need to think outside of the box. I think I need to do the same. If the spirits can help, I welcome it. The dark side of Ballard is growing stronger. I don't think John will be able to control him much longer. He challenged me the day of Katie's wedding, and I know he meant what he said."

"How will he come?" Jessie wrapped her arms around her body.

"If only I knew, I could plan. As it is, I am walking into the situation blind. I do like to think of all of these spirits as my reinforcements. I have a feeling I'm going to need them."

Peyton continued to watch the heightened supernatural activity around her. That's when she saw Kathryn standing outside the store looking at her. Pictures began to flood Peyton's mind. Kathryn's memories of seeing Ballard outside eating lunch one summer afternoon. She saw the battle that warred around him. Light and darkness battled over the core of the man. Kathryn saw the many days that the battle raged around him until one day she knew that his heart had changed. Darkness prevailed and walked with him more often than the light. That's when people began to go missing among the poor and the disabled. The atmosphere at the hospital changed as if a dark cloud hung over it. She noticed coming to work that there were places on the property where the fresh ground had been turned. Each day she found it harder to force herself to go to work. The light seemed to be snuffed out of the building along with the compassion and regard for the people in their care. The deaths from the Spanish Flu pandemic had been sad enough, and she carried the grief and felt it daily when she went into the building to work. But the other presence sucked the life out of the makeshift hospital and from all who worked in it. With her memories shared Kathryn smiled at her great-great-granddaughter and told Peyton that she wasn't alone. Love always wins, and good trumps evil in the end. Peyton knew when Jessie came to stand beside her. Kathryn's final words to them were, "I, my dears, have seen the light and the power of love. You'll know it too when you need it the most."

Peyton hugged Jessie. "Did you see and hear her too?"

Jessie nodded, and her tears were the only answer that Peyton needed. They both reached for the box of tissues at the same time and laughed.

Chapter 47

Later at Matt's house, they lingered over dinner and discussed their latest ongoing theories of how the case would end. Jaxon surprised himself by keeping it together in the face of a situation with enough twists and turns to bend his mind. Something didn't add up to him. No matter what angle he approached it from there seemed to be a missing key. "What I want to know is how has the doctor traveled through time? How has he managed to escape death?"

"Good questions. I have one to add. Did he travel in our time or did he find a portal into an alternate dimension?" Peyton added her question to the group around the table.

"I have no idea what any of you are talking about. All I know is when you were pushed forward in time, I got caught in the ripple effect." Mary pointed at Peyton. "I'm here, and I'm the same age as I was in nineteen-eighteen."

"Mary, why didn't I think of that?" Peyton slapped her hand to her forehead. "It has to be some kind of energy field. I wonder—did he accidentally create one during his experiments? Whatever happened seemed to preserve him and his work through several generations. Having said that, I believe the field is breaking down. His world is shattering. Since the raid on his research lab, he hasn't got what is needed to maintain the chemistry of his existence. The war is raging inside of him. He knows his time is fading away, and he is planning to go out in his own determined way."

"The question is does he have enough left in him to do any real harm?" Matt asked.

"Remember what Kathryn said to us about seeing the light and the power of love?" Jessie squeezed Peyton's arm.

"I'll never forget. Why?"

"He has sustained himself on the deaths of others. It has empowered him in some odd way. The one thing that darkness can't tolerate is…"

"The light!" Peyton shouted jumping up.

Jaxon thought he must look as confused as he felt. Again, another clue way out of his wheelhouse. Too far out for his logical brain. He was happy the cousins understood what they were talking about because he had no idea. While the women continue to talk details excitedly, he went into the living room followed by Matt.

"Did that make it any clearer for you?" Matt sat in his favorite recliner.

"No, I can't say that it did." Jaxon sat on the couch. "Maxwell emailed me earlier with more details from Heisenberg's file. The drugs and elements that Frank's dog found also turned up in some of the bones found on site, as well as the patients that were transferred to the hospital. They were different levels of nerve agents that depending on the dosages could build and become toxic over time. Some of the chemicals were untraceable without the most sophisticated equipment to detect and some were unknown compounds. A few were lethal enough to kill in a single drop the size of a pinhead. At least this evidence I can understand even if I can't wrap my head around the scope of it."

"Hell." Matt raked his hand through his hair. "What is he planning? How did he get others invested in his scheme?"

"Tom said the interviews begin tomorrow."

"Boy, would I like to sit in on that."

"Maxwell said we could come. I think we should. It might give us a clearer picture of the extent of this crime."

"Count me in. Kip and Gary can babysit the girls for a few hours." Matt reached for the remote. "Does this ever make you think that being a cop isn't what it used to be? The bad guys seem to be one step ahead of us. Now they're even coming in on energy fields." He turned the TV on to the sports channel.

****

The store was busy between the mystery book club, the ghosts, and customers. Peyton hardly had any time to think about the case. Kip and Gary's presence reminded her though. When Reba walked in the door with Sadie, she knew the day was about to get even more interesting. "Hi, Grams." Peyton kissed her grandmother Sadie's cheek. "What are you two up to?"

"Hi, dear." She smiled at Peyton and waved at Jessie waiting on a customer. "Reba saw all the action over here and had to stop by on our way to lunch. You know how she is. Once she gets a thought in her head it's like a bee in her bonnet."

Peyton leaned close to her grandmother and whispered in her ear. "Kathryn was here again yesterday, and both of us saw her." She went on to tell her about the visit.

"How I would love to see her," Sadie said wistfully. "I guess those days are over for me."

"What days are over?" Reba led her over to the nice comfy leather chairs.

"Seeing." Sadie sat in the chair, crossing her legs at the ankle.

"Why do you think I brought you here? You must be in this store at this very minute, that's all I know. And so we are here." Reba placed her purse beside her on the chair. "Peyton, why don't you get us each a cup of tea. My treat." Reba reached into her purse to give her the money. "Buy us one of those lovely lemon bars to share too."

"Only one?" She glanced at both women.

"Yes, dear, only one. We don't want to eat too much before lunch. Thank you, sweet girl."

As Peyton waited for her order, she couldn't help but wonder what Reba was up to. It seemed a bit scary to have Sadie anywhere near the store right now. Who knew when John would lose the battle raging inside him and come after her or Mary?

Molly handed her the bag. "Thanks, Molly." Peyton dropped a tip in the big jar. As soon as she stepped over the threshold into the store, she knew something was happening. Jessie sat on the arm of Sadie's chair with a tissue box, and both had tears in their eyes. And that's when she saw her. Peyton sighed. Sadie was able to see Kathryn too. The circle of life. It started with Kathryn, passed on to Evelyn, down to Sadie, and on to Jessie and herself. She sat on the other arm of Sadie's chair, and the tissue box was passed to her.

"Kip, do you know what's going on with them?"

Gary pointed at the four women.

"I have no idea. Women—who can figure them out? They cry at the drop of hat." Kip shook his head. "But they're awfully nice to look at."

"Hell, yes." Gary smiled.

****

The day had been enlightening. One suspect after another with their fancy lawyers tried to sidestep any questions thrown at them, until the last man figured out he didn't want to be in prison for the rest of his life. Not a person of consequence, he had the most to lose and he knew it. He got pulled into the scheme through a friend as a great retirement investment. He was promised a quick return on his money once the product got traded on the market. He had already made money as the potential interest grew. Supposedly, Heisenberg had created a weapon that could change the face of war, making it more humane.

He had met the doctor on several occasions and saw one demonstration by way of a simulated video. Heisenberg could be extremely moody if questioned in any way. They were supposed to attend another in-person demonstration next week. When asked how he felt about the doctor and his invention, he told the agent he was beginning to have doubts. To him, the doctor didn't seem stable. Heisenberg had told them the weapon was designed to kill hundreds on the battlefield painlessly in a few moments after activated. He was never upfront about how that would be accomplished or what would happen to the people who deployed the weapon. The man ended the interview with the fact that he had pulled his original investment out. He told the other investors to keep any money he had made.

Something was off about the whole thing.

"What do you think?" Matt asked Jaxon as soon as he closed the car door.

"Something tells me that guy was lucky not to see the in-person demonstration of the doctor's weapon. He'd be a dead man. The raid on Heisenberg's lab may have shut down his project, but I have no idea what he's still capable of." Jaxon leaned his head back against the headrest.

"All those men enabled the doctor knowing he was creating an unknown germ pathogen to be weaponized. In place of nuclear capability, it gives a whole new meaning to the word 'dirty bomb.' " Matt frowned. "They're guilty in my book."

"My thoughts exactly." Jaxon latched his seatbelt and texted Peyton to see if she was okay. "The question still is how do we stop him? I wonder if Jeremy has any ideas. Energy force fields might be right up his alley." Jaxon chuckled.

"Those who grew up with the space movies can appreciate we are seeing some of the things from those movies becoming reality. I read the other day a man in a jetpack flew in front of a landing jet. I wonder if someday we'll all be strapping them on and taking off." Matt turned onto the highway back to Blue Cove.

"Makes you wonder, doesn't it? Peyton told me the other night I might have to think outside the box on this one. I'm afraid she's right. I'm not sure I know how to do that." Jaxon glanced at the text that Peyton sent him. She was fine, and now he was too.

****

His strength waned. Not able to drink the mixture, he couldn't regenerate himself. The time he had left diminished in front of his eyes. It didn't matter whether he lived or died at this point. Thankfully the monster inside him had been quiet for a while. Without the magic liquid, the beast seemed to have reduced in strength. Needing to conserve his energy, he lay down, stretching out on the grass. Closing his eyes, he found images swirling around him. There was one that brought a sweetness with it. He could almost hear her voice and see her face. Peace. How he had missed these quiet moments of reflection. He slept.

By nightfall, the battle returned with a vengeance. The darkness enveloped him almost choking out his life and bringing him to the brink of death, followed by a bright light that pushed against the darkness holding it at bay. He gulped for air, and the weight lifted off his chest. The darkness came from within his body and out of his mouth forcing the light to retreat from his view. Cursing and filth spewed out of his mouth twirling around him in the dark mist. In the center of the darkness, a tiny light in a beating heart grew until it forced the dark to recede into the shadows and out of his sight. In the middle of the heart was the face of an angel and memory from his past. "Mary." He cried out her name before sleep claimed him once again.

Chapter 48

She might be a newbie when it came to the gift passed down from her great-great-grandmother, but Peyton knew something monumental had happened a few moments ago. It felt as if the atmosphere shifted around her. What that meant for the case she had no idea. The doctor's accusers were in Blue Cove to testify against him. Would Ballard escape, or was this the time he would have to face all the pain, suffering, and deaths he had caused by his actions? She hoped it would be the latter. Straightening the book table, she helped Jessie get the store ready to close. Mary had gone over to Reba's to rest and for dinner. Reba had taken a liking to the woman. The truth was that if Reba liked her she couldn't have a better someone in her corner. Peyton waved at Jaxon and Matt when they pulled up in front of the store.

She went out the door to meet Jaxon as Matt rushed in the door to find Jessie. "How did your day go?" Peyton asked.

"I learned a lot, but I still have a few questions and loose ends to tie up." Jaxon pulled her into his arms and hugged her.

"As in all of your cases." She pulled her head back to look at him. "Have I told you lately how handsome you are?"

"I can't recall you saying that in the past few

days." He rested his chin on her head. "I like hearing it."

"I've thought it many times. I should have told you." She snuggled in his arms. "Today was enlightening to me too."

"Why don't we go to dinner and you can tell me all about it." He smiled when she ran her fingers through the hair on the base of his neck.

"You read my mind." She pulled out of his arms and walked with him into the store. "I need to help Jessie finish closing the store. We have to go back to Matt's to get a car unless Jessie lets you drive hers." Even the suggestion made his eyes light up.

****

"Man, this is a sweet set of wheels." Jaxon ran his hand over the paint job on Jessie's car. "I heard you restored it with the help of your brother, Matt, after it was riddled with bullets. You did an awesome job." Jaxon opened the door and looked at the interior. "Beautiful."

"Thanks," Matt said. "I find working with my hands is good therapy for me. Enjoy your dinner. We'll pick up Mary. See you at the house later." Matt pulled Jessie into his side, and they walked in the back door together.

Jaxon glanced at Peyton. "What sounds good to you?"

"I was going to ask you the very same thing." She smiled at him. "Tell me what sounds good, and I'll tell you the best place to go."

"After the day I've had I want a cheeseburger and a malt. No judgment. Not the healthiest, but you asked."

"There's one place that's the place for what you

want, and that's Sally's in Seaside Village."

Later, while stretched out on the bed Jaxon went over the conversation that he had with Peyton earlier that evening. Two things stood out to him. Sadie seeing Kathryn was a definite highlight. Peyton's eyes got misty as she told him the story. He couldn't imagine how it impacted Sadie to see her grandmother along with her two granddaughters. The other thing that stood out to him was Peyton knowing something would happen soon. She described the atmosphere change. What could it mean?

Pulling out his laptop, he finally got the chance to read the information Jeremy had sent him on the questions he had asked earlier. In the email was info about an energy force field in chemistry. Jaxon couldn't understand most of what he read. Chemistry wasn't one of his strongest subjects in college. The part of the email that did interest him was on the force field in speculative fiction. It was known to readers as an energy shield, or deflector shield. The shield was made of plasma or particles. The force shield served to protect the person within the field from attacks and intrusions. Jaxon reminded himself to think outside of the box. Jeremy added a brief note of his own.

—As crazy as it seems you might what to take a look at fictional technology to explain how Ballard remained untouched through all the years. Teleporting, cloaking devices, and tractor beams don't sound so farfetched when I think of Peyton and Jessie. Maybe in one of the doctor's chemistry experiments he stumbled on to it. In all fiction, if the shield is infiltrated or breached, you know from reading or watching sci-fi movies what that would mean. It would be a seismic

shift when it comes to the doctor.—Peyton had said the same thing.—*Buckle up, it sounds like you're in for a ride to the finish on this one.*—

****

Peyton got up early after tossing and turning most of the night. Hopefully, a shower would help her. Drying her hair took a lot of her energy. A glance in the mirror was proof enough that she needed concealer and foundation to make her look alive. The dark circles under her eyes told the story. Come on, concealer, do your magic. She topped it off with a touch of blush and lip gloss. She frowned at her image. At least the extra effort on her hair was worth it. Routine—exactly what was needed most for her at the moment. It made everything seem right, even when she knew that it wasn't.

How crazy and yet amazingly wonderful her life had become since her trip to Arizona. What a drab existence she had lived before. She realized yesterday with Sadie and Jessie what a great treasure it was to share a life-changing event with people you love. Those were the memories that gave meaning and purpose to life.

Something smelled good. She walked down the hall and into the kitchen. "Wow, every girl's dream—a guy that can cook and is a total hunk in the kitchen." She sat at the counter. "It smells delicious."

"Good morning, sweetheart." Jaxon turned down the burner. "I make a perfect crepe if I do say so myself. I hope you're hungry." He poured her a cup of coffee.

"I am." She smiled at him. "I never pictured you in the kitchen. What brought this on this morning?"

"Probably the same thing that got you up early and looking like a million bucks. Therapy, routine, or whatever you want to call it. Maxwell told me this morning there are some seedy folks who are really bad dudes aligned with the group of investors. They were in line to buy the product and use it in a terrorist operation. They're not in custody yet and might have gone underground. Maxwell warned me to be on guard. News like that makes me edgy especially when I know what these guys are capable of."

"For me, it's the doctor. He's coming, and he's resigned to the fact that he's dying. It's the unknown factor of what he will attempt to do on his way out that frightens me. There's a battle raging in him, and I have no clue how it will play out. From my research, I believe in the beginning he extracted stem cells in the blood and bone marrow for research using techniques advanced for his time. Somewhere along the way he simply murdered the victims outside of the hospital as his need and greed grew. He used it in a potion to regenerate."

"I guess we should enjoy this moment of calm. We may be in for a rough day." He put two crepes on a plate and placed it in front of her. "One is strawberry, and the other is ham and cheese. Enjoy."

Peyton took her first bite. "Oh my, this is wonderful." Her tongue touched a spot where a tad bit of powder sugar landed on her lip. "I had to taste the strawberry first. I do love strawberries." She answered his question before he could ask. "You know the life is short, eat dessert first theory. But I'll leave the rest for after I finish this one." She pointed at the ham and cheese.

"Sweetheart, you can eat whatever you want first. I'm happy you're enjoying them." He grinned.

"Of course I am, and I like that a man is making them and waiting on me." She smiled back at him.

Jaxon and Peyton soon were joined by the others, and the crepes along with the coffee were polished off in no time. After breakfast, Jaxon dropped Peyton and Mary off at the bookstore on his way to the station. Earlier Peyton had overheard Jaxon tell Matt about his emails from Tom Maxwell and Jeremy. It left her with questions she wished she would have asked. Anxious, she helped her cousin open the store. One thing she knew for sure—she didn't want Ballard anywhere near the store or the people she loved. How could she get him to follow her somewhere else?

As different scenarios played out in her mind one major theme kept resurfacing. Jaxon needed to know how she felt. She had a good idea where the guys were that Tom had warned him about. She sent him a text and got to work when a customer came into the store.

****

Jaxon caught up on his texts right before lunch. After he read Peyton's text, he ran out of the station and headed to Jessie's store. He called Matt and filled him in on what Peyton had texted him. "I'm going to take Peyton and Mary away from Jessie and the others for a while. Peyton is worried about putting others in jeopardy."

"I'll go to the store and hang out. Where are you going to take them?"

"My best bet is to let Peyton tell me where we need to be. I'll call you as soon as I know." Jaxon pulled into a spot near the store. The first thing he noticed when he walked into the bookstore was the children present. They sat in a circle around a chair where Sadie sat reading to them. He could understand Peyton's concern.

"Hey Jessie, I want to steal Mary and Peyton for a little bit. Does that work for you?"

"Of course. I can handle it." Jessie smiled and nodded.

"I see you got my message. Can you see why I'm concerned?" Peyton asked.

"Yes. I would have been here earlier, but I just read your text. Get Mary, and let's go."

Peyton reached behind the counter for her purse. It felt heavier than normal with two books inside. "Mary, we need to go. I'll explain on the way."

Relief filled Jaxon when he had both of them in the car and drove away. He could see Matt's car in his mirror pull into the space he had just vacated. It didn't negate the fact that both women's lives were in peril. He most likely was too since he was with them.

"Where to?" He glanced at Peyton.

"To the place where it all began for me." She held tight to her purse.

"Pinedale? The area is off-limits." Jaxon stopped at the light.

"No, not the school. The path to the marina where the murder took place. It has to be somewhere between the inn and that spot."

"Are you sure?" Jaxon drove toward the inn calling Matt to tell him they might need backup.

"I'm as sure as I can be." She frowned. "It has to be there. That's where he showed himself and challenged me. He'll be waiting." She clutched her purse in her hand.

"We stay together, Peyton. You don't do this on your own. If your premonition is true, we have to have help. We need to wait." He turned onto the road that went back to the inn. "I mean it. We wait." The knot in his stomach tightened.

"I know." Peyton reached for the door handle but didn't open it.

What seemed like a lifetime had been less than five minutes when several police cars pulled up beside and behind Jaxon's car. Jaxon reached Peyton's side before she could rush off. He could tell she wanted to.

Chapter 49

The threat real, Peyton prepared for the fight even though a part of her wanted to flee. The adrenaline began pumping through her bloodstream. She took quick, short breaths in response to her increased heart rate. She readied herself to take the monster on. She knew what she had to do, but she had no idea if it would work. “We need to get going.” She paced, feeling the energy pulsating through her. She could hardly stand still.

“Slow down, sweetheart. These guys have to know what’s about to happen.” He latched onto her hand which clutched his tight.

“They need to keep their eyes on the men with him and the bag in his hand. If he reaches into it, shoot him. We can’t let him release that pathogen into the air. I will challenge him. If he drops the bag, grab it. Don’t let anyone else get the bag. Please don’t let anyone else get their hands on that bag.”

“You heard her.” Jaxon issued a few more commands. “They will be armed. Stay alert.”

Another car approached the others. Matt jumped out of the car. “I couldn’t let you have all the fun.” He slapped Jaxon on the back. “Don’t worry, Peyton. I have someone with Jessie and Sadie.”

Peyton started walking toward the cottage. The closer she got the stronger the sensation became that he was near. She reached inside her purse for the two books. Dropping one of them, she knew the other was the one she needed. Jaxon followed close behind her. The others had fanned out and were moving behind the trees and under cover. Mary walked beside Jaxon with a look of sheer terror on her face.

As soon as her foot hit the path away from the cottage, Peyton knew he was waiting. "He's here." She glanced at Jaxon behind her. "He's been waiting for this moment. His self-aggrandizing makes him vulnerable. Keep Mary hidden until I tell you to let him see her." She pointed to a clump of trees.

"I can't let you go on alone." He pulled her back against him.

"You have to. If he sees you first, all hell will break loose. We might all be killed." She stroked his cheek with the back of her hand. "It has to be this way. I knew the day of Katie's wedding that this wouldn't be a normal fight. It has to be done on a different level." She glanced one more time before she turned her back on him and began down the path. Ballard waited for her. Several men stood a short distance away.

"I've been waiting for you. I knew you wouldn't let me down." He pointed at her. "I'm about to show these men my little experiment. I felt sure you'd want to see it."

"I'm wondering who I'm talking to at this moment. The weak John Ballard or the egomaniac Dr. Heisenberg. Neither one of you are that impressive to me. I've learned a lot about you and the people you have tortured and killed over the years. I'm not sure the world will want to remember you. If they do, it will only be with contempt." She sensed the anger rising in him. “Before you display your greatness, I have someone you might want to see.” She continued to approach the group. Some of the men pointed their guns at her. She kept moving closer toward him. “Mary, John would like to see you.” Mary started down the path toward her.

The doctor’s reaction was swift. “Mary, my sweet Mary.” His face contorted shifting from love to hate, from longing to anger. Regret followed loathing only to be replaced by pain. It happened so fast that he twirled around like a whirling dervish, sending out strange ripples in every direction. The men standing near him began to run in fear when the waves hit one of them and knocked him to the ground. Peyton flipped the pages of the book that had been the basis of his dual persona, and the shield around him began to visibly crack. Peyton kept flipping the pages until he dropped to the ground in a heap. When she looked around her, the men had been gathered up by the officers and Jaxon had the black bag in his hand. Thank God.

“He has a pulse.” When Matt went to cuff him, John disappeared. “What the hell?”

She put her arms around the sobbing Mary. “I can’t believe you asked that after working with Jessie all this time.” Peyton’s hands started shaking. “I need to sit down.” She sat in the spot where she had been standing. It was either that or her legs would buckle. “I can’t believe it worked,” she whispered.

“What worked?” Mary sat down beside her. “For a moment I know he recognized me.” She gasped. “I still can’t believe what I saw.”

“Yes, he did. You were the distraction that I needed. I’ll try my best to explain it to you as soon as I calm down enough to think clearly."

****

As soon as the men were booked in jail, Jaxon and Matt were on a conference call with Tom Maxwell.

"I can't believe you got them all. How did it happen?"

"Peyton had the idea that he would put out the call that he had moved up the demonstration before the news got out about the others' arrest. She was right of course." Jaxon leaned his hip against Matt's desk.

"I'll be there with another agent to transport them. You've got some dangerous men in your custody. I don't want the news to get out about them. No telling what might happen. I believe it's safe to say all the investors and Dr. Heisenberg will have 'traitor' added to their charges."

"We don't have John. You'll have to wait to hear what happened. I'm not sure any of us could tell you, and we were there."

"I'll be there as soon as I can get there. How many are we moving?"

"Seven all total," Matt answered.

"Something tells me I'll find the story hard to put in my report." Tom chuckled.

"I'm sure of that. It'll be right up there with UFOs," Jaxon told him.

"Relegated to a top-secret file locked away for another generation to scratch their heads at when they read it."

Later, after agents had transported the men to a federal jail, Tom joined them at the Chowder House. The meal was on him. As soon as the group was seated and orders taken, Jaxon put his arm around Peyton.

"The floor is all yours. Tell your story. We all agreed to hold our questions until later."

****

"Before I do, I want to introduce you to Mary, Tom. She was John Ballard's wife back in 1918." She smiled when she saw Tom's face. "How she found her way here is where my story begins." With a steady voice, she started with the day of the murder and the challenge from the stranger. She explained about the book in the attic and her travel through time. "That's where I first learned of John Ballard.

"It was Kathryn's visit to my cousin's bookstore and her pointing out this book"—she pulled it out of her purse—"that explained the situation that we were dealing with a man who had traveled through time somehow with a dual persona. The one thing we had on our side was that he was fighting within himself."

"What happened today? How did you know what to do?" Tom asked.

"I woke up this morning knowing this was the day. Ballard was getting more unstable. I knew the book was part of the answer, but I didn't know how. I also thought seeing Mary would impact him. It was overhearing Jaxon talking with Matt at breakfast this morning that gave me an idea." She glanced at him and smiled.

"What did you hear?" He squeezed her shoulder.

"You talked about thinking outside the box and speculative fiction. It hit me that some kind of protective energy force was how Ballard had survived all this time. How he stumbled onto it I don't know."

"Matt mentioned reading in Ballard's notes that there had been an explosion in the lab that brought about a great discovery. He detailed the incident. The answer has to be in there." Jaxon glanced at her.

Peyton continued. "John had almost perfected the pathogen with an untraceable footprint which made it perfect to weaponize. He was going to sell it and live out his days as a wealthy man hoping to move forward again. The raid on the lab pushed up the date of the sale. He needed to go there to keep regenerating. He was willing to risk the formula's imperfections and to go out on his terms. Seeing Mary sped up the shattering of the dual persona inside him, sending out energy waves and impacting the suspects. When I started flipping the pages of this book, the shield of protection or whatever you want to call it cracked, and he fell stunned to the ground. He simply disappeared because he no longer existed." She frowned. "The final chapter of his life is still to be written. He was a monster and needs to be seen that way even if the facts of his death remain shrouded in mystery."

"I have lots of questions." Tom proceeded to ask them.

"History has happened and can't be changed," Peyton explained. "Just ask the poor souls who suffered at his hands. They had gathered to accuse him. I'm sure he faced them in the end."

Maxwell stood. "Jessie, you might have to write the article that speaks of the death of the doctor and the end to the Pinedale research institute. You'll figure out the angle and get approval before it's printed. I'll make sure you get the names of the men involved. The investors and the thugs. This was a hell of a day. We got lucky with this one." He laughed when both Jaxon and Matt shook their heads.

"Not luck, sir. It took ghosts, time travel, and a whole lot of girl power to solve this one." Jaxon stood next to Peyton. "Face it, we would have never seen it coming until it was too late."

"Damn, when you're right you're right." Tom followed them out of the restaurant.

Peyton and Jaxon walked hand in hand to her car. "It's so nice to be able to drive this again, but I want you to drive it tonight. I'm tired." She dropped the keys into his open hand. Once in the car she laid her head back and closed her eyes. "I'm not sleeping." She smiled. "I'm just resting my eyes and inhaling the new car smell."

"You do that, sweetheart. You've earned it. This is by far the strangest experience I've had in my career." When he stopped at the light, he squeezed her hand. "I have plenty of questions to ask you but not tonight. I hope you remember that I've planned a special night for us tomorrow. I'm glad the investigation won't interfere with it. The one thing I want to know is if you have the answer to how the inn fits into the story." He smiled when she gave him an eye roll. "You can tell me tomorrow."

Chapter 50

Jaxon walked through the garden to the cottage. Stopping to look around filled him with peace. His mind still reeled from the craziness of the past several days. Through all of it his one bright spot, his north star, the one whom he sought out, was Peyton. They made a great team. He couldn't wait to see her tonight and spend time getting to know her better. He hadn't been looking for a relationship until she walked into his life and challenged everything he knew. He still hadn't recovered and didn't want to.

When he arrived at the door, he didn't need to knock. She stood quietly inside the open door watching him. "Have you worked it all out, or do you need to think some more?" She smiled at him.

"What gave me away?" He grinned at her.

"Only the intense look of concentration on your face. You looked like you were about to force down something you didn't want to eat."

"That bad, huh?"

She nodded. "Except for your occasional sigh of contentment."

"Excuse me, I don't sigh." He smiled.

"Of course, you don't." She chuckled. "Whatever you call those strange noises you were making, I hope some were because of me."

"Thinking about you is my favorite pastime." He

opened the screen and pulled her into his arms and hugged her tight. “This is what I think of when you come to mind.” He framed her face with his hands and kissed her gently, deepening the kiss when he felt her response. “Are you ready?”

“Yes. Give me a minute. I need to get my purse.” She walked back into the house.

“You look beautiful.” He raked his hand through his hair. “You always do. I love that dress on you. I can still recall the night you walked out the door of the resort wearing it. You took my breath away, and I couldn’t respond for a few minutes. I stood there like a dummy as every coherent thought left my mind. You were ready to turn around and go back inside your room. I knew at that moment I was in deep trouble. You sneaked your way into my heart, and I intend to keep you there.” He reached around her to make sure the door was shut and locked. Placing his hand on her back, they walked through the garden to the car.

“You remember that night?” she asked when he got in the car.

“I sure do. I remember how the sun caught the red in your hair making it look like liquid fire falling over your shoulders. And the way that dress clung to every curve on your body. You took my breath away.”

“I had no idea. I was mad at you that night in case you hadn’t noticed.” She laughed.

“Oh, I noticed all right. I deserved it because I was doing everything in my power to push you away. Nothing worked. Each time I saw you I fell a little deeper under your spell.”

“Where are we headed?” She glanced out the passenger window as he turned onto the highway. “If it's a surprise you don't need to tell me. If you have any questions you still want to ask, we should talk now. The subject will be off-limits from dinner on."

"Sounds good to me. Did you ever figure out how the inn fit into it?" he asked.

"I did. Katie will flip out when she hears about it. The kitchen of the inn is all that is left of the original building sitting on the property. There was a small inn there in nineteen-eighteen. John and Mary honeymooned at that inn and spent time at the cove. She told me they were some of the most blissful days of their marriage. They loved it here and bought a small house on the edge of town. It isn't there any longer. Another mind numbing fact to add to all the others you have stored up in your head. This place has quite a history that I'm only beginning to understand. One of the owners had, shall we say, less than a stellar reputation. But that's a talk for another day."

"Wow, that's something. I would have never guessed. It makes sense though. If he loved Mary, John would return to a place filled with happy memories for him. What you're telling me is the inn could still be a hot spot."

"You could say that, but who knows." She turned in her seat to look at him. "Sorry, there wasn't a lot of logic in this case for you to work with." She patted his arm. "Who knew a simple murder could turn out this weird."

"Murder is never simple. And believe it or not, this case had more logic than you would think. Most crimes boil down to the lust for power, money, and passion whether that is love or hate. John Ballard was a narcissist who gave in to his lust for power in the persona of Dr. Heisenberg. For the investors, they became traitors for money while the buyers had a passion for hate. Even the energy field made some logical sense because of chemistry. I have to admit seeing him spinning with his face contorting seemed a bit over the top for me."

"You and me both. At least for now we can put this to rest, and I don't want to think about another incident for a long time. Although I can't wait to see what my cousin does with the story. With you going back to Arizona my life should settle down. My immediate plans involve finding a job. Not at Pinedale, obviously."

"It'll be time for you to testify at the trial of your shooter before you know it. That, and meeting my parents. They'll love you." He got into the turn lane.

"I'm looking forward to meeting them. They must be awesome folks to have raised a man like you."

"Thank you. Matt told me this is a great place." He got out and opened her car door.

Matt had chosen well. The place overlooked the ocean, and Jaxon had reserved a table with a window. The music in the background was perfect and the lighting made it romantic, which was the mood he was in. The best part was the dance floor. He patted his pocket to make sure he had remembered to put the gift he had bought her. He couldn't help noticing all the eyes following his stunning date. His hand went possessively to the small of her back.

"Perfect." She reached across to take his hand after they were seated and the waiter had taken their orders. "Detective Kincaid, you've managed to surprise me with your thoughtfulness once again." She glanced at the couples dancing. “I remember the night of your friend’s engagement party. I had such a great time.”

“Until you were shot.” He thanked the waiter when he poured the sparkling wine into their glasses.

“Not a good memory, but our first dance is. One of my all-time favorite moments is when I’m sure I surprised you with a less than sisterly kiss.” She sipped her wine meeting his gaze over the glass.

“Ah, one of my favorites too. I wasn’t sure how you felt about me until that moment. I also remember I didn’t sleep well that night.” Jaxon heard her chuckle and smiled at the sound. “I may be wrong, but I think that was the whole point.”

“I’ll never tell.” A rosy glow tinged her cheeks. “There isn’t much I don’t like about you, Kincaid, but I think I’ll always like you best as the hunky cowboy of my dreams.”

The night was for discovering new facets about each other. They ate, talked, and gazed into each other’s eyes. Their hands touched often across the table. When the plates were cleared and the bill paid, Jaxon reached for her hand. “The first time I saw you that day at the pool I wasn’t trying to be rude. When you turned those gorgeous hazel green eyes of yours on me, I couldn’t remember anything. Of course, I had to interview you again. I had botched it so bad the first time. I’m glad that I did.”

“I got the impression you didn’t like me at all.”

“My poker face worked.” He grinned. “After you told me about what you saw at the scene, I was sure I could walk away from you and not look back. But you stayed in my mind, messing with my thoughts, and worked your way into my heart.” He saw her smile.

"And it was those dimples of yours that sealed the deal. You're a beautiful woman, Peyton. Inside and out."

"Thank you." She reached in her purse for a tissue.

"When I saw this in the store window, I knew I wanted to see it around your neck." He placed the small box in her hand. "Thank you for opening my life to see new possibilities I never could have imagined. I read speculative fiction growing up and still couldn't think outside the box until I met you."

She opened the small box and saw the beautiful necklace inside, a jade stone with a diamond on each side. "Oh, Jaxon, this is beautiful." She reached for his hand again. "Thank you." She slipped her treasure from the box and latched it around her neck.

"It's like I imagined it would look on you when the jeweler showed it to me. Do you know that depending on what you wear your eyes change colors?" He saw her nod. "When you wear a certain color of bluish green your eyes become a beautiful shade of jade. That's when I think of you as my green-eyed girl." He stood and moved toward her. "May I have this dance?"

"I thought you'd never ask." She took his hand, and he led her onto the dance floor.

"Have I mentioned you are a perfect fit?" He pulled her into his arms.

"I think you might have said that to me once or twice before, but I don't mind if you tell me all the time." She gazed into his eyes as they moved to the music.

"That's good because I'll probably tell you every time I hold you in my arms."

"I find it strange that I can't remember any of the songs we danced to before. I knew there was music, but

I could never tell anyone the name of the song. But tonight is different. I will remember this song for the rest of my life."

"Why this song? Why tonight?" He tightened his hold on her, loving the way she rested her head on his shoulder, anticipating her answer.

"The song is romantic, but what makes it memorable is that this is the night I've finally decided to stop running and to trust you." She snuggled closer in his arms. "I've wasted enough time worrying. I want to believe that love is possible."

Jaxon took her by the hand and out the door to the walkway by the waterfront. Under the canopy of the stars and with the witness of the moon he pulled her into his arms and kissed her, thankful to be the man who was lucky enough to be in the right place at the right time when she decided to take a chance.

A word about the author...

I am a multi-published Amazon best selling author who writes romantic suspense with a touch of the paranormal. I enjoy writing fiction. The character development, their stories, and the twists and turns in the plot intrigue me. Once I let the characters loose I can't wait to see where they take me. I'm hooked from the first words on the paper and I have to keep writing to see how the story ends. Layer by layer I build it until I come to the happy conclusion.

I live in Colorado with my husband and family. I am a member of the RMFWPAL (Rocky Mountain Fiction Writers Published Authors League) and have enjoyed becoming involved in my community as one of the many authors living in Colorado. I invite you to read one of my Blue Cove Mysteries and see for yourself why Blue Cove is a special and unusual place. http://www.ionamorrison.com

Thank you for purchasing
this publication of The Wild Rose Press, Inc.

For questions or more information
contact us at
info@thewildrosepress.com.

The Wild Rose Press, Inc.
www.thewildrosepress.com

www.ingramcontent.com/pod-product-compliance
Lightning Source LLC
Chambersburg PA
CBHW050031030726
47506CB00001B/226

9781509237579